The Cryptid Dossier: Confidential Case Files 1-4

(The Complete First Series)

by

Quelle von der Umbra

'The Cryptid Dossier: Confidential Case Files 1-4 (The Complete First Series)'

KDP Paperback Print Edition (First Edition 2024)

This work is a collection comprising of the following four previously and separately released copyrighted novella Kindle e-books authored by Quelle von der Umbra:

> 'Rise of the Dogman – The Cryptid Dossier: Confidential Case File 1'
> 'The Return of Broken Fang – The Cryptid Dossier: Confidential Case File 2'
> 'The Ghost in the Beast – The Cryptid Dossier: Confidential Case File 3'
> 'The Dogs of Budapest – The Cryptid Dossier: Confidential Case File 4'

cryptid-dossier.com (Home of Quelle von der Umbra)

Author's note on this 'combination' edition...

This work comprises the collected four separate novella-length installments originally released on the Kindle platform as part the first series in the 'Cryptid Dossier' collection of stories (pictured above).

The response to those first four novellas detailing Sarah Shaw's fascinating entanglement in an ongoing inter-cryptid conflict has been very encouraging. It was quickly suggested that some readers might appreciate the series being arranged into single e-book and print book editions—The result being this novel-length work published as *The Cryptid Dossier: Confidential Case Files 1-4, (The Combined First Series).*

The previously published e-novella titled *Rise of the Dogman* naturally comprises 'Part 1' of these combined editions, followed by the three subsequent novellas in the series charting Sarah Shaw's terrifying journey into cryptid hell; i.e. *The Return of Broken Fang*, *The Ghost in the Beast*, and *The Dogs of Budapest* respectively.

A second *Cryptid Dossier* series centered on Sarah Shaw's continuing paranormal adventures is currently underway, so please do leave any reviews or comments you may have on Amazon if you enjoy this first series of tales; it's always very much appreciated. Until then, happy reading...

Quelle
June, 2024

Contents

Author's note on this 'combination' edition... 3
Part 1: Rise of the Dogman 6
Epilogue to Part 1..76
Part 2: The Return of Broken Fang............................79
Part 3: The Ghost in the Beast 159
Part 4: The Dogs of Budapest 254
About the author... 352

Part 1

Rise of the Dogman

The Cryptid Dossier: Confidential Case File 1

An ancient feud,
two legendary cryptids,
a woman caught between.

****

1

"...please tell us about your encounter now; give us every last detail that comes to mind..."

Vic Cundiff, *Dogman Encounters Radio*, Episode 397.

America's Pacific Northwest; the encounter...

It's like it's happening all over again, every time I remember...

I curse under my breath as I trudge along the forest trail. This was supposed to be a fun day hike with my friend Dana. But at the last minute, she bailed, leaving me to choose between hiking solo and wasting the drive to the trailhead.

Against my better judgment, I decided to do the hike alone. The Pacific Northwest forests are so beautiful in autumn, and it seemed a shame to turn back around. I'm an experienced hiker having spent virtually all my childhood walking the mountains of Oregon, just seeing if I could spot my favorite wildlife in their natural habitat; I'd say I'm a child of the forest; always been most happy when surrounded by the scent of fresh pine and the clear mountain air.

Now, as the afternoon light starts fading towards dusk, I'm questioning my decision. The remote trail, which had seemed peaceful and enchanting earlier, takes on an ominous feel. I shudder, unable to shake the creeping sensation that I'm being watched.

Stop it, I tell myself. You're freaking yourself out over nothing. But I can't ignore the prickling on the back of my neck. The shadows between the tall firs and cedars grow steadily deeper. I pick up my pace. I just have to get back to my car before full dark sets in.

My unease amplifies as the last traces of sunset filter through the branches. I glance over my shoulder frequently, scanning for any sign of movement. But nothing seems out of the ordinary—just endless silent trees. And yet, something is there...

Nearly running now, I round a curve on the winding path. I slow to a stop, my heart pounding wildly. There, lurking among the underbrush just ahead, hulks—something—like an enormous, shaggy creature.

My breath freezes in my lungs. It's like nothing I've ever seen, something that cannot be unseen: If it stood, it would be eight feet tall at least, covered in reddish-brown fur that looks like matted hair. Its eyes reflect the fading light, glowing with a distressing intensity, somehow looking at me; no, through me... disturbingly human-like...

The creature seems intent on peering cautiously past me as if on guard against something even more threatening. Then a voice begins to resonate inside my mind, softly but insistent, repeating over and over: "Be quiet...*he* is near... Be quiet... *he* is near..."

I stand paralyzed—Who is *he? Who is near?* I can't tear my gaze away from the dreadful thing crouching before me.

My mind reels as I stare at its massiveness, this impossible creature mere yards away. This can't be real. Bigfoot is just a myth. But every detail of the hulking beast is burned into my vision—the shaggy fur, immense shoulders, and intelligent eyes reflecting the dusk light. And those eyes... *so human...*

"Who's here?" I inexplicably find myself calling out, searching the shadowy trees for the source of the voice in my head. But the voice in my head keeps on, more urgent than before... "Be quiet... *he* is near..."

Completely unnerved, I take a fearful step back, a twig snapping loudly under my boot. The Sasquatch's glowing eyes snap onto me as if this is the first time it has actually seen me, its lips baring flat yellowed teeth. Adrenaline floods my veins—it could tear me apart effortlessly.

Then, as the creature unperceptively shifts its vast bulk, I glimpse a smaller form clinging to its leg—her infant child. Its wide eyes peer at me, more alarmed than threatening.

The mother—for she must be the mother—makes no move. Instead, her body language shows the same wariness and fear that is gripping me. She glances away furtively through the trees as if anticipating something even more dangerous...

And the voice in my mind keeps repeating its insistent warning: "Be quiet...*he* is near."

I'm stunned that I'm even capable of rational thought. Bigfoot isn't real, that's just a legend. I've never believed in or prepared for something like this. Yet here one stands, unbearably real.

I become aware that the mother continues peering out into the dark trees behind me, its muscles tensed. If she thought I was any kind of threat, I know she could easily rip me to shreds, but instead, I feel like I'm being warned—telepathically if that were possible. Her fear and focus are on some unseen threat out there... I'm not her enemy, and it's as if she is as wary of me as I am of her.

I realize I have no idea what she senses approaching in the darkness, and renewed fear floods through me. But the palpable dread I can see reflected in her almost too-human eyes makes me tremble the most—the kind of trembling that comes with shock! Something is very wrong here, and getting closer by the second.

"*Sarah...*"

I'm jolted as the voice in my head speaks my name. When did I tell it my name? I never even thought of my name, yet somehow it knows!

"*Sarah...*" it repeats relentlessly.

I see the Sasquatch's eyes boring into mine. She *knows my name*, but that is not what she is telling me. Her eyes widen.

"He... is here."

Icy fear trickles down my spine. I slowly turn...

Two points of red light flare in the darkness of the woods. Eyes. Watching me hungrily.

My heart seizes as a form detaches itself from the blackness. It slinks forward, towering and lean, canine-like, but far larger than any wolf. It's up on two legs—a fantastical sight—its lips peeling back; its teeth as if created from the dawn of time purely for tearing flesh from bone. Its dog-like head is enormous, with pointed ears, and its sleek, shining fur covers it down to sloped yet powerful-looking shoulders. Lean and long muscular arms, reaching down to its knees, end in distended, raccoon-like hands—yes, it has *hands*... and I'm losing my mind!

I open my mouth to scream, but only a choked gasp emerges, dying in my throat as an overwhelming wave of malevolence emanates out from the creature's snarling visage. My every instinct screams for me to run, but my limbs won't obey. Its eyes pin me in place, peering through flesh and bone into the core of my being.

This is nothing ordinary, no common animal. Its towering, dominant form seems merely a vessel for something far more sinister—an ancient, insatiable evil given physical shape in a world in which it doesn't belong.

I watch, transfixed, as the creature's lips spread wider as if savoring my terror. Its demonic grin belies a hunger that goes beyond flesh and blood. I can feel its thirst, a yearning for the utter annihilation of hope and light, its craving for the corruption of innocence into dark despair. I can feel all these things as sharply as I know that those gnashing jaws could tear my body apart. But it is the feeling that I am in the presence of a warped, almost otherworldly psyche that genuinely terrifies me. There is an uncanny animalistic, high intelligence of malign intensity radiating like a black aura about it.

It stands there, reveling in its gloom. The shadows around the creature seem to deepen, clinging to its glossy fur like writhing dark tentacles. Everything about it exudes wrongness. Everywhere that its gaze touches, the forest withers, vitality leeching away.

Behind me, it's as if I can feel the Sasquatch press her young one closer, protective, her thoughts pleading with me. But against this vortex of primal darkness, I have an overpowering fear that we are overmatched. I watch as the wolfish creature's snout bares rows of jagged teeth; it knows its prey is cornered. Malevolence pours from its twisted form in suffocating waves as it begins to stalk steadily nearer, poised to devour us body and soul... stalking closer, its wickedness floods my mind. I brace for its attack, knowing I stand no chance.

All I remember is a deafening, guttural *WHOOP!* that seemed to shudder the air. My vision blacks out as the sound hits me, echoing within every cell in my body. I have a faint sense of being lifted, flying.

I regain fuzzy awareness and find I'm lying in a dry riverbed, coarse sand grinding against my back. The sunlight is harsh on my eyes, and I see figures in uniforms rushing towards me.

Someone shouts out, "She's alive!" And another voice asks, "What's your name, miss?"

I rasp my name, disoriented. The rescuers begin checking me for injuries. My head pounds, thoughts all jumbled.

One says, "You've been missing nearly a week. Your family is worried sick."

I... a week? That can't be... I try to sit up, bombarded with questions that mean nothing to me.

"The Sasquatch?" I mumble, feeling my words slur. "Her baby... are they okay?"

I see these people I don't know exchanging concerned looks. I glance down, finding I'm nearly naked, my clothes and gear all gone.

I begin demanding answers, realizing I'm miles from where I saw the creatures. I can't understand... How did I get here? What happened?

Exhaustion overwhelms me, and I'm vaguely aware I'm being stretchered to a helicopter. Darkness retakes me as the medics sedate me, checking my body for trauma and injuries, and inexplicably finding nothing wrong, I drift into oblivion...

Sarah stared out the hospital window, lost in thought. The endless sympathy from family and friends was suffocating. She knew they had meant well, but none of them understood. How could they, when she couldn't even grasp the truth for herself?

The doctor had said it was a miracle she survived out there for five days, five days that she simply could not remember. He had claimed the tests showed no physical trauma—but it must have been some form of exposure and hypothermia that caused her memory loss and disorientation. Sarah had nodded along, feigning grateful relief.

But the doctor's patronizing rationalizations didn't align with her scattered recollections. Flashes of impossible creatures... and a bone-chilling sense of malevolence that haunted her dreams. And those people she had been catching glimpses of, two of them, like observers lurking in the hallway; scrutinizing her silently from afar... Did they know something? Sarah would catch the doctor shooting what looked like wary glances at them as if needing some kind of permission.

Sarah began to worry that questioning the doctor's explanation would only validate any concerns they might have about her mental state. At this point, she just wanted to go home and sleep in her own bed, so she buried her doubts deep down. Sarah just wanted to get through this, get over it, and get away from the questions, the constant blood pressure tests, the probing, even if it was all for her own good.

At one point, a detective from the town police department asked questions; could she remember anyone else out there—not the creatures, obviously—but anyone she might have recognized? She asked the detective why the police were involved, but he reassured her it was just routine in cases where people have gone missing for extended periods of time.

Eventually, satisfied that Sarah had not been abducted—at least not by anything human—the detective left. But Sarah saw him stop and talk with the two people who had been looking in on her occasionally but who had never spoken with her. They were a man and a woman, official-looking people in dark suits, and they came with that officious swagger that screamed 'government.' The detective said a few things to them out of Sarah's earshot as they listened carefully, and Sarah had a perturbed feeling out of it all, like they were openly talking about her but she was never going to know what they were saying.

Once the staff cleared her for discharge, the doctor recommended she follow up with a counselor and provided her with a referral. Sarah accepted it politely, knowing she could never reveal the truth if anyone were to take her seriously ever again.

"Her name is Dr. Andrea Cooper," the doctor said in his professionally concerned manner. "She's new in town, but she comes highly, highly recommended."

Sarah thanked him for the recommendation and assured him she would carefully consider it. For now, she just wanted to take each day one at a time. The doctor reassured Sarah that he was available any time she needed and wrote her out a script for something to help her sleep over the next couple of days.

"You know," he had said, "not many people go missing for as long as you did and come out so well. You seem like a very resilient young woman." He had given her a reassuring smile but had turned severe quickly. "Just be careful, Sarah, because these kinds of things have a way of sneaking back up on you—reach out if you need to."

Outside, as the taxi taking her home pulled away, Sarah finally exhaled. The fresh air cleared some of the fog from her troubled mind, but doubts still lingered—something sinister was out there, back in the forest. She prayed that whatever happened in those missing days would stay buried, or at least reveal a rational explanation. But in her heart, she knew this was only the beginning. Sarah felt a gut-wrenching pang of panic when the taxi passed a darkly wooded park, and she knew then that her world had changed forever.

A few days later Sarah sank onto her couch, bone-tired after another shift at work but too restless to sleep. Ever since getting back, her nerves had been on edge. She had hoped throwing herself into her job might help, that time spent at the animal shelter, where she worked with a range of lost, injured and abused animals, would somehow change the traumatic memories of coming face to face with something inexplicable.

But shadows now seemed to have a way of jumping out at her from every corner, and some of the larger stray dogs at the shelter had triggered apprehensive feelings, which was a tragedy for someone who loved animals.

She knew she was safe, especially here at home—it was just a residual paranoia she was experiencing that had been carved into her psyche by the trauma. But rational thought provided little comfort when her mind constantly flashed back to a set of glowing eyes stalking her in the darkness. And it didn't help that she lived alone, though that was her preferred lifestyle. However, she was loath to let a bunch of bad half-memories start dictating how she should live her life.

Sarah sighed, glancing at the animal shelter calendar on her fridge, filled with pictures of happy dogs she had helped adopt out. Could she really go back to that life of happy contentment? Sarah had decided early on that working with animals would be her thing. She had trained as a veterinary assistant and then found work at the local animal shelter. Coupled with her great love of the outdoors, Sarah had treasured her job from the first day. But now, after the last few weeks, so much still remained unanswered about those missing days. Before, sasquatches had not even been on her radar, let alone whatever that other wolf-like creature had been!

2

Sarah found herself thinking about a guy called 'Demon,' or 'Daemon' Skinner, a weird kind of guy who worked at the county's animal control unit. Skinner wasn't into animals; Skinner was into cryptids and other assorted crazy stuff, and most of Sarah's colleagues and workmates had made him the butt of their jokes whenever he had brought impounded dogs and other animals to the shelter for processing—Sarah included! She didn't know him well but knew that everyone saw Skinner as the town's local nut job, especially after he did an interview with the local student radio station claiming he had seen a *werewolf*.

Sarah felt ashamed with how she had laughed and played along with her co-workers, all at Skinner's expense; what would they think of her if she ever told them what she had seen... what she now knew lurked in the forests...

A knock interrupted her brooding. She opened the door cautiously to find Deputy Tim Rogers standing there, badge-emblazoned hat in hand. "I just wanted to check in and make sure you're doing okay," he said with an easy smile.

Sarah managed a polite nod, tamping down her annoyance. Tim's tireless interest in her had always felt more ego-driven than genuine care, but she couldn't deny that his concern was comforting after weeks alone.

"Those reports say you claimed to see some pretty wild stuff out there," Tim said, helping himself to a seat at her kitchen table.

Sarah's heart sank. The last thing she needed was someone like Deputy Rogers poking around in her affairs. If it ever got out what she had claimed had happened to her...

"Tim, I would appreciate it if you kept that stuff to yourself," she sternly warned him, hoping he would get the message that she was not in the mood to talk.

"*Aw*, I wouldn't put too much stock in it," he said jovially, her severe look sailing over his head. "They say hypothermia can cause all kinds of hallucinations."

Sarah decided to stay silent. She expected disbelief from anyone who might hear her story and knew that Tim meant no harm by his somewhat patronizing words—but only she could know the stupefying reality of what was haunting her dreams. All she could do was brace herself, be aware that others would have their doubts, and try to move on from the living nightmare she was going through as best she could.

Sarah found herself standing up, her posture firm. She didn't want to be rude but could no longer bear talking to the deputy. "I appreciate you checking on me, Tim, but I'm fine," she said, holding the door open for him to leave. "I just need some time alone to think things through."

Deputy Rogers might have been one of those overly persistent suitors that women often have to deal with, but he was not one to overstay his welcome. He touched the brim of his hat. "Well, if you need anything..."

An abrupt clattering from the yard made them both jump. Rogers' hand went to his holster. "Stay here, I'll check it out."

Sarah watched anxiously as Deputy Rogers approached the overturned bins. A raccoon leaped out, teeth bared, claws swiping viciously at Rogers' shoes. The lawman startled back, cursing in surprise.

"It's only a raccoon!" he called back to Sarah, barely suppressing his relief. But she stood paralyzed. The raccoon's snarls and aggressiveness triggered vivid flashbacks of the dog-like creature's otherworldly malice. As the raccoon reared up on its tiny hind legs, front paws dangling like twisted hands, Sarah felt the same overwhelming sense of danger emanating from its glaring eyes. Its snarling chirps seemed alarmingly wolf-like, full of rage and primal menace.

Sarah only belatedly realized Rogers was making some kind of joke about arresting the thing. But she was frozen in place, her pulse racing as she stared transfixed at the diseased-looking claws trying to tear into Rogers' stout boots. Nothing was amusing about what was happening to her, and for the first time in her life, Sarah felt hatred towards an animal–*irrational hatred*!

"Please, thanks, but just could you go," she finally managed, tightly, willing herself not to completely break down till he left. She quickly shut the door, pressing her back against it, using all her strength to keep the shadowy nightmares outside. *It was just a raccoon!*

Later, after a warming cup of chocolate had helped Sarah calm down, she leaned back from her laptop, rubbing her tired eyes. She had spent hours every night since getting home scouring the internet for clues about what she had seen. It had sucked her into a deep rabbit hole of cryptid sightings, myths, and contested evidence.

She had learned that Bigfoot was now considered by many to be an evolutionary cousin to humans, with thousands of witness sightings and accounts littering the internet. Most reports emphasised the famous cryptid as a wild man of the forest, both dominant and frightening. But Sarah could only shake her head, remembering the mother sasquatch and its infant's sad, frightened eyes—like they themselves were as much prey as any other creature of the wilds.

Be quiet... he is near...

Finding information on the gaunt, frightening wolf-like creature was far more complex, however. But the descriptions Sarah found rang eerily accurate to the lanky beast that had stalked her. As she absorbed one description after another, Sarah had begun to feel an immense sense of relief, realizing that others had seen similar creatures and lived; that she wasn't crazy after all.

3

Over the next few days, Sarah sifted through a labyrinth of mythical beasts—werewolves, skinwalkers, and lycanthropes. But the descriptions and images never quite matched the towering, primal thing she had encountered; other accounts painted images of something far too humanoid for what she had seen.

Sarah then stumbled upon a niche podcast discussing a cryptid called 'the Dogman', and that's when she felt the chill of recognition. The harrowing eyewitness accounts of this particular cryptid echoed her trauma in vivid detail, capturing the essence of its lean, canine shape and the alien malignancy in its eyes.

To her relief, Sarah finally had a name for the beast: The *Dogman*. It was like she now had conclusive proof that she wasn't insane, that others had survived encounters with creatures like this! Sarah knew most people would still scoff but didn't care. However, she wondered if even fellow believers would believe she had seen a Sasquatch and a Dogman together. By all accounts, that was unheard of. But Sarah knew what she had seen and somewhere there had to be answers to how she had been caught up in something beyond her comprehension.

Sarah glanced around her small cabin. It was nestled quietly off the road and backed into the woods. It had always been the kind of place she had wanted to live in. Embracing solitude had been a part of Sarah's personality since childhood, preferring the company of animals over most people. Now, she would use that sense of independence to take the space and time she needed to pursue an understanding of her own experiences, to find out what had happened to her and why she had lost five days from her memory.

Sarah had noted that the online 'Dogman community' stressed seeking professional help in dealing with the severe trauma that could come from a dogman encounter. However, many also cautioned against the mainstream medical profession's tendency to still view such experiences as purely psychological. It seemed to Sarah that most people in her situation had been forced to deal with the kind of mild condescension she had encountered with the doctor at the hospital.

Sarah considered her options but finally relented after one particularly fitful night in which the Dogman creature again vividly reared up in its nightmarish malevolence to invade her dreams. She made an appointment with the psychologist her doctor had recommended the next day, pleased that she had kept his referral card. Sarah had been avoiding fully processing the ordeal—especially the missing time from her memory. It was time to face her fears with the help of others, one-on-one. She comforted herself that knowledge was power and that this was a positive sign she was done with being afraid.

Feeling a little better, Sarah was nursing a latte a few days later while enjoying a rare lunch outing with two work friends. The conversation steered clear of Sarah's ordeal, giving her a semblance of normalcy.

As they got up to leave, a familiar voice called out. "Fancy running into you here!"

Sarah stifled a groan as Deputy Rogers strode over. Her friends tittered, well aware of his interest.

"Mind if I borrow her for a quick chat?" Rogers asked them with a wink. Before Sarah could object, he guided her aside.

"I've been doing some research into Bigfoot sightings around here," Rogers said eagerly, handing her some photocopied reports. "I thought you could look these over and see if they match what you saw."

Sarah skimmed the official-looking Bigfoot reports with thinly veiled impatience. "I'm not sure this is what I saw," she finally said, handing back the pile. Rogers looked crestfallen. "And I thought I told you I didn't want this to get about!"

"Oh, sorry," he said, shuffling the papers back into their folder. "I just thought... and when I saw you there..."

"But thank you for taking the time," Sarah butted in gently. She smiled politely before rejoining her curious friends, resigned to fielding their questions about 'her deputy.'

Sarah watched Rogers out of the corner of her eye as he dejectedly slunk back to his cruiser, pretending to take an urgent radio call. She winced as he tore out the parking lot, siren blaring unnecessarily. It was all bluster, and she wondered if his bruised ego would likely come back to haunt her someday. But she couldn't deal with his unwanted advances at this time and hoped he might get the message.

A couple of days later, Sarah left her house to go to her scheduled appointment with the psychologist. Looking up, she noticed an expensively clean-cut black SUV with tinted windows parked along her quiet street. Odd to see something like that in this neighborhood, she thought absently before continuing to her car, dismissing its presence as a visitor calling in on one of the neighbors.

On arrival, Sarah glanced at the nondescript office building that housed Dr. Andrea Cooper's psychology practice. The receptionist, a thin elderly woman with a friendly face, politely guided Sarah through filling in the standard intake forms. Sarah hoped the impersonal questions the forms asked would not indicate how the sessions would be handled. She was here to directly ask about and discuss her encounter, not get some bland reassurances that she was making improvements, whatever that might be!

Dr. Andrea Cooper's office had a comfortable yet efficient feel. Sarah took in the many diplomas and credentials displaying the psychologist's impressive achievements despite her relatively young age—somewhere in the mid-thirties, Sarah thought.

Dr. Cooper was smartly outfitted in a well-cut suit and satin blouse that conveyed success but little flair. Something about the polished, proficient aesthetic nagged at Sarah, stirring hazy memories she couldn't place.

During their first session, Dr. Cooper's manner was open and non-judgemental, something Sarah greatly appreciated. She asked thoughtful questions about Sarah's background and interests, establishing a warm rapport.

At the hour mark, Dr. Cooper gently ended their first meeting and scheduled Sarah for a full session next week. Sarah hid her disappointment at what she thought was a lack of progress, but as she left she made up her mind to see things through. She decided that she liked Dr. Cooper and looked forward to their next session, feeling that talking about things with another person might actually be making a difference.

Over the following few appointments, Sarah tentatively brought up the creatures she had seen. But Dr. Cooper steered the conversation towards 'healthier coping strategies.' By never dismissing Sarah outright, the psychologist managed to maintain Sarah's trust. She would say, 'I can understand why such an ordeal could lead to vivid memories' or 'We'll unpack those memories when you're ready.' Sarah liked how Dr. Cooper steered the focus of their discussions toward coping techniques but never outright dismissed Sarah's claims. Her patient approach allowed Sarah to open up further in each session, carefully building the trust that Sarah knew was necessary. It wasn't really that much different from how Sarah and her colleagues at the animal shelter coaxed renewed feelings of trust from the traumatised animals that came into their care.

It was not until the fourth visit that Dr. Cooper broached Sarah's missing time gap. "Your records indicate you have no memories from several days of your ordeal. We might try to recover those using hypnotic regression if you feel ready."

Sarah eagerly agreed, finally feeling that she was being heard. She had read a bit about this technique, usually in stories covering criminal trial cases in which witnesses underwent deep hypnotic trances to access repressed memories and images. It excited Sarah that she might finally have some answers on the one part of her scary experience that she had no recollection of.

A few days later, Sarah was walking downtown when a commotion drew her attention. Across the street, she thought she recognized Daemon Skinner, the animal control worker with the weird werewolf tales. He was wrestling and cursing in an effort to subdue a large and snarling stray dog. Sarah watched uneasily as the young, unkempt man roughly forced the struggling animal into a cage in the back of his van, the whole episode fraught with a level of violence that would be unacceptable back at the animal shelter.

Glancing up, Skinner's penetrating gaze locked with Sarah's, his expression chillingly unreadable. It reminded her of those dreams where someone recognizes you, but their intentions are unclear. Then, for an instant, the dog also turned its vicious glare in her direction, its snarls evaporating into a strangely calm yet intensely territorial challenge. At the periphery of the dog's glowering stare, Sarah picked up a disturbing yet knowing grin breaking out on Skinner's sweat-stained face...

In that brief but tense moment of shared focus, Sarah felt a flash of some buried memory stir, too fleeting to grasp. Unsettled by Skinner and the dog's unspoken warning, she broke away and hurried off, struggling to ignore the nagging sense of familiarity that had been sparked by the chance encounter. She could feel as if the dog's glaring eyes were still boring into her back all the way home...

4

The scheduled regression session coincided with a day heavy with rain. On her arrival at Dr. Cooper's practice, a shadowy black SUV cruised past as Sarah parked outside the office, its tinted windows pitted with running raindrops and the dappled glare of the storm-laden skies. She glanced after it, a faint unease prickling at her senses as she raised an umbrella to shield out drizzle, and then she hurried inside, preoccupied with what lay ahead.

As Dr. Cooper's soothing voice guided her into a hypnotic state, Sarah's limbs grew heavy, her thoughts drifting...

Brief images flashed—a dark forest, glowing eyes flashing in the shadows, silhouettes of a hulking, hairy creature, and a tall, fur-covered form. There were human voices, but she could not make out what was being said... like words in a foreign language. Then a stench filled Sarah's nostrils, and a swirling darkness quickly enveloped everything.

Abruptly, Dr. Cooper's distant voice broke through: "Sarah, wake up now!"

Sarah surfaced, blinking. Dr. Cooper loomed over her, her face bloodless. With a trembling hand, she helped Sarah sit up.

"What did you find?" Sarah asked groggily, but hopefully.

"N-nothing, it didn't work," Dr. Cooper stammered, avoiding Sarah's eyes. She started gathering her things with jittery motions.

Sarah tried to clarify what was happening, but Dr. Cooper insisted on ending their session, making a flimsy excuse about another appointment coming up. She urged Sarah toward the door while calling for the receptionist.

The receptionist looked as confused as Sarah by Dr. Cooper's agitated state as they were both shuffled back into the hall.

"When can I come again?" Sarah inquired, still flustered at the abruptness of the session's end.

"Call my receptionist," Dr. Cooper said absently as if her receptionist was not standing there with them.

"You'll tell me then?" asked Sarah, almost pleading.

But Dr. Cooper was already back in her office, the door crashing shut behind her.

"You were in there for quite some time," said the receptionist, trying to soothe Sarah's growing disquiet over Dr. Cooper's behavior. "I'm sure everything will be fine—she's very good, you know?"

Completely flustered by the turn of events, Sarah gave the receptionist a vague nod.

"So, I'll call you to make another appointment... tomorrow?"

"That'll be fine," smiled the receptionist as she gently ushered Sarah out of the practice.

Needing to clear her head, Sarah wandered to a nearby coffee shop. What had happened after the inky blackness swallowed her during the session? She strained to recall any glimpse of what Dr. Cooper might have found that had made her react so peculiarly. Again, those swirling shadows encroached on Sarah's mind, merging with the stray dog's baleful stare she'd seen with Daemon Skinner a few days before.

Sarah gulped from the large flat white steaming in front of her, its acrid taste biting into her thoughts. But it was to no avail, the maelstrom of thoughts assailing Sarah's mind now threatening to overwhelm her when an unexpectedly foul, meaty stench suddenly assaulted her senses. Gagging, Sarah fled the coffee shop in a panic. The phantom reek seemed to cling to her all the way home, though she thought it had to be in her mind. But what had awakened it?

What did you find Dr. Cooper?

As perplexed over Dr. Cooper's conduct as Sarah was, she became even more concerned over the next week as Dr. Cooper obviously began dodging Sarah's calls and emails. Determined, Sarah decided to confront her at the office, only to find it completely vacant—stripped of all furnishings and accoutrements, and with a large rental sign in the window.

Sarah stood staring in shock. How could Dr. Cooper have abandoned her practice so abruptly? Is it something to do with me, Sarah thought? And, if so, what could have rattled this woman so profoundly that she would uproot her entire practice and disappear entirely? Sarah enquired with the building's management but got no answers other than that the practice had ceased operating—which was obvious.

Back on the street, the heavens opened up, and Sarah found herself splashing her way to her car. She was becoming agitated, and things didn't help when an SUV drenched her legs as it passed by through a deep puddle. Sarah yelled at it defiantly... it was black. It had tinted windows...

Wet, distressed, and angry at how the regression therapy session had turned out, Sarah drove the distance to her home through the driving rain, her windscreen wipers giving off an eerie monotonous screech as they battled the deluge.

Sarah's hands gripped the steering wheel tightly as she drove through the storm. Dr. Cooper's bizarre behavior rang alarms in her mind. Had she unearthed something dangerous during their session? And if so, wasn't it Sarah's right to know?

Sarah shuddered, rain obscuring the lonely road ahead.

Hypnotic images began flickering precariously into her memory—glowing eyes, massive shadows. Sarah tried focusing on the pavement lines to calm her nerves. She had to slam on the brakes at a stop sign she nearly missed. Breathless, Sarah watched as the windshield wipers squealed over the glass, smearing the view in streaky shards of rain. As it cleared, a tall, wolfish form appeared wetly under a close by solitary streetlamp... and glowing impenetrable red eyes fused with hers.

Sarah's breath caught, and a deep dread crawled up her spine. It can't be... She watched as the windshield blurred again with rain. When it wiped clear, the creature remained, steam rising from its drenched gloomy fur. Sarah's fingers trembled over the car horn as a wave of primal terror washed over her.

Then headlights turned the corner behind her, bleaching her car's interior with cold blue light. When they illuminated the streetlamp, nothing was there. Nothing was there! A hoot from another car got Sarah's stunned brain moving again. She drove past the stop sign in shock, but Sarah knew—somehow, *he is here... he has found me...*

5

Sarah barely slept that night, terrified and certain that the creature from the forest had returned, sure that *it was here.* When she called in sick, her boss sounded skeptical. Sarah didn't care—the boss be damned; she wasn't going anywhere after what had just happened.

Taking a furtive look outside her kitchen window, Sarah saw that the black SUV was back, parked at the end of her driveway. Sarah's pulse quickened. Too many sightings of one car to be a coincidence. Who were these people? Definitely not visitors calling on her neighbors!

Against her better judgment, Sarah thought about calling Deputy Rogers. She was loath to give him false impressions of her feelings towards him or her need for his protection. Still, the sight of the black SUV and the sighting of the loathsome dogman the night before made Sarah incredibly uncomfortable, and frightened.

"Well, hey there! This is a pleasant surprise," he chirped, answering after the first ring. "What's going on?"

"Look, Tim, I didn't want to bother you at work, but I've been noticing a strange vehicle parked outside my place over the last several weeks, and I wanted someone to check it out," Sarah explained. "I would do it myself, but..."

"*Aw*, I'm sure it's nothing to worry about," Rogers replied breezily, cutting her off. "I'm only a few minutes away, so I'll come and check it out for you just to be on the safe side—all part of the job!"

"I feel a bit silly having to ask," Sarah admitted.

"Nonsense! Happy to help in any way I can. But if you just wanted an excuse to see me, you could've just said so," Rogers added clumsily... and entirely inappropriately.

Sarah rolled her eyes, already regretting calling him, but stayed silent and sucked it up. After hanging up, she wondered if she'd made a serious mistake, that she was giving Deputy Rogers fuel for the torch he bared. But it was too late now and Sarah needed some answers.

A few minutes passed, and Sarah found herself nervously watching as Rogers' cruiser pulled up a little later, with the swaggering deputy making a show of getting out and approaching the SUV. Her eyes widened as a stern woman in a dark trench coat stepped out of the SUV, flashing a badge back at the deputy. Rogers' cocky stance shifted immediately to deference as he scrutinized the woman's identification, and Sarah had a weird feeling this was not the first time she had seen this woman.

At the same moment, Sarah's attention was distracted as the SUV's driver emerged and strode directly towards Sarah's door, ignoring Rogers. He was a large man, and as he neared, Sarah made out that the man's windbreaker jacket was emblazoned with the words "HOMELAND SECURITY."

Sarah met the government agent at her door with trepidation. "Ms. Shaw," he stated. "We need to have a discussion about certain... concerning matters. May I come in?" His tone brooked no argument.

Sarah wordlessly stood aside, heart racing, a queasy feeling of anxiety dripping into her stomach. She regarded the agent coldly. "I don't believe I caught your name?"

"Agent Murphy," he replied briskly, flashing an ID too quickly to read before pocketing it.

"Agent Murphy..." Sarah repeated. "First name?"

He hesitated. "That's not required."

Sarah's eyes narrowed. What kind of Homeland Security agent couldn't share their first name?

When she persisted, he reluctantly gritted out 'John.' His caginess instantly put Sarah on edge. She didn't like egos like his.

"So, *John* Murphy," Sarah said, emphasizing his name. "What exactly brings you here unannounced and sitting outside my home spying on me?"

"If you may, Ms. Shaw, I'll ask the questions," Murphy said sharply.

Sarah bristled at the officious manner. Whatever this man wanted from her, she was determined to not to make it easy for him, her dislike being immediate and absolute. She narrowed her eyes as he launched into interrogating her about calling the deputy.

"Let's start with why you felt the need to involve local law enforcement," Murphy said. "You should know that we're here on a federal matter."

Sarah bristled at the imperious tone. "Maybe because a strange vehicle is parked outside my home, which seems like a *local* matter, and it made me feel vulnerable." She hardened her eyes to a squint. "I've been through an ordeal so I'm a bit jumpy, not that I think I want to be sharing my problems with you!"

Sarah pictured the shadowy figures at the hospital after her rescue as she spoke. With dawning unease, she realized one had been this Murphy character.

"In fact, now that I think about it, you were at the hospital after my... incident," she said, eyes narrowing further. "Why exactly is Homeland Security involved in a local hiking emergency?"

Murphy's face tightened. "That's classified. Now, about this call to the deputy—"

"No, I want an explanation!" Sarah pressed. "Why were you at the hospital?"

Standing her ground, Sarah folded her arms and waited for the agent to answer.

"An appropriate agency representative was dispatched once your case displayed certain... irregularities." Murphy was neatly sidestepping the question. "Nothing for you to concern yourself with; we just need to get some things straight."

But the man's caginess only increased Sarah's suspicions.

What are you really investigating?

"By staking out my house?" she frowned, incredulous. "You're getting things straight by staking me out like some criminal or terrorist?"

Murphy's jaw tightened, but he redirected the line of questioning. "Let's discuss your relationship with Dr. Andrea Cooper and her recent disappearance."

Sarah paused, surprised by the shift. Was Murphy's interest more about Dr. Cooper than herself? Sarah chose her following words carefully.

"My, you do have quite the disarming manner—My sessions with Dr. Cooper, as someone like you would know, are confidential," she said evenly. "I was referred to her by my doctor, and she was helping me deal with the trauma of my ordeal, as any psychologist would."

"So you claim no knowledge as to why she suddenly cleared out her practice and vanished?" Murphy asked pointedly.

Sarah stayed silent as she considered her response. The agent clearly suspected a link between her and Dr. Cooper's disappearance... something Sarah herself suspected. But how could she explain to this brutish oaf what she herself barely understood?

Sarah realized that Murphy was studying her closely. "Since you won't elucidate your relationship with Dr. Cooper, let's discuss your recent internet activity. We've been monitoring it... for your safety and the safety of others."

Sarah stiffened, anger flaring at this revelation. "You've what?" she recoiled. "If there is one thing I know about the law, it's that monitoring my internet activity is a clear invasion of privacy!"

"We have an obligation to keep tabs on citizens who may have encountered... sensitive situations," Murphy replied evenly.

"You mean like researching cryptids after encountering one of the things?" Sarah challenged, her blood beginning to boil. "Clearly the *modus operandi* of your average criminal or terrorist—Do you even have a warrant for spying on my online activity? Or does that no longer apply when it comes to so-called sensitive situations?"

"Actually, you're the one who invited us in and agreed to cooperate," Murphy said, the condescension of a born bully starting to really show through.

"Then I'm afraid I'm also the one who is going to disinvite you; this chat is over until I speak to my lawyer!" Sarah had tired of this agent and whatever he wanted from her. It was time someone gave her information that she wanted!

As Sarah turned to grab her phone, a motion outside caught her eye—Murphy's female partner was approaching with a police dog.

Sarah whirled back. "What is your partner doing?" she demanded.

But before he answered, Sarah had already recognized Murphy's partner as the woman she had seen with him during her stay in the hospital. It sobered her, confirming that these two agents had been surreptitiously interested in her for some time.

"I told you, this is for your own protection," Murphy replied smoothly.

"I don't need or want your so-called protection!" Sarah snapped, storming towards the door.

But it was too late—the agent already had the dog sweeping the outside perimeter of Sarah's house, nose glued to the ground.

Sarah fumed, watching the warrantless trespass helplessly. She noticed Deputy Rogers was now striding up the driveway, taking in the scene with concern.

"Tell your partner to restrain her dog at once!" Sarah called back at Murphy. She took some satisfaction in seeing the surprised look on Rogers' face at her outburst.

Rogers approached cautiously. "Everything okay here, Sarah?"

"As my partner surely explained to you, Deputy, this doesn't concern you," Murphy said brusquely. "Official Homeland Security business!"

But Sarah stepped forward. "Actually, Deputy Rogers is a respected law enforcement officer of the community—you know, someone sworn to serve and protect people like me?"

She stared hard at Murphy. "Anything you say to me can be said in front of him."

Rogers looked surprised and then seemed to stand a bit taller. Emboldened, he turned to Murphy. "I'm going to need some answers about what exactly is going on here, sir."

Sarah allowed herself a small smile. Deputy Rogers was proving surprisingly helpful against the intimidating agent. She met Rogers' eyes briefly, something unspoken passing between them. His defensive posture relaxed into an easy confidence, and Sarah gave him a subtle grateful nod in return. Murphy coughed and shifted impatiently, but neither Sarah nor Rogers acknowledged him. An understanding had taken root between the two of them... no pretense or assumptions, just something like friendship...

Abruptly, the police dog began whining and cowering, tail tucked submissively between its legs as it was led toward the property's treeline. The female agent struggled to restrain it as the dog scrambled back from the trees.

Murphy's head snapped up, hand instinctively going to his holstered weapon. "What is it? What's wrong?" he called sharply.

The other agent looked baffled by her highly-trained dog's behavior. "I don't know... he's never reacted like this before."

"I thought you said dogs were the best way to deal with *these things*?" Murphy said back cryptically, but with a tightness in his voice that hadn't been there before.

"That's what I was told," Murphy's partner said defensively. "I was also told we should have secured a specialist dog handler as part of the team."

"Budget wouldn't allow for it," Murphy retorted.

Sarah and Deputy Rogers looked at each other fleetingly, unspoken questions filling the space between them.

Murphy stalked over to his partner, where they conferred in hushed, tense tones. Their eyes kept darting towards the treeline. "Let's check the perimeter," Murphy said finally. Hands placed tensely on their guns, they moved to sweep the area, the cowering dog dragging behind despite the agent's urging.

Sarah met Rogers' eyes again and saw her unease reflected there, his hand hovering over his holstered sidearm as they watched the agent's dog. Sarah had seen this kind of thing before at the shelter, where abused and frightened animals often came in exhibiting the same kind of behavior. She knew that whatever had sparked such a primal fear response in the animal was either lurking somewhere in the shadows or had left traces of itself—traces that the keen senses of other animals could pick up where humans could not.

A familiar chill was now running up and down her spine. Sarah recalled the prior night's drive when she'd glimpsed the creature that still haunted her nightmares, its malevolent eyes and hulking form now etched into her memory. Could it be stalking her even now in the treeline? The dog's terror seemed to confirm her worst fears. Sarah's heart quickened as she pictured the Dogman's demonic gnarled claws and salivating jaws, its coiled body resting, hidden, watching from behind the dark tree trunks.

As she watched, the agents cautiously moved along the treeline that marked the edge of her property—almost too cautiously. Their fear was palpable, and it had Sarah fighting a rising panic. Her mind kept flashing back to those unearthly eyes that had gazed at her with that incomprehensible, twisted intelligence. The agents may have weapons, but they were all prey against the kind of hellish thing she had seen. She could feel it out there, biding its time... *He is near...*

The agents completed a perimeter sweep, finding nothing obviously amiss in the encroaching twilight. Their dog still whined and resisted on its leash as they returned.

Sarah observed the agents carefully as they reconvened, noting their rigid posture and eyes that scanned back over the tree line. Though they hid it well, their tightly controlled movements gave away an underlying disquiet. Whatever they suspected was out there rattled them despite being armed. She knew they knew more than they let on about the darkness she was suffering.

Rogers stepped forward. "Now that you've finished accosting my friend here, and finished with your legally questionable property search, mind telling me what this is really about?"

The agents exchanged an annoyed look. "We'd like Ms. Shaw to accompany us to the location of her... disappearance," Murphy said tightly. "To clear up some inconsistencies in her account."

Sarah bristled, her dislike for Agent Murphy only intensifying. "I'm not going anywhere with you alone," she said.

"Very well, the deputy can escort you," Murphy conceded. He gritted his teeth. "We'll rendezvous at the coordinates tomorrow near dusk—say seventeen hundred hours?"

"Do I have a choice?" Sarah asked with a surly incline of her head.

The agents said nothing, so Sarah nodded reluctantly. She was not convinced in the slightest that these people had her best interests at heart, but she thought it was better to get this over with on her terms.

"Okay, it's set then," Murphy said gruffly, stealing another quick glance over his shoulder at the treeline.

Final arrangements for the meet were tersely confirmed before the agents took their leave, the dog almost dragging its handler to the SUV. Sarah watched them go with a mix of anger and dread. But the most unsettling thing about their unwelcome visit had been witnessing a robust and powerful police dog being turned into a whimpering puppy scared of its own tail... and the fact that these two Homeland Security agents had been there at the hospital during her recovery... watching her...

After the black SUV from Homeland Security had mooched off out of sight, Sarah turned to Rogers. "I don't trust them or their talk of inconsistencies. They seemed more interested in my psychologist, Dr. Cooper."

"Why would they be interested in your therapist?" Rogers asked, puzzled. "When they brought the dog out, I thought this had something to do with drugs." He looked at her and then gave an easy smile. "But knowing you, Ms. Sarah, that made no sense *whatsoever*."

Sarah smiled at Rogers, who gave a big, friendly shrug in return before Sarah turned serious again.

"After treating me, Dr. Cooper suddenly shut down her practice and vanished without explanation," Sarah explained. "Her office is now completely abandoned, and no one knows where she went!"

Rogers' brow furrowed. "Well, I guess that is a bit strange. I haven't heard anything about a missing person case involving Dr. Cooper or anything else that might be related." He pondered Sarah's information. "I'll tell you what, I'll run full background checks on them all and see what I can find." He paused, glancing back at the treeline uneasily, suddenly alert.

"What is it?" Sarah asked, turning.

"I thought I saw a face in the trees," Rogers said dismissively. But it's gone now… but I'm sure…"

"What did it look like?" Sarah pressed, trying to follow where Rogers' line of sight had been.

"Huge. Human-like features but massive, behind that tree." Rogers shrugged it off. "Just shadows playing tricks on me." He laughed half-heartedly. "Been reading too many Bigfoot reports it seems."

But Sarah was now feeling an odd sense of reassurance wash over her. The face hadn't been that of some hellishly monstrous dog; there was something else there. As if feeling it deep in her soul, Sarah knew what, or rather who lingered in the forest. With an almost magical sense of relief, she felt as if an old ally was watching over her.

She stifled a smile as Rogers turned to leave, and she followed him down the driveway to the street where his police cruiser was still parked. They confirmed their meeting for tomorrow, with a perturbed Deputy Rogers still shaking his head at what he thought he had seen. But, as she waved him goodbye, Sarah felt an absolute comfort embracing her over what had just happened. Though she hadn't seen the face in the treeline that had startled Rogers, Sarah was feeling a reassuring presence that she could not quite put her finger on, a feeling that she was not as alone as she had been over the last few weeks. Something, or *someone*, was out there, keeping watch... and then it happened! The voice returned...

"Sarah... careful... he is near..."

6

On the drive out the next day, Rogers gave Sarah an update: "I haven't been able to dig up anything substantial on those Homeland Security agents or your Dr. Cooper yet. It's concerning."

Sarah was pensive despite having had the first night of natural sleep in weeks. The voice in her head had gone as soon as it had come, followed by mellow warmth that had enveloped her soul. Looking at Rogers beside her, his hands nonchalantly steering the big police cruiser to their destination, she decided to chance her arm and let him in closer, let him know what she was thinking about.

"I've been thinking, what if the regression session revealed something critical or sensitive about my missing days?" Sarah speculated. "Maybe Dr. Cooper learned things they wanted to be kept secret. That's why the agents were so interested in her."

"What's an *aggression* session?" Rogers asked innocently, his brow arching suspiciously as he focused on the road ahead.

Sarah had to smother a laugh.

"*Re*-gression," she corrected him. "It's when they hypnotize you so they can ask you questions about things buried in your subconscious."

Rogers was thoughtful.

"You mean like they do in serial killer cases with witnesses?" He nodded grimly. "Cool!"

Sarah looked at the strapping deputy. He was a physically solid man who, until recently, had been all bluster and unattractive male ego as far as she was concerned, a persistent social irritant who couldn't seem to take a subtle no for an answer. But here, in his expansive police cruiser, she decided she liked him, but strictly as a friend. How fate can pick your friends from the most unlikely candidates was strange, Sarah thought, but she liked how things were turning out.

"I get this feeling that everything that's happened to me has to do with those missing five days," Sarah said quietly. "Five days that I just can't remember."

Rogers gave her a quick glance. "Then let's hope these guys find some clues today." He turned his eyes back to the road, but his thoughts were obviously elsewhere. "But I have to tell you, Sarah, I don't like this one bit." He checked his gun instinctively.

"Don't like what?" Sarah asked pensively.

"I don't like being told I'm restricted–" he looked at Sarah again, his mouth pinched and bothered. "–Restricted from being told what I want to know!"

"Yeah," said Sarah, softly. "I know the feeling. It's concerning."

The familiar forestry parking area was just ahead, a lonely clearing some ten miles deep into some of the densest woodland in the county. As Sarah and Deputy Rogers pulled in, an ominous silence permeated the trees around them.

Sarah felt her uneasiness return as Rogers pulled onto the deserted forest trail that led to the parking area. It was too quiet, and only their vehicle disturbed the silence. She shivered, memories of that creeping fear that had consumed her during that fateful hike blinking back into her mind.

“Place gives me the creeps,” said Rogers. He rested his hand on his holstered gun as they spotted the lone parked black SUV belonging to Agent Murphy and his partner.

Rogers steered his police cruiser toward the Homeland Security vehicle and stopped about twenty feet away. He and Sarah got out together and approached the SUV from the rear, its black-tinted windows dully reflecting the dark woods around them.

“Doesn’t look like anyone’s home,” Rogers muttered as he and Sarah made for the driver’s side.

They found the doors were unlocked, keys still inside. Sarah hesitated before looking in the backseat. She recoiled—the male agent lay crumpled face up on the floorboards. His throat was savagely torn open, dried blood coating his shredded clothes.

“My god...” Rogers whispered, instinctively reaching for his radio to call it in.

While he turned away, Sarah found herself inexplicably hurrying to the SUV’s rear cargo area, opening its back hatch door and rooting around. There, as if she were meant to find them, was a box of files clearly labeled with Dr. Cooper’s name, with an additional subheading showing another name; ‘Sarah Shaw!’

Rogers was having trouble getting through to his dispatch operator when he belatedly realized what Sarah was doing. He scolded her, yelling something about her contaminating a crime scene, but Sarah was too intent on reading her inscribed name on the box of files to heed him. She held up the box to Rogers.

“It’s got my name on it!” she said breathlessly.

"I don't care!" Rogers shouted. "You've got to put it back where you found it!"

"But this could—"

"Hang on!" Rogers cut her off, panic starting to set in. "There's two of them... where's the other one, the government chick with the dog?"

Rogers looked wildly about them, but Agent Murphy's partner was nowhere to be seen.

"Maybe she didn't come," Sarah suggested nervously, her eyes darting back and forth.

"That's not how these government types operate," Rogers shouted. He tried his radio again, but only static greeted his efforts. "I can't get anything..." He fruitlessly stabbed the device with his fingers.

Rogers then took out his phone.

"What!" he spat, holding his mobile up and out, reaching for a signal. "Nothing! No connection!"

But Sarah was getting something, some connection from within: *"Sarah... leave...not safe..."*

Then it came; a bone-rattling *WHOOP!* echoed from the forest, followed by multiple agonized wails like a woman being murdered. Sounds of monstrous destruction carried on the wind—trees snapping, earth trembling. Then a woman's scream, penetratingly urgent, abruptly silenced!

Rogers blanched, stumbling back. Sarah's blood ran cold as the voice in her mind repeated: *"Leave now...not safe."* She didn't argue, nor did Rogers. They both fled to the cruiser and took off, the sounds of carnage fading behind them. Sarah didn't dare look back, the voice in her head getting weaker the further they drove away. But Rogers did take a look back in his rear mirror—

"What the—!" he blurted out, his voice a strangled octave higher than usual.

"What?" shrilled Sarah, her eyes locked on the deputy's face as he wildly slammed his foot down on the cruiser's accelerator.

"Just drive!" he scolded himself as they lurched forward, the car gathering speed as the trees began to blur on either side.

"What did you see?" Sarah demanded, oblivious to the new danger Rogers was putting them in as he recklessly careened down the forest road.

"Nothing!" he bawled. "I didn't see *nothing*!"

"Tim!" Sarah screamed. "Slow down, or you'll kill us!"

Sarah's words somehow found their way into the deputy's panicked brain. He started to decelerate, but his nervousness came out in a torrent of sweat dripping down his forehead. He flicked it away and gave Sarah a glancing look of sheer fright.

"Some dog!" he stammered. "I saw some dog coming up behind us!"

"Some dog?" Sarah spluttered back, a sickening feeling dripping down into her bowels. "What kind of dog?"

But Sarah already thought she knew the answer...

"A big dog—Huge! Biggest I've ever seen!" Rogers looked at her again, the horror in his eyes clearly visible. "I've never seen anything like that in my life..."

"Like what?" Sarah asked, that sickening feeling now in her throat.

Deputy Tim Rogers seemed to take an eternity to answer, but when he did, there was raw fear in his voice. A tear rolled down his cheek.

"It was a huge black dog... Chasing us... Fast! It was running on *two* legs... Like a human... But fast!" Rogers shook his head violently as if to shake the image out of his brain. "I saw it running on two legs, Sarah."

They drove in shocked silence for another five minutes—it could have been hours for all they knew—when Rogers' police radio spluttered into life. Rogers reacted like a snake had just bitten him.

"Dispatch calling Unit 231, come in," came the static heavy voice over its speaker.

Rogers fumbled at the receiver: "Where *the hell* have you been, Dispatch?"

Sarah flinched at the intensity in Rogers' words.

"Come again, Unit 231?" the voice replied.

"I've been trying to get through," Rogers hissed back into the radio's mic. We have a situation out at the car park at the end of forest road number 31! It's a government agent *down* kind of situation!"

"Units responding now," confirmed the voice. *"Advise on current status?"*

"*En route* with a witness," advised Rogers with a glance at Sarah.

"Roger that, Unit 231," the voice replied, signing off with a crackle.

"A witness?" Sarah queried, looking sideways at Rogers as he barrelled the police cruiser through the forest. "You expect me to tell people about what we just saw... what we just heard?"

Rogers shook his head again like he had burning wax in his ear.

"No, Sarah," he said, trying to lower his voice to something that might sound like he was in control. "There's a dead government agent out there, and we are the two people who found him." He looked at her again, a pleading expression taking over his face. "That's what you *and me* are witnesses to."

Sarah immediately regretted her terse, even self-centered response.

"His throat was ripped out," she whimpered.

"I know," said Rogers. "Hella'va way to die!"

Sarah thought back to the scene; the body of Agent Murphy stuffed into the rear floor space of his SUV, blood soaking everything. And then it hit her: She looked about herself madly but couldn't see it.

"What's wrong?" Rogers asked anxiously.

"It's not here!" Sarah shouted. She turned to Rogers, her eyes pleading. "We have to go back!" she implored him, hysteria threatening to overwhelm her.

"No. Way. On. God's green earth are we going back there!" Rogers barked emphatically, looking like he was about to burst into tears.

Sarah burst into tears.

"But... the box!" Sarah begged. "I dropped the box of files... it had my name on it!"

Rogers turned to her, his breathing heavy, ragged, and labored.

"It's evidence, Sarah!" He tried a reassuring smile, which looked more like he was trying to swallow something nasty. "If I can, I'll find out for you what's in that damned box."

The weather was turning ugly again, spots of dark rain hitting the police cruiser's windshield hard. They drove on.

7

"It's for your own safety, Sarah. Just one night."

Sarah had begun to loathe that phrase.

When Sarah and Rogers had finally pulled up, the Sheriff's Department building had been a hive of urgent activity. Drenching showers had started washing over the building, and a distant, delicate sound of thunder had roiled the horizon as dusk had given way to the blackest night.

Rogers' insistence on protective custody grated on Sarah's frayed nerves. But glancing at the deputy's exhausted, pleading eyes, she relented. The day's trauma haunted him, too.

The holding cell was sparse but secure, with officers always nearby. Sleep eluded Sarah as nearby police radios crackled incessantly with muted reports that she strained to comprehend. Words like 'savaged' and 'unnatural' reached her ears.

Dawn finally came, and with it, a break in the weather. Rogers arrived, uniform freshly pressed, but dark circles under his eyes telling a different story of a night fraught with fear.

"Hey," he said gently. "The sheriff wants us back at the scene. More questions, I'm afraid."

Sarah tensed. "Do we have to?"

Rogers nodded regretfully. "Afraid so. But we'll get through this."

She saw the same dread in his eyes that gripped her chest at the thought of returning. But they had no choice.

Their drive to the scene was quiet, the unspoken memories hanging heavy between them.

The remote parking area was now a hive of activity. The night's rain had muddied things up, but there was an unnerving freshness to the place that had not been there the day before. The morning sun hurt Sarah's eyes as she took in the scene. A white tent shrouded the black SUV as a crime scene unit went about it, still collecting samples and doing other things crime scene units do.

Sarah thought about the box of files with her name on it. It was nowhere to be seen.

Rogers guided Sarah through the hustle and bustle of law enforcement personnel, and Sarah was alert enough to spot 'FBI' emblazoned on the windbreakers of a couple of important-looking men observing the situation. One of the men was a tall fit looking individual with a military-like haircut. He seemed intent on watching Sarah and Rogers from behind dark sunglasses. He gave Sarah the creeps.

"Word is this whole thing is going to be handed over to the Feds once us local guys get through doing all the hard work," said Rogers as he sensed Sarah's questioning glance at the presence of yet more Federal agents. "The US Park Police have jurisdiction here, but they need us to secure the area and make preliminary inquiries... The usual interagency pissing contests."

Sarah nodded her understanding but was perturbed by how things had escalated from a matter of a local missing person to something now increasingly in the hands of the United States government—and involving murder!

With reassuring hands on her shoulders, Rogers brought Sarah to a makeshift station littered with communications gear and other equipment. State troopers and sheriffs' deputies eyed them curiously but kept their distance. Rogers stood sentry as an older man in a rumpled suit introduced himself as Senior Detective Mark Lee, the lead investigator from the local sheriff's department.

"He's a good man, but he plays it by the book," Rogers cautioned Sarah quietly.

"I take it you have already given your statement," said Lee to Rogers.

"Yes, sir. Detective Andrews is processing it as we speak."

Turning his attention to Sarah, Lee began by asking about events the previous evening, acknowledging that she had already made her own statement at the Sheriff's Department headquarters. He had a kindly manner in the way he asked his questions and listened intently as she answered. Sarah gave him the same general rundown on how she and Rogers had come across Agent Murphy's body. As she struggled with the memory of the ghastly scene, Sarah thought again of the files with her name and couldn't help herself.

"I saw a box of files with my name on it," she blurted out.

Rogers looked like he was going to have a heart attack, but he kept quiet.

"A box of files?" queried Lee, his interest heightening, but only slightly. "What kind of files?"

"There was a box of files in the back of the SUV. I saw them... with my name on it; Sarah Shaw!" Sarah asserted again.

The detective looked mystified.

"We didn't find any files, Ms. Shaw," he drawled, far too casually for Sarah's liking. "Are you sure about this? After all, you've been through quite a bit."

Sarah glanced at Rogers, who met her eyes with an imperceptible shake of his head. Bile whelmed in her throat, but she realized she was pushing things too far, maybe getting them into trouble.

"Could be," she conceded, casting her eyes downwards, defeated.

"Could be what?" insisted Lee.

Rogers gritted his teeth in the face of Lee's badgering tone, but he kept his cool.

"Could be I made a mistake," Sarah relented.

Sarah felt her persistence over the box of files had nearly turned into a dangerous moment, and she regretted her outburst. She looked at Rogers apologetically, but he gave her a reassuring smile, and she dutifully repeated the final details of her original statement concerning their discovery of Agent Murphy's body. As she finished up it seemed all to the satisfaction of Detective Lee.

Sarah had made no mention of the sounds of forest destruction and the animalistic screams that had driven Sarah and Rogers to flee the scene, let alone Rogers' sighting of a huge dog-like creature chasing them on its hind legs; Sarah now realized more than ever that some truths, it seemed, were far too dangerous to share if you wanted life to remain uncomplicated.

Afternoon eventually brought their release from Detective Lee's inquisitiveness. He had finally asked Sarah if she had seen anything out of the ordinary upon discovering Agent Murphy's body, like any large predatory animals; bears or wolves and so on. But she had played it dumb.

As Sarah and Rogers walked to his cruiser, she heard one of the deputies remark, "Ain't no animal I know did that. We're damn lucky whatever's out there didn't pick us off one by one last night."

Rogers tensed at the words but didn't respond as he went to open his cruiser's passenger door for Sarah. There were no words for a situation like this, only the shared trauma between those who know.

A burst of activity brought them up short at that moment. A group of law enforcement officers emerged from the darkened treeline with shouts, summoning the detective and his people. They were being urged to come and see what had just been found.

"They've got something," said a state trooper nearby to Sarah and Rogers.

"Something about a woman, I think," said another trooper, his head straining to pick up on the kafuffle of noise that now swirled about the investigating officials.

Sarah and Rogers looked at each other. Without saying anything, both knew this had something to do with Agent Murphy's missing female partner.

"I want to see," Sarah said to Rogers as most of the gathered law enforcement people drifted anxiously towards where the officers had emerged from the forest.

"Are you sure?" Rogers asked, wary of what Sarah was asking. "Could be bad after what we heard."

"And what did you hear, deputy?" said a voice from behind them.

It was one of the men with FBI written on his jacket; the tall, fit military-looking one. His sunglasses reflected Sarah and Rogers dully in the encroaching forest gloom.

Rogers and Sarah started, their worn nerves jumping at the intrusion. Rogers looked at the FBI man seriously.

"What you probably just heard," Rogers said earnestly. "That they've found something!"

The FBI man gave Rogers a stiff stare and then sauntered off to join the others moving towards the new discovery. Sarah gave Rogers a cagey smile, impressed by how he had rescued the situation. He smiled back sheepishly.

"This is not to say that I endorse lying to the FBI, Ms. Sarah Shaw," he drawled. "But sometimes..."

Sarah let out a small laugh but quickly remembered the seriousness of their situation.

"To answer your question, yes, we have to see what they've found."

"If you insist, Ms. Sarah," Rogers said dubiously. "But don't say I didn't warn you."

Sarah and Rogers followed the investigators through the dense forest to a small, gloomy clearing. As they walked, Rogers whispered into Sarah's ear: "Don't worry; I'm getting that sour gut feeling, too. It happens to virtually everyone in these situations if they're honest about it."

Even so, Sarah could feel the hand of terror crawling up her spine as they drew nearer to what awaited. The police had formed an irregular ring around a small clearing, their hushed voices and darting eyes revealing unease. After a solemn nod from the lead detective, the officers slowly parted to allow Sarah and Rogers into the scene. Detective Lee, professional to the last, observed Sarah's reaction on seeing what lay before them.

Sarah's hand flew to her mouth, choking back bile. The female agent, or what was left of her, lay splayed on her back, arms and legs sprawled unnaturally wide. She had been stripped entirely naked, her clothes torn violently away.

Her torso had been sliced open from throat to navel with bizarre precision, and the skin and muscle peeled cleanly back to expose the empty ribcage within. All organs had been removed, leaving only a vacant cavity lined with glistening bone.

Yet there was no blood pooled anywhere. The body and surrounding earth were oddly colorless. The excisions had been performed with meticulous care, severing arteries with seemingly laser-like perfection.

Nest to the supine agent, her stomach and entire digestive tract had been carefully arranged in a coil, like a nest of dead snakes. Sarah could see other organs had been placed in an arcane pattern radiating out from the body.

Sarah's basic veterinary training told her that the visible cuts to the woman's body were impossibly smooth, with no tool marks visible. No blade Sarah could conceive of could inflict such flawless incisions. It seemed so artificially unnatural.

Looking at the agent's lifeless face, Sarah could see that it was frozen in a rictus of primal fear, lips parted in a silent scream. Her eyes had been surgically extracted, leaving empty sockets grotesquely staring into a blind infinity.

Sarah was aware of the investigators around her speaking in stunned, hushed tones, unable themselves to comprehend the bizarre scene. This area had supposedly been searched multiple times already, yet, only now, had the body been discovered, staged for all to see with disturbing ritualistic purpose. How? Recriminations were building between the various agencies represented at the scene.

Among the mystified local police, a quiet panic had begun to build. This was beyond anything any of them had ever experienced—the work of cults, aliens, or forces outside their understanding? Dark possibilities were whispered just out of hearing...

Rogers placed a shaky but comforting hand on Sarah's shoulder, equal parts protective and grateful not to be alone in this nightmare. Unable to tear her gaze away, Sarah knew—the answers she sought surely waited in the malign shadows around them if only someone, even herself, dared to ask the question.

But Sarah was not ready to ask the question.

"I need to get out of here," she whispered, trembling.

Rogers nodded, guiding her back through the maze of stunned officers. As they headed for his cruiser, Detective Lee deftly intercepted them.

"Not so fast," he said. "We will obviously need more answers about your ties to the victims."

"Later," Rogers insisted, steering Sarah past him. "She's done for now... Sir!"

The detective nodded, recognizing that Rogers had a point. He courteously gave way, waving them on with a kindly yet thoughtful look.

The gathered investigators' low voices faded as Sarah and Rogers emerged from the trees. But then, a blood-chilling howl echoed out of the forest depths.

The law enforcement officers around them all rushed to grab weapons, eyes darting about. The sound was unlike the cries Sarah and Rogers had heard the day before—they were deeper, more primal.

Rogers quickened their pace, leaning in close. "That's no ordinary wolf or dog making that noise," he murmured shakily.

Sarah shuddered. She whispered back, barely able to hear her own voice. "Tim... *He* is near..."

A stern voice interrupted. "Who's near, Ms. Shaw?"

It was the same FBI agent again, but with his sunglasses removed. He was studying Sarah keenly with a set of deep and unkind eyes, eyes that bore no empathy. But before Sarah could reply, a thunderclap split the sky and the heavens unleashed a deluge of rain. It was as if the full force of Mother Nature had caught them all napping.

Sarah looked skywards. It was close to dusk, and that familiar feeling of unknowing horror was again seeping into her consciousness. An overpowering smell of putrefaction filled the air, and Sarah began to panic.

"Do you smell that?" she asked the FBI agent, but Rogers intervened quickly.

"Something stinks! And we gotta go!" Rogers declared, hustling Sarah into the cruiser.

The agent watched them depart, water streaming down his intense yet impassive face.

As the clambered into Rogers' cruiser Sarah felt the bite of the rain soak through to her skin. Whatever dark forces were gathering, she thought, now was the time to go. She looked about her and grimly wondered for how long they could play this game before things finally caught up with them...

8

Sarah and Rogers returned to Sarah's cabin as the weather closed into a steady downpour. Rogers gathered some equipment from the trunk of his cruiser. Sarah noted an overnight kit—standard for most police units—and Rogers' police radio. Besides his sidearm, Sarah also realized Rogers had brought a police-issue shotgun, complete with a muzzle-mounted flashlight—he was bringing it into her house. Usually, this would be a total no-no, but she thought about the circumstances and decided not to make a big deal over it—at least not this time!

"I'll take the couch," Rogers said, glancing around nervously as they entered Sarah's house. "No arguments—I'm staying over. Whatever's going on, you shouldn't be alone."

Sarah nodded, finding herself unusually comforted by another person's presence. Before, anyone telling her that one day Deputy Tim Rogers would be spending the night in her home would have been laughed off into next week. But things had changed in ways that not even the most gifted fortune-teller could have ever envisioned.

"Thank you," she said to Rogers. "I know this goes beyond your duty, so I appreciate it."

Rogers gave a good-natured shrug. "That was some pretty messed-up stuff back there..." He hesitated. "What you said back there, about 'he is near'—can we talk about that?"

Sarah thought about his request for a moment, the image of the mutilated female agent still playing on her mind, but then decided that it was time Rogers knew—time someone really heard what had happened weeks ago in a forest glade while out on an autumn hike.

“Let me get us a couple of mugs of coffee, and then we can talk,” she offered.

“Best idea I’ve heard all day,” Rogers breezed as cheerfully as he could.

Sarah brought their coffees, and the two sipped lightly as Sarah gathered her thoughts and strength. Eventually, she put down her mug, took a deep breath, and began describing her original dogman encounter—its towering height, muscular wolf-like appearance, and malevolent intelligence.

Rogers' face paled as she recalled the creature he had seen the day before, its pointed ears and massive clawed hands vivid in his memory. Sarah could see his mind flashing back to the giant canine form running on two legs that he’d seen in the rear-view mirror. Sarah’s intense account matched that brief glimpse all too closely. Rogers listened intently, cold dread creeping through him as she detailed the creature's unnatural speed and vindictive gaze.

When she finished, Rogers sat in silence, stunned. Sarah’s experience aligned with his own run-in with the seemingly impossible creature. He ran a hand down his face. Just what had they stumbled into?

“I’ve heard of predators bearing grudges over lost kills,” he said. “If it thought that the sasquatch you saw was its prey, and then you got in its way...” He shook his head in disbelief. “But to keep pursuing you this long? It’s unnatural.”

Sarah nodded, her mind reliving the frightening events from a few weeks ago over and over.

"There's something peculiar about this creature," Sarah insisted. "It won't stop until..." She trailed off, chilled by the unspoken thought.

Rogers attempted a reassuring smile. "Hey, we'll be fine. I've got my guns and my training. Imagine how popular I'd be if I made the first-ever arrest of a dogman." He laughed at the thought. "I could even run for sheriff... if I did that." He chuckled again, but his eyes betrayed his lingering doubts.

Sarah hoped Rogers' weapons would prove needless. She had heard and read enough tales and accounts by other witnesses stating that dogmen were no ordinary animals to be deterred by bullets. But, given the nature of what seemed to be out there, all they could do was wait. The depths of the night were now closer than ever... maybe a night of reckoning...

"There is one other thing I would like to tell you," Sarah said softly, a hint of trepidation in her voice. "I've been getting voices in my head..."

She trailed off, but Rogers gave her a nudge.

"Go on."

"...It started when I saw the Sasquatch and realized it had a child with it..." She trailed off again, worried that she was about to stretch Rogers' incredulity to breaking point.

"Sarah?" he prompted. "Go on."

"Look," said Sarah. "The first time I heard the words '*he is near*' was when I first saw the Sasquatch."

She felt an urgent need to convince Rogers of what she was saying.

"I think the Sasquatch was communicating with me... warning me." She looked at Rogers, a desperate need to have him believe her. "I think it was the Sasquatch that saved me!"

Rogers didn't do anything for a long time.

"Are you saying that this Bigfoot Sasquatch spoke to you, all telephonically-*capathically*, or something," he murmured in hushed, disbelieving tones. "...And then it saved you from that... *thing*?"

Sarah stared at Rogers.

"Fine! Laugh if you want! But I thought you would be interested to know—considering everything that's happened in the last couple of days!"

Rogers held up his hands apologetically, quickly trying to douse Sarah's flare-up.

"No, no, no," he said, imploring her to hear him out. "I totally understand what you're saying, and I think it's totally possible—even cool! Like you said, how could I not with all the crap that's gone down lately." He lowered his hands, his voice taking on the best conciliatory tone he could muster. "I'm actually a pretty simple guy when it comes to most things, Sarah. And this stuff just has me all confounded and stuff."

Sarah considered his words.

"I don't want you shooting sasquatches thinking they're a dogman!" She declared, her fists bunching up in frustration, the entire situation suddenly unbearable.

"Okay, okay," accepted Rogers. "I get it; sasquatch good, dogman bad."

His latent gift for the flippant was now starting to annoy Sarah, just like he had always done.

"Tim, I'm going to bed!" She gave him a disproving look. "Try not to ventilate the entire cabin with your guns if something goes bump in the night."

Sarah turned and stalked off to her room, leaving Rogers to give the cabin that 'what did I say?' look.

Sarah lay on her bed, the light turned off, reviling herself for getting angry at Rogers. After all, he'd been there for her when the now dead Homeland Security agents had come harassing her, and he had been there to support her during their awful discovery of agent Murphy's body... and everything that had happened since then. Sarah chastised herself again, the tiredness of the day's events causing her mind to drift. She thought about going through to apologize to Rogers...

... And then something went bump!

9

Sarah was startled awake by a dull thump outside, like something heavy had just landed on the soft earth by her room. Pulling the curtain back and peering tentatively out the window, she was struck by the stillness of the night. The storm had passed, leaving only a full moon shining brightly over a blanket of mist. But it was the quietness of the scene that unnerved her, an abnormal silence that was more still than any photograph.

Something moved...

Sarah could see two orbs of light drifting in tandem among the trees at the edge of her property, about where agent Murphy and his partner had searched with their dog two nights before. The orbs were basketball size, but as she was processing the strangely calming phenomenon, she heard an urgent whisper from Rogers coming from the kitchen—"Sarah! You gotta see this."

She tore herself away from the floating lights and hurried to the kitchen where Rogers was also watching the orbs from a different angle, their luminosity more ethereal than actual. Sarah saw Rogers had his shotgun in hand. "What do you think those are?" he asked excitedly. "Some kind of alien UFO things or something?"

But Sarah sensed a familiar presence. "It's here to help us," she whispered back.

If Rogers heard her, he didn't let on. He seemed bamboozled by the free-floating lights.

Sarah thought about the many witness accounts she had read where people often talked about encountering glowing orbs shortly before Bigfoot sightings.

As Sarah and Rogers watched, the orbs were joined by a third, smaller light. But it quickly faded out. Sarah felt a stabbing pain touch at the edges of her mind and was quickly immersed in a dark vision—the flash of violence, a child Sasquatch screaming.

"Her child is dead," Sarah murmured.

"A child? Dead?" spluttered Rogers, his eyes still absorbed by the dimly lit phenomenon outdoors. "Who's child?"

Rogers started to ask Sarah again, but then a massive form emerged from the trees. Sarah had to hold up a restraining hand to stop Rogers from raising his gun. She could feel only calm certainty as the giant shape of the Sasquatch approached the window, its face eerily lit by the moon.

"My god, he's huge!" Rogers said, stunned by its nine-foot stature and its deep-set eyes. "*Aw*, man! That's the face I saw the other night... it's him!"

"It's a female," Sarah corrected him, her own sense of calmness almost frightening her as the Sasquatch drew nearer. "It has boobs."

"Oh," was all Rogers could say, unsure whether to be embarrassed or avert his eyes. He still fingered his shotgun fretfully, though.

The Sasquatch stopped with its face close to the window's glass pane. Its breath fogged the glass as it peered in, and Sarah felt like it was looking deep into her being.

"She can't see us," she managed to say to Rogers. "The moonlight outside is too bright, and the window is reflecting her own image back to her like a mirror..." She faltered. "But she can hear us."

In Sarah's mind, a gentle voice resonated, tinged with mournful acceptance: "*My child is gone; you are not to blame. Paths cross for a purpose.*" Sarah closed her eyes as the maternal spirit in her mind soothed her guilt. Now she knew that this Sasquatch had been the one that had saved her and that her infant had been the price. It hurt to finally confirm what she realized she had always somehow known... always felt...

"What?" Rogers interrupted, seeing that Sarah had dropped into a trance-like stare. "Is it doing that head thing you talked about?"

Sarah listened, initially ignoring Rogers and then nodding as the Sasquatch continued peering intently into its own reflection. It then put a hand up to the window, and Sarah knew it sought a more meaningful contact. She raised her hand, and an astonished Rogers watched as both females touched palms together, only the glass between them.

"She's telling me," Sarah breathed, "she's telling me... that—*he is here!*"

The Sasquatch turned abruptly, a strange pulsating glow forming at the bottom of Sarah's driveway. Sarah and Rogers watched in terrified awe as the pinpoint of light expanded, its blooming shape starting to resemble a tunnel-like structure. *Like a portal*, Sarah thought.

And then a shadowy, muscular form started to writhe within the hypnotic entranceway. The beast's movements were at once frenzied and unnatural as it struggled against the clinging luminescence. Its sinuous writhing to break free suggested the actions of a partially birthed creature.

The creature then tore itself free with a disturbing defiance of gravity, dropping heavily to the ground on all fours.

Sarah's blood turned to ice as the hulking beast rose on its hind legs. Memories flooded back at the sight of the creature's pointed ears, robust frame, and baleful gaze radiating absolute *vindictiveness*!

It had returned!

The Dogman cometh...

"The shotgun? Now?" Rogers asked urgently. He raised his weapon to take aim.

"Bullets do nothing to them!" Sarah gasped.

Rogers experienced a stultifying moment of indecisiveness—should he even attempt to blow the thing away, or...

The Dogman wavered, snarling as if scanning for its prey. Sarah and Rogers retreated a couple of steps from the window in terror.

Only then did Sarah realize that the Sasquatch had vanished as if it had never been there. She desperately searched the treeline for the orbs, but they, too, were absent.

"She's gone!" she hissed urgently at Rogers, his face reflecting her horror.

"Well... what do we do?" Rogers spluttered, spittle spraying everywhere.

The Dogman's ears pricked up, its keen senses latching on to Rogers' words. It bared its fangs, focusing on Rogers' voice behind the flimsy glass plane where Sarah and Rogers stood. Its ears now flattened against its enormous dog-like skull, like some monstrous vicious Doberman poised to attack. Sarah caught her breath as the vile creature again dropped to all fours, its latent speed and power bristling through its shiny black fur. But then, a deep hooting erupted from the dark trees, followed by branches crashing.

Before Sarah could react, an ear-splitting crack resounded as a massive tree was ripped from the earth and hurled up into the night sky. It carved out an arc through the air, its trajectory bringing it down on the Dogman's position. But the creature narrowly dodged the improvised missile as it skittered and demolished Rogers' parked cruiser, shooting splinters in all directions.

"My car!" Rogers yelped in dismay.

Sarah watched terror-stricken as the Sasquatch stepped halfway into view, its enormous bulk glistening in the moonlight, its massive feet pounding the ground as it howled violently. The Dogman whipped its head around towards the commotion, distracted from its initial prey.

Like a scene out of *Gotterdammerung*, the titans sized each other up, muscles rippling beneath fur and sinew, hair and hide. The Dogman's ears flattened as the Sasquatch's chest swelled with a booming hoot. For a moment, the Dogman hesitated, torn between the defiant prey before it and the vulnerable humans inside. Hunger won out—it turned to stalk the retreating Sasquatch.

Seeing her chance, the Sasquatch cautiously withdrew back into the woods. The dogman bounded after it in an instant, vanishing between the darkened trunks of the trees. A crashing of trees and branches became a tumult of agonized howls and ear-splitting shrieks.

Before Rogers could react, Sarah flung the kitchen door open and made to pursue the creatures.

Rogers' desperate shouts of warning faded behind her as Sarah stumbled into the forest. Thrashing and roars of combat rang through the darkness. She glimpsed flashes of fur, claws, and snapping jaws locked in mortal combat. She was close, but her human eyes simply could not resolve the dark maelstrom of mortal struggle taking place mere feet from her.

The unwieldy beasts crashed deeper into the woods, the sounds and quaking impacts receding, but a now familiar stench of rotting eggs mixed with decayed fish lingered. Sarah desperately wanted to go on, chasing the carnage, but felt Rogers' hands pull her back.

"Sarah, wait!" Rogers shouted after her. "We can't fight that thing even if we've got a Bigfoot on our side!"

But Sarah called back, "I have to try something—She saved me before!"

Rogers struggled to restrain her. "It's too dangerous! What if it's that dogman thing that comes back?"

"Please, trust me!" she implored, breaking loose again.

But she only moved a few more feet before she realized the craziness of what she was doing. She stopped, crouching in the darkness, listening, nearly sobbing. Rogers came up behind her again, his shotgun in hand.

"They're gone," he said quietly, his words coming in heavy breaths. "But if you want, we can wait here... see what's happened.

Sarah nodded, the thick trunks of the trees around them providing a sense of cover for them both.

They waited together, anxiously, inside the treeline, looking for any sign of the battle's victor. But now, the unnatural silence had returned. No birds greeted the dawn as it finally appeared, the quietness chilling Sarah more than the dawn's frigid light.

"It's getting cold," Rogers eventually said. "We should get back inside, and I can call in some help."

“What about helping her?” Sarah asked testily, flinging her hand out in the direction the running battle had faded away to.

But Rogers had his eyes on the trees. They widened.

“Oh. My. God!” he said breathlessly, and pointed.

The hulking form of the female Sasquatch lurched into view, not more than twenty feet away, the trees hiding most of its great shaggy body in the shadows. It met Sarah’s relieved eyes with a look of profound mourning. But Sarah felt she could also feel a sense of life, though she knew it was she who should be most grateful to be alive now. Sarah blinked, and it was gone, its vast bulk disappearing again into the primordial world from which it had come.

“I’ll never doubt you again,” Rogers whispered to her. “That... that Bigfoot really seems to like you.”

Sarah stood for a moment, her thoughts willing a message of thanks in the wake of the creature’s departure.

They returned to the house and surveyed the cruiser’s caved-in roof and shattered windows. The massive tree lay overturned beside it, roots jutting skyward.

“So, uh, a tornado...?” Sarah suggested, her sense of the absurd not entirely lost to the night's events.

Rogers shook his head, wondering how he would ever explain things to his boss.

10

As the dawn turned to early morning, a bunch of deputies arrived, about three of them with a van from the county's animal control agency. They eyed a dishevelled Deputy Tim Rogers with more than askance looks. After supposedly spending the night with a woman they knew he was sweet on, the deputies were amused to find Rogers looking like hell. However, the man from animal control knew Sarah from the animal shelter and had the sense to know that when a woman had that look on her face, it was best to keep one's thoughts to one's self.

One of the deputies chided Rogers, "We had some noise complaints from the neighbors." He was an older guy and probably Rogers's senior.

"Yeah," laughed another deputy, who looked fresh out of college. "Some real *animal* noises they said was going on over here," he grinned salaciously as the other deputies smirked and giggled in a high voice.

Sarah groaned inwardly, but Rogers was having none of it. He shouldered his shotgun, which made the deputies step back a bit.

"If any of you reprobates can tell me how a twenty-foot tree can end up planted upside down on top of a Sheriff Department's cruiser, then maybe, just maybe, I'll tell you all about last night," he snapped. "—Not that any of you would have a clue about what went down here last night, even if it turned up and slapped you silly six ways from Sunday!"

The deputies all stiffened, looking wide-eyed at the offending tree as if they had only just now noticed it.

"Well, hang on there, Timmy," the older one said, taken aback by Rogers' outburst. "We was just joshing—"

"Save it, *Steve*," Rogers bit back. "Now get your animal guy to take a look in the woods back there and see if he can find anything that might explain these noise complaints the county Sheriff's Office seems so keen on investigating!"

The gathered deputies were indecisive, wondering whether to take offense, maybe call Rogers to order. Sarah saw them look at Rogers' hard-set eyes, and saw them all decide against it. Sarah couldn't help smiling at their discomfort, but she gave the animal control worker as friendly a wave as she could as he was summoned to take a look at the tree line. He gave her a nod in return and then went about his business.

Rogers turned to Sarah, and she could see his eyes were still burning.

"Sorry about that," he apologized. "Some guys never grow up!"

Sarah gave him a pleased look, but he bent in closer to her, his face only inches away from hers but carefully angled away from his colleagues.

"Don't tell these apes *nothing*," he advised her earnestly. "They'll only make fun of us behind our backs." He gave them a quick glance to make sure none were in earshot and then continued, "Believe me; I know what they're like!"

Sarah nodded her understanding, marveling at the change in Deputy Tim Rogers. But then, a shout from the animal control worker broke the moment and took everyone's attention. The group moved towards the treeline as the grim-faced man waved them over. He pointed to the apparent destruction amongst the trees, the broken limbs and branches, but he mostly pointed at a patch of blood-soaked earth littered with tufts of black fur. A rancid stench rose from the patch, making one of the deputies gag.

"Been one hell of a fight gone on in here," the man said, giving Sarah a surreptitious look.

Sarah strained to look closer and caught her breath when she saw what looked like a large broken piece of tooth. It was a canine tooth... like a dog's, but larger... much larger.

"Whadda you reckon then?" the deputy called Steve asked, poking at some of the fur tufts with his booted toe. "Bears? Wolves? Some big cats going at it?"

The man hunched his shoulders and again gave Sarah an inquiring look. Sarah kept her face as neutral as possible, dreading what he might say.

"Hard to tell," the man said. "But whatever it was, it was a brawl to write home about."

The deputies looked at each other, then at Rogers, and then back at each other. The animal control man kept looking at Sarah, but then gave her an understanding nod when he saw the look of concern in her eyes.

"I guess we'll never know," the man continued, his eyes still on Sarah. "They're long gone now."

Sarah couldn't hide her relief that the man wouldn't make things difficult by asking a lot of inconvenient questions. She knew this man—he was Daemon Skinner, a man with a reputation for harboring unconventional views about some of the more unexplained happenings in the animal kingdom. She knew that he would suspect something out of the ordinary had happened. But right now, all she knew was that she was grateful he had chosen not to air any suspicions in front of the deputies.

"Okay then! Case closed!" Deputy Steve announced. "Just a couple of animals taking a dislike to each other—at least that's what's going in the report."

Deputy Steve gave a nod to Rogers, who returned it cagily.

"I'm not sure how you're going to explain that ol' mess, though," Deputy Steve said to Rogers, pointing at the upside-down tree sitting on top of Rogers' police cruiser. We've had some nasty weather of late, maybe a tornado or something?" he offered, a dry smile curling the corners of his mouth.

"Or *something*," Rogers confirmed after giving it some thought.

Both men knew that this part of the country didn't get tornados, but only Rogers knew what the 'or something' actually was, and he was not about to share his knowledge with Deputy Steve.

As the deputies made their way back to their own cruisers tut-tutting and muttering, with Sarah and Rogers quietly willing them on their way, Daemon Skinner soundlessly stepped up next to Sarah. She had almost forgotten he was still around.

Skinner held up the broken, jagged canine tooth from the remains of the animal fight to her. "A souvenir, eh?" he said with a wicked look in his eye. "Maybe worth something to the Tooth Fairy, huh?"

Skinner dropped the brutal-looking tooth into Sarah's reluctant hand, and she stood there staring at it. There was a jagged split that ran the length of the tooth, its serrated edge giving off a cruel glint in the morning sun. Skinner got into his van to drive off, a sly smile on his face.

"But we all know that the Tooth Fairy doesn't exist, right?" His smile disappeared. "Talk to me anytime, Ms. Shaw... Anytime you need to."

The tooth felt like dead weight in Sarah's hands as Skinner drove off. She had a sudden desire to fling the thing back into the trees, away from her. But she didn't.

"What was that all about?" a concerned Rogers asked her as they moved back into the house.

Sarah had taken on a slightly chastised demeanor as if dealing with an unpleasant memory. She turned the broken dog tooth over in her fingers, a definite unpleasant smell of rotten meat wafting up from it.

"That's Daemon Skinner, a guy we used to all laugh about at the animal shelter," she confided to Rogers. "We treated him as the local nut job, into conspiracies and UFO stuff." Sarah looked at Rogers, shame behind her eyes. "I remember how we all laughed and teased him when he claimed he had once seen a real werewolf."

"A werewolf?" said Rogers sardonically looking back along the road where Daemon Skinner's animal control van was drifting off into the distance. "Well, I guess I've heard everything now!"

Epilogue to Part 1

The man gazed contemplatively out the airplane window at the vast northern forests unspooling below. From this height, the swathes of untouched wilderness seemed to go on forever. He mused how easy it would be for a cunning apex predator to remain hidden in such remote reaches if it did not wish to be found.

He turned from the window with a bemused shake of his head, grasping the briefcase handcuffed to his wrist. It contained sensitive documented evidence from his latest assignment, an unusual case gathering evidence related to the killing of two US government agents. His superiors were now rushing him to one of the most secure facilities in Europe for processing and archiving.

The plane touched down smoothly at an undisclosed location. The man disembarked and was soon making his way through stark concrete hallways to a reinforced concrete evidence room. He presented the briefcase to the clerk, who inspected his credentials.

"We've been expecting you," the clerk said as took the case and looked the tall and supremely fit looking man up and down. He unlocked the cuffs and meticulously cataloged the contents—a single box of files. "I'm to inform you that your skills are needed again back in the States."

The agent shrugged, unsurprised, his unkind eyes betraying no emotion. He was a man accustomed to his work being of a highly fluid nature. It gave him a distinctly military air to his presence.

As he began to shed his FBI windbreaker, the clerk continued, "You'll need to keep that," he said indicating the windbreaker. "You're going back undercover immediately to continue surveillance of the suspects in the ongoing Agent Murphy case—to ascertain exactly what the exposure is concerning the involvement of the cryptids in his and his partner's deaths."

'Cryptids'—the word made the man smirk. He'd been called on to deal with far more dangerous things in this shadowy profession as far as he was concerned. "I can do FBI again," he replied casually, and pulled the FBI windbreaker back onto his shoulders.

The clerk finished logging the items and handed him the box. "Deposit this in archive aisle X42."

As the man turned, the clerk stopped him and handed him a collection of papers and identification documents.

"Before I forget, your new FBI credentials!" the clerk said.

"And who am I this time?" asked the man without even a look at the documents as he took them.

"Special Agent John Smith," the clerk replied. "There's a flash drive included with a detailed brief on your assignment—to be destroyed as soon as you have memorised it."

The man's smirk widened into a grin.

"'John Smith?'—how original," he said. He then gave the clerk a chilling smile. "I can be a 'John Smith'."

The newly minted fake FBI Special Agent 'John Smith' stuffed his identification papers into the inside of his fake FBI windbreaker and then proceeded down a maze of corridors. They were lined floor to ceiling with shelves holding identical boxes to the one he carried. Finding the correct aisle, he slid the box into a gap in the shelves. As he did so, he noted the labels on the box one last time—'Dr. Andrea Cooper'... and 'Sarah Shaw.' Two more names to be filed away in obscure secrecy.

Part 2

The Return of Broken Fang

The Cryptid Dossier: Confidential Case File 2

How do you *make peace* with a Monster?

****

11

Radio Interview Transcript: Daemon Skinner's Werewolf Encounter

[Intro music and sounds fade out]

Host: Welcome back to Oregon Night Talk, the program dedicated to exploring mysterious creature sightings and paranormal phenomena reported around Beaver State and beyond. I'm your host, Derek West. With me today is a rather colorful local figure who claims to have had a run-in with the legendary werewolf. Let's give a warm welcome to Daemon Skinner.

Daemon: Happy to be here. Thanks for having me.

Host: So, Daemon, why don't you tell us about when and where you had this supposed encounter with a werewolf creature?

Daemon: Right. It happened about two months ago in the northeastern part of the state off Highway 37 in the Mount Hood National Forest area. I had stopped my truck to check something out around dusk when this massive canine-like beast emerged from the treeline about 50 yards away.

Host: You say "canine-like."—What exactly did this thing look like? Was it just a big wolf that you mistook for something supernatural in the poor light?

Daemon: No, it was far too large and tall to be a regular wolf. This thing stood at least seven or eight feet tall on its hind legs. It had muscular front legs that almost looked more like twisted human arms with clawed hands and shiny black fur covering its entire body. The wolf-like head sat on very broad shoulders, and its whole frame seemed to ripple with power, like some gigantic bodybuilder or something. But it was the eyes; they glowed red when it turned my way. Those details are burned into my brain. I can tell you, this was no ordinary animal.

Host: Right, no ordinary animal. I'm sure our listeners are just enthralled.

Daemon: They might be enthralled, but I was paralyzed by... like a wave of intense dread... The worst part was the blood-red eyes that seemed to be looking into my very soul. It was like it was full of malevolent animalistic intelligence. And there was this rotten stench surrounding it—overpowering stink! I felt helpless and overwhelmed beyond anything I'd experienced before or since.

Host: Now, you work in animal-control, isn't that right, Daemon? You must deal with aggressive stray dogs and such quite a lot in that line of work.

Daemon: That's true. It's part of the job.

Host: So, isn't it possible spending so much time capturing dangerous canines could have affected your judgment at this moment? That your mind exaggerated a stray wolf or large dog into some kind of monster?

Daemon: As you've pointed out, I work in animal-control, so I'm trained to know the difference between dogs and wolves and what I saw. No dog or wolf stands and moves like that thing did, or gives off such palpable evil. I still have nightmares about those eyes. At the time, I was so... shocked, I guess, that I couldn't even reach for my phone to get proof; I was kinda frozen by some kind of primal dread. And people can believe me or not, but after that encounter, I know werewolves exist whether society accepts it or not.

Host: If you say so! Of course, we only have your word for all this. Did anyone else witness this creature? Do you have any evidence beyond anecdotal?

Daemon: There were no other cars or people around. And it happened fast—the creature took off back into the woods moments later. I know how it sounds without proof, but I know what I saw. Native American legends warn of shape-changing beasts in those forests. Maybe those stories aren't so crazy after all.

Host: Hmm, well, as entertaining as your tale is, Daemon, our listeners can draw their own conclusions. Just be careful when spreading wild claims—you don't want to damage your reputation or work up public fears over a stray dog sighting now!

Daemon: Actually *Derek*, I don't care about my reputation—I care about warning people. Something sinister is in those woods. So, go ahead and laugh, but the truth will come out eventually, no matter how much some cling to their safe worldviews. This encounter changed me forever, and I have to make people aware, even if I'm mocked for it. If just one person takes my account as a sign to be extra careful in those forests after dark, then it's worth it.

Host: I'm sure you believe that's true. Well, thank you for providing such a...stimulating account tonight! Up next, we examine haunted lighthouse legends along the Oregon coast. Stay tuned!

[Closing theme music]

[End of Transcript]

Sarah clicked off the audio file, shaking her head in frustration. She recognized the interviewer's dismissive, even sarcastic tone all too well. It uncomfortably reminded her of the ridicule she herself had indulged in at Daemon Skinner's expense.

But now things were different. After her own harrowing encounter with a dogman and subsequent near-death confrontation with the vile thing at her home, Sarah knew now that Daemon had been telling the truth about seeing a werewolf-like creature. The supernatural dangers she had heard him describe were now all too horrifyingly real. She felt ashamed for ever having dismissed him.

Sarah's hand went instinctively to the tooth necklace she now wore—a jagged fragment from the dogman's jaws that Daemon himself had gifted her. Fashioning it into a talisman had somehow given her a sense of power over the traumatic memories that still plagued her nights. But deep down, keeping such a spiritually charged object from a living creature troubled her. She worried about her ignorance of the traditions held by indigenous peoples who respected the reality of such creatures; that possessing such an item may only further endanger her.

Closing her eyes, Sarah allowed her mind to replay snippets of that fateful hike - the towering dogman materializing in the shadows, its red eyes glowing with preternatural intelligence as it stalked her. Also, its fierce battle with the noble sasquatch, another legendary cryptid that continued to visit Sarah's dreams with cryptic warnings. And then there was the memory of waking to find herself miles from the initial encounter, with no memory of how she got there.

She shivered, her fingers clasping the tooth tighter. So many unanswered questions lingered about her missing memories, the creatures' origins, and the shadowy forces that seemed to be monitoring her from afar. Forces she was sure had silenced others who came too close to the truth.

Sarah was beginning to accept that she and Daemon were clearly bonded by their harrowing encounters with a realm that defied explanation. She debated reaching out, wondering if pooling their knowledge could help fill the gaps. Perhaps the time had come to connect with the one person, other than Deputy Tim Rogers, who might sincerely understand.

Sarah's determination hardened. She would call Daemon to share her story and the proof of his claims. But first, she had to catch up with Deputy Rogers and see how he was doing. They hadn't spoken in the weeks since their lives had been saved, saved from a monster that Sarah believed was the very same beast that Daemon Skinner called his *werewolf...*

12

Sarah pulled up to the modest ranch-style house on a quiet side street where she knew Deputy Rogers lived. She sat in her idling car, suddenly unsure of herself. It had been weeks since she had seen or spoken to Rogers after everything they had endured—that shipwreck of shattered assumptions that had changed how they saw the world.

Taking a deep breath, Sarah got out and rang the doorbell. She heard footsteps approach before Rogers opened the door, astonishment flashing across his face.

"Sarah! This is a surprise. Wasn't expecting to see you here," he said, looking both pleased and awkward to see her.

"Hey Tim, hope I'm not catching you at a bad time," Sarah replied, feeling strangely nervous. "Just thought it was past time we caught up, you know...after everything?"

Rogers nodded solemnly, understanding her implied meaning. "Of course, where are my manners? Come on in."

He stepped aside to let Sarah enter the sparse but homey living room. She sat gingerly on the sofa while Rogers occupied an armchair. An uncertain silence hung between them.

"So, how are you holding up after all the craziness?" Sarah finally asked.

Rogers frowned, searching for words. "Honestly, I'm still processing it all. I'm questioning everything I thought I knew. It feels like the world shifted under my feet."

He gave her a knowing look. Sarah exhaled, relieved he could voice the turmoil she also felt.

"Yeah, I get that," she said. "Hard to go back to normal life after coming face to face with...well, whatever that thing was. At least we got through it."

Rogers smiled. "That's an upside for sure. As far as facing supernatural beasts, you're the one person I know that truly gets what it's all about."

Sarah hesitated before asking her next question. "Speaking of going back...how are things at work?" Sarah watched for a reaction. "Is Detective Lee still looking into the agent murders?"

Rogers' face took on a saddened look. "I thought you might be after some information about all that," he said.

Sarah felt the sting of Rogers' near accusation, that she was only there to use him for his connections with the county sheriffs' office.

"I'm sorry Tim," Sarah said trying to sooth his hurt feelings. "But this is important for both of us."

Rogers perked up at that and he gave her a rueful smile.

He said, "The official investigation has now been taken over by the Feds. My department's been instructed not to discuss the case details."

"Oh," Sarah replied, trying not to sound as frustrated as she felt. She had hoped to glean something from Rogers about the mysterious files she'd seen at the scene of the killings, the files that had clearly shown her name on them.

Rogers frowned, seeming to debate something internally. Finally, he spoke in a low voice. "I probably shouldn't say anything more..."

He glanced around as if making sure they were alone and Sarah leaned in closer.

"But between you and me, there are rumors about things the investigation uncovered that don't seem to add up, such as peculiar forensic evidence."

Sarah raised her eyebrows, intrigued. Rogers held up a hand.

"That's all I can really say about it. Detective Lee made it clear this is a Federal matter now. No good will come from stirring things up by speculating. Best we kept things to ourselves."

He gave her a significant raising of his eyebrows, and Sarah understood his unspoken warning. She would have to find answers through other means. At least now she knew the violent deaths of the two Homeland Security agents were more mysterious than authorities were letting on. That gave her a place to start digging.

"I appreciate you giving me that heads up, vague as it is," Sarah said sincerely. "I'll be careful not to take it any further."

Rogers nodded, looking relieved he hadn't been too indiscreet with confidential information.

Sarah tucked away the new questions raised by what Rogers had hinted at concerning the agents' murders. She instinctively felt that those deaths were the key to solving the larger mystery of her missing memories. After all, why else would they have been surveilling her and asking about her relationship with the now missing Dr Andrea Cooper?

But more importantly for Sarah, Rogers' revelations bolstered her feeling that their shared experience had formed an enduring bond between them—one that gave

Sarah the courage to reveal her true intentions in dropping in on the Deputy Sheriff.

"I heard Daemon Skinner—the animal-control guy who came to my place the morning after the dogman-sasquatch thing—talking on the radio about his werewolf encounter," she began, feeling for the raw, broken dogman tooth that now dangled from her neck beneath her autumn sweater. It felt dangerously uncomfortable, like the single fang was poised to pierce her heart.

Rogers' eyes widened in surprise. "That dog-thing was what Crazy Daemon saw?"

"So he claims," Sarah said, internally bulking at Rogers' unkind description of Daemon Skinner as 'crazy'. It reminded her of her own unkind dismissiveness towards the man.

"I didn't believe him at first either," she continued. "But he described a towering wolf-like creature in the forest with muscular arms and glowing red eyes. Sound familiar?"

Rogers shuddered involuntarily as Sarah continued.

"I want to contact Daemon and compare our accounts, but I don't want to approach him directly at his place of work." Sarah paused a beat. "But if he truly saw the same beast, maybe he knows things that could help explain what's going on."

Rogers looked doubtful but contemplative. "I gotta admit, it does line up with our experience. As crazy as they say Daemon may be, we at least owe it to him to reach out."

Sarah nodded gratefully. She had known that convincing Rogers might have proved difficult given his natural skepticism, but he was showing her a far more mature side than she had expected.

"I appreciate you keeping an open mind," she said. "I know it's asking a lot, but I think we've been given a glimpse behind the veil of what the real threats out there might be... if you know what I mean?

Rogers held her gaze, but his eyes were elsewhere. He was recalling the frightening spectacle of canine viciousness that he had seen appear out of some weird and unexplainable light on Sarah's driveway. Then, he seemed to snap out of it.

"You're right. We started down this rabbit hole together, so we should see it through," Rogers said, returning his focus to Sarah. "I can help contact Daemon if you think it will give us answers."

Sarah gave Rogers an appreciative smile and they parted with the promise to stay in touch about what they learned. Sarah hoped that both Daemon Skinner and Detective Lee's ongoing investigation would give her some peace of mind and she left Rogers feeling more upbeat than she had in quite a while.

Sarah was lost in thought as she drove home later that evening from visiting Rogers, rolling the possibilities and variables over in her mind when the ring of her mobile interrupted her brooding. She quickly pulled over and parked to take the call.

"Hello, Sarah Shaw speaking," she answered.

"Ms. Shaw, this is Detective Mark Lee," said the gravelly voice. Sarah first thoughts were to why Detective Lee would call her at this time, especially right after she had just been talking to Deputy Rogers about the investigation into Agent Murphy's killing. Was this just a coincidence?

"Sure, Mr. er, Detective Lee," she half-stammered into her phone. "What can I do for you?"

Detective Lee's disembodied voice scratched down into Sarah's ear over the connection.

"I'm sorry to bother you, Ms. Shaw, but I need you to come to the station tomorrow. Got a few follow-up questions for you concerning the case of the dead Homeland Security agents, the ones you had some interactions with."

Sarah's imagination quickened. "More questions? Anything to do with those files I saw... the ones with my name on them?"

There was a pause on the other end which set Sarah's teeth on edge. She realised she had made another mistake in bringing up the subject of the files again.

"Nothing specific, Ms. Shaw. Just a routine follow-up on your connections to the victims," Lee replied vaguely. "We're being thorough."

Sarah hesitated, unsatisfied. "But what could I possibly add at this point?"

"Standard procedure, ma'am," Lee said. "Let's just say some new information has come to light that warrants revisiting your statement." He paused to let Sarah process his words. "Does ten in the morning tomorrow work for you?"

Sensing no way out, Sarah reluctantly agreed and hung up. She sat parked on the side of the road, filled with fresh unease. Lee's cryptic words hinted at new and exciting revelations concerning the case, but Sarah felt a chill in that she might not be ready yet to confront new information.

To her dismay, Sarah realized she had been absently fingering the necklace hanging around her neck with the dogman's tooth, all while speaking with Lee. Sarah had never been a 'fiddler,' disliking the wearing of jewellery in general. Still, the urge to touch the tooth seemed to her to be overwhelming, especially during times of stress.

Starting her car, she pulled away towards home. It was only when she braked at the next stop sign that Sarah realized where she was—the exact same place where she had experienced her second terrifying encounter with the Dogman several weeks ago.

Sarah recoiled at the memory of the fateful encounter, bile and panic searing the back of her throat. It had happened on a drenched rainy night after Sarah had left the mysteriously and abruptly vacated offices of her former psychologist, Dr. Cooper. Her heart lurched as she recalled the tall wolfish shadow that had appeared spotlighted under a lone streetlamp that night, those malevolent glowing eyes searing her soul. She found herself gripping the steering wheel, half expecting the apparition to reappear. But only an empty, clear evening looked back at her.

Shaken, Sarah accelerated quickly through the intersection, leaving the ominous memory behind. She began speculating as to what dreaded truths Lee might have unearthed about the murdered government agents in his investigation. An unwanted distrust began to shroud her thoughts, and she wondered whether Deputy Rogers had played a role in Lee's serendipitous call. It would be a long night before ten o'clock in the morning rolled around.

13

Sarah sat rigidly in the interview room at the Sheriff's Office, awaiting Detective Lee's arrival. It felt more like an interrogation room, and she jumped when the door opened. Lee walked in holding a plain manila file folder.

At the sight of the folder Sarah felt an involuntary rush of adrenaline, wondering if this was information from the box of files she'd seen with her name on it; the box of files Lee had claimed didn't exist? She strained to read the tab on the folder Lee clutched but couldn't make out the words.

Seeing no outward indication of the folder's contents, Sarah tempered her hopes. Lee had given no hint that they'd discovered the mysterious files. This was, as he had claimed, likely routine paperwork and notes for the interview. Still, she was speculating—what if Lee was finally ready to address the files she saw?

Lee placed himself across from her, putting down the folder on the table between them with a dry papery smack. Sarah resisted the urge to glance directly at it, feeling she had to be careful not to reveal too much.

"Thank you for turning up, Ms. Shaw," Lee began in his gruff voice. "I know this is difficult, but we appreciate your continued cooperation with the investigation into Agent Murphy's death."

Sarah nodded warily, thoughts still on the folder. "Of course. Though, I believe I've told you everything I know already."

Lee looked at her searchingly. "Perhaps, but some new information has surfaced that requires clarification on a few points."

He opened the folder and rifled through it. "Now, I can tell you that this case has been declared a federal matter, but they've asked me to conduct these follow-up interviews as a courtesy—because I already know you and the others who are also connected."

Sarah stayed silent, unsure where this was headed.

"I'll get right to it then," Lee continued. "We have reason to believe your previous statements, and those of Deputy Rogers, may not have been... entirely complete."

Sarah stiffened but said nothing. Lee held her gaze.

"It's best for everyone if we get all the facts. So I'll ask again - did anything seem peculiar or unusual when you and Rogers discovered Agent Murphy's body?"

Sarah's mind flashed to the mutilated body of Agent Murphy's female partner, her remains splayed grotesquely in the forest clearing. The woman's torso had been brutally sliced open, the organs removed with bizarre precision. Sarah suppressed a shudder at the memory and couldn't help recalling the eerie and shocking sounds that had echoed through the woods shortly after, sounds that had driven her and Rogers to flee in primal terror. But outwardly, she maintained her composure. Only then did she realize something, and it really bothered her: Sarah had no idea what the name of Murphy's partner was—it seemed callously thoughtless of her.

"What was her name?" she asked Lee. "The woman whose body was found... Agent Murphy's partner?"

"You don't know?" said Lee, his eyebrows arching slightly.

"I only ever spoke with Agent Murphy when he came to my house," said Sarah.

"That the time when you called Deputy Rogers to check out their presence..." Lee consulted his file. "... a suspicious black SUV with tinted windows that had been following you, eh?"

"Yes," said Sarah, disappointed that Lee's file was obviously the Sheriff's Department's case file on her, not on the missing files she so desperately wanted to know about.

"She brought a dog with her to sniff around my house the last time I ever saw her. Agent Murphy never made a formal introduction."

"Her name was Special Agent Samantha Meyer, seconded to Homeland Security from the FBI," said Lee, leafing through some papers in the file. "But it's about your discovery of Agent Murphy that is important here—was there anything unusual, even peculiar, when you found his body?"

Sarah's mind pictured the high-precision carnage of Special Agent Samantha Meyer's damaged body one more time and contrasted it with Agent Murphy's savaged corpse found in the back of their government SUV. Being aware of both agents' names now made it seem all the more horrifying.

"No, nothing beyond seeing his body that I can recall," Sarah said evenly, hoping her face didn't betray the chilling recollection.

Lee studied her for a long moment before moving on. "And what do you make of Dr. Cooper's sudden disappearance right after one of your appointments with her?"

Sarah tensed at the overt mention of Dr. Cooper's name even though it was constantly in the back of her mind. Vivid memories of their interrupted hypnotic regression session raced through her mind—the way the doctor had abruptly ended things, her cryptic refusal to explain what she had unearthed from Sarah's repressed memories. Sarah swallowed hard, grasping for an appropriately vague response, mindful that Lee had led her into potentially dangerous legal territory.

"I was as shocked as anyone when she suddenly shut down her practice and left town," Sarah replied evenly. "She didn't provide me any explanation for why she left."

That was true, though Sarah suspected her recovered memories had been the catalyst for spooking the doctor into her hasty departure. She hoped her face didn't betray the swirling speculation tearing at her mind. But Lee was studying her closely again.

"No idea where she went or why?" he pressed.

Sarah shook her head. "None at all. I tried calling but never got an answer. Her office was totally cleared out."

"Have you had any concerns about Dr. Cooper's treatments, or have you discussed with her your concerns about any other doctors who have treated you at any time?"

"Excuse me?" said Sarah, nonplussed by the turn Lee was taking in his questions.

"Did you have cause to complain about any form of treatment Dr. Cooper had administered to you or the treatments of any other doctors, for that matter?" Lee reiterated.

"No," said Sarah. "Only that she left without telling me why..."

Let the detective make of that what he would Sarah thought. She wasn't about to voice her 'conspiracy-theory' belief that murky forces had silenced the doctor. At least not until she fully understood what was going on.

The detective stared at her silently as if trying to divine an elusive truth. Finally, he closed the folder, appearing displeased but resigned.

"Very well, Ms. Shaw. That will be all for now. But we may require additional interviews as new evidence comes to light." His tone made it clear she was being dismissed, for the moment at least.

Detective Lee had been far too watchful for Sarah's comfort. She knew that if she revealed to him the whole truth of what she had gone through, that he would think she was crazy or lying. And Sarah knew the repercussions of spilling the full truth could lead to losing her job and her standing within the animal care community.

Sarah stood to leave, eager to escape Lee's piercing gaze before he noticed anything more amiss. She believed she had succeeded for now in concealing the disturbing reality of what she was dealing with. Still, one never knew when it came to a law enforcement veteran like Detective Mark Lee.

However, as she left the county Sheriff premises she felt a sense of morbid irony over her situation. The kind of reserved skepticism Detective Lee had displayed towards her must have been exactly what Daemon Skinner had endured—ridiculed and dismissed by people like Sarah herself when he had tried to share his own seemingly unbelievable encounter.

Sarah couldn't blame the detective over his suspicion that her story remained incomplete, but that didn't make holding back the stark truth any less frustrating. She was torn between the urging of her conscience to make a full disclosure of everything that had happened to her and the fear of becoming a pariah like Daemon Skinner.

But the meeting with Detective Lee had deeply unsettled Sarah. She knew she had to be even more cautious than ever now regards whom she trusted with her incredible story. The authorities were clearly either not ready to accept the reality of what she had witnessed first-hand, or simply unwilling to give credibility to her story. Sarah decided it was best to turn her thoughts to what she would say to Daemon Skinner as the best way of getting the answers she needed, answers from the kind of person who might actually believe her.

Later that day, Sarah's phone buzzed with a text message. She saw it was from Deputy Rogers, which contained a phone number with the words "Daemon Skinner" beside it.

Taking a deep breath, she dialed the number. After two rings, a man answered grumpily.

"Yeah? Who's this?"

"Hi, is this Daemon Skinner? My name is Sarah Shaw; I'm not sure if you remember me..."

"Sarah Shaw?" Daemon interrupted. "The vet-tech from the animal shelter?"

"That's right," Sarah confirmed, surprised he even remembered her connection to the animal shelter.

"Well, this is unexpected. To what do I owe the honor?" Daemon asked sarcastically.

Sarah hesitated before continuing. "This will sound strange, but you gave me a broken tooth, like a big dog's tooth, when you were called to my place several weeks ago... it's now part of a necklace I... anyway, I think we may have had similar..." Sarah's words were coming out all flustered. “You know, similar-type experiences in the forest—And you said we could talk anytime I needed to...”

There was a long pause on the other end before Daemon spoke carefully. “Sure, but not the kind of thing I talk about over the phone anymore. We should meet.”

“Of course! When do you have in mind?”

“Tomorrow, about two in the pm. Java Moon coffee shop downtown.”

“Okay, see you there,” Sarah agreed, slightly reluctant, before Daemon brusquely hung up.

14

The next day, Sarah entered the coffee shop nervously. She still worried about how it would look for someone in her position to associate with the town eccentric. If her co-workers at the animal shelter found out she had been talking with the infamous Daemon Skinner, well–

Daemon stood before her like he had just appeared. “Hi,” he smiled, almost apologetically. “It’s good to meet you.” He pointed to a vacant table at the back of the coffee shop. “Let’s take a seat before we order.”

Sarah studied him. He looked to be in his early twenties, and his unkempt appearance reflected his work in animal-control. His dark hair was shaggy and overgrown, while his clothes looked rumpled and stained. An air of weary resignation clung to him.

In person, Daemon gave off an impression of high intelligence but low concern for social conventions and appearances. His intense gaze took in everything around them with casual hyper vigilance. The man was clearly accustomed to scorn and isolation, regarding the world about him with a bitter wariness for someone so young. Sarah again felt a pang of guilt for ever having being one of the people who had dismissed his claims. She felt a deep loneliness existed beneath Daemon Skinner’s gruff exterior.

As Sarah sat, Daemon leaned in and spoke in a low voice. “I’m sure you’re aware that associating with the likes of me does no favors for one’s reputation in this town.” He grinned out a smirk. "Yet here you are, willing to be seen talking to the resident crazy man'"

When Sarah didn't answer, he gave her an appraising look. "That's why I wanted to meet here rather than speak over the phone. To see if your need for answers outweighs the inevitable social stigma of being connected to me—particularly when it comes to someone like you who works at the animal shelter." Daemon paused. "They don't like me there."

Sarah shifted uncomfortably, knowing Daemon had accurately recognized the nature of her hesitancy. She inwardly cursed herself for being so obvious.

"So, let's talk plainly to set the right expectations here," Daemon continued. "I need to know that you genuinely encountered what you claim and aren't merely curious or seeking thrills at my expense." He eyed her carefully. "This is not entertainment for me; it's deadly serious. I trust you understand my position?"

Chastened, Sarah met his gaze. "You're right, I'm sorry. I assure you my experience was as real, and as terrifying as yours. I only want to understand what's happening. You have my sincere word."

Daemon studied her momentarily before giving a satisfied nod and relaxing in his chair.

"Sarah... can I call you Sarah?" he said.

"Sure," said Sarah. "That's my name—"

"—Then it seems we've got a bit to discuss, you and I..."

Daemon broke off to go order a couple of flat whites—the best in the county, he assured Sarah—and when he returned with them, the steaming aroma of good coffee softening the atmosphere, they got down to dogman business.

Sarah pulled out the necklace with the jagged tooth hanging from it. "This is what you gave me. It came from the creature, didn't it?"

Daemon's eyes widened in recognition as she handed it to him. "Do you know how rare physical evidence is? Most encounters never leave anything to collect as samples." He leaned in eagerly. "Tell me exactly what happened in those trees where I found this tooth."

Sarah found it hard to start at first. Still, she was soon recounting her eerie hike, the appearance of the gigantic dogman, its glowing red eyes, and the intervening sasquatch. Daemon listened raptly, nodding.

"A dogman and sasquatch together is nearly unheard of," he murmured. "Did you encounter this dogman again after this incident?"

"Yes, once near an intersection while I was driving home, and then it appeared outside my home one night a couple of weeks later." Sarah paused on the memory of the dogman's arrival. "I say appeared because it seemed to step out of some weird light that came out of nowhere."

"Wow," Daemon breathed, taking a sip of his coffee. "That's skinwalker-type stuff. Interesting."

"Skinwalker?"

"Skinwalkers are manifestations of shamans who have decided to take a walk on the evil side." His grin broadened. "The shaman takes on the shape of an animal, usually a wolf, and becomes this evil spirit-like being that brings all kinds of bad." Daemon continued, pleased at showing off some of his knowledge. "The First Nations people have a deep history with skinwalkers."

Sarah shuddered. “This thing had the same nasty eyes I saw in the forest. I believe it’s been stalking me ever since the initial event.”

“Fascinating! Daemon said. “You seem to have gotten its attention somehow, more than anything I’ve experienced.” He shrugged his shoulders. “But I don’t think it’s a skinwalker. More likely the classic Type-One dogman.”

“Type-One?” Sarah’s lips pursed. “How many types of these things are there?”

“Technically, there are three,” said Daemon. “At least three... with the Type-One being the version that really spooks people out on account of its size, its wolf-like appearance, and its ability to run upright—it’s the type of dogman I mistook for a werewolf, which would be the Type-Three variation. The Type-Three looks too human for most people to deal with—a lot of people seem to confuse this type of dogman with Bigfoot.”

“Then what’s a Type-Two dogman?” asked Sarah, morbid fascination taking hold of her.

“The Type-Two dogman is basically a large, powerful-looking dog that runs around on all fours; it is mostly associated with cattle mutilations.” Daemon smiled. “Pretty cool stuff, huh?

Sarah gestured at the tooth, impatient to maintain a specific focus on her own story. “I thought this might be some kind of key to what’s going on. You gave it to me—why?”

Daemon stared at the broken fang, the jagged split along its length glinting dully in the café’s light.

“When they called me out to your place, and I saw the ruckus that had gone on in the trees by your place—the uprooted tree dropped onto the cop car, and all—I knew this was no bears or cougars causing that." Daemon lowered his voice. "The tooth is a very rare find, very special—but it's also the kind of physical evidence that has a way of disappearing when someone like me finds it."

Daemon gave a knowing tap to the side of his nose that made Sarah shift uncomfortably.

"You know; men in black, government agents, *et cetera.*"

"I'm not sure I buy into conspiracy theories," Sarah said.

"'Conspiracy theory' is just a term for what the government doesn't want you to know," Daemon replied indifferently. "I'm just saying; better I don't keep any cryptid artifacts, given my history." He fixed Sarah with a meaningful smile. "But I did grab some of the hair samples, which I've passed on to people who know what to do with that kind of DNA. In the meantime I figured you could keep a hold of the tooth."

Sarah didn't like the sound of what Daemon was implying.

"So you thought *I* could keep the tooth for a while—to keep it out of what you think are the wrong hands?" she said, gripping her flat white tensely. "What? Were you going to come round one night and try and steal it back once these people you know wanted it?"

"Of course not!" Daemon retorted, taken aback by the implied accusation. "I just wanted to know where the thing was so the government couldn't get at it."

"What if I had thrown it away?" Sarah asked, an incredulous arching of her brow crinkling her forehead.

"Why would you do that?" Daemon responded, his turn to look incredulous.

They stared at each other for a moment, not sure what came next.

"Look, Daemon, here's the thing," Sarah said, her tone turning deadly earnest. "I have five days missing from my memories, a dogman thing that's taken to stalking me, and which is probably also going to go after Deputy Rogers—"

"—Deputy Tim Rogers?" Daemon interjected.

They stared a each other for a couple of beats.

"*The* Deputy Tim Rogers," Daemon reiterated incredulously. "The world-class blowhard and legend in his own lunchtime?"

"Yes," said Sarah. She was as offended by Daemon's characterization of a man she had come to respect as a friend as she had been by Rogers' own offhand appraisal of Daemon's mental state.

"It was his car you saw squished under the tree that the Sasquatch threw at the Dogman!"

"You mean Deputy *Timothy* Rogers was there that night, and not just part of that squad of deputies I saw at your house?"

That knowing smile Sarah had seen on Daemon's face the day he gave her the tooth returned, but with the addition of an unwelcome salaciousness.

"You and the Deputy got some kind of thing going?"

Sarah thought about tossing her flat white in Daemon's grinning smirk.

"He was there offering to protect me," she hissed. "He's also seen the dogman and... Oh, what's the point!"

Sarah made to get up, but Daemon held up his hands to stop her.

"Okay! Sorry!" he said, penitently. "It's just that me and the county sheriff have a bit of history." Daemon hushed his words. "Go on, Sarah; so you, the deputy, and me have all seen this same nasty-as dogman, huh?"

Sarah, partially placated, sat back and folded her arms.

"The main thing, Daemon, is that I have crucial gaps in my memory from this whole ordeal. I'm missing nearly five days from when the encounter happened to when I was found." Sarah stifled a tear. "And I need to find a way to get this thing to leave me alone, or at least be prepared if it returns."

Sarah took the tooth back and clutched it desperately. "This is the dog I have in this fight, and I was hoping you might have some answers about that beast, this tooth, and what happened to me—Do you get it?"

"I got it," Daemon answered, his eyes showing renewed understanding.

"I can't help but think this tooth is some kind of key to everything," Sarah continued, her eyes boring into Daemon's. "A few weeks ago, I had never heard of anything as crazy as a dogman, so I'm on this massive learning curve about something so crazy that it's threatening to tear my life apart!"

Sarah stopped for a moment, her mind seeming to drift off as Daemon watched her take a sip of her coffee with shaky hands.

"I need help!" Sarah said finally, avoiding Daemon's eyes in recognizing the fact.

Daemon looked at her for a while as if trying to decide on something, and then he took out a small notebook from his trouser pocket. He scribbled something on one of its pages, tore it out, and pushed it towards Sarah.

"Sarah, there's a war going on that nobody around here has a clue about," he said quietly. "Sightings of creatures like the one you and I have seen are on the up." He looked around as if to doubly make sure no one was listening.

"People who take this stuff seriously say that these dogmen are encroaching on traditional sasquatch territory, and that things are getting ugly."

"Ugly?" Sarah asked, pensively returning her eyes to Daemon. "How ugly?"

"Let's just say that many of the more aggressive sasquatch sightings that have been reported lately..." Daemon paused to gather his words. "Let's just say that people are more likely seeing dogmen instead of good 'ol Bigfoot when these encounters turn bad."

Daemon tapped on the piece of paper he had passed across the table. It had an address written on it.

"Come to this place on Saturday, early morning, just after sunrise," he whispered. "There's someone I think you should meet... probably the best person to give you the answers you need."

Sarah took the piece of paper, looked at the address, and memorized it before putting it in her pocket. It was an address for a place in the country, about an hour's drive away.

"Thanks, Daemon," she whispered back. "And I want to apologize–"

"No apologies needed," Daemon cut in. He smiled at her, but this time, it was a smile with compassion. "This is the real deal, and I can see you know what I'm talking about."

They left without finishing their coffees... neither noticing a man sitting casually at a window table watching them intently as they walked out.

15

When Saturday arrived, Sarah drove slowly through the dawn along a winding dirt road, following Daemon's directions to the secluded home of a man called Morning Star. She was relieved when she spotted a weathered hand-painted sign read "Morning Star Outfitters - Guide Service and Spiritual Readings."

Daemon was already waiting outside a rustic cabin as Sarah parked. He waved in greeting.

"Morning Star is expecting us. I told him you were looking for answers to do with dogmen, and he's good with that." He gave Sarah an encouraging smile. "This guy is a true shaman. He helped me deal with my own dogman shtick when I needed it most, and I'm sure he can do the same for you."

Sarah was already aware that most people in the cryptid community held the indigenous perspective in high regard when it came to these matters. However, this would be her first experience coming face-to-face with someone as spiritually connected as this man called Morning Star. She had done her due diligence in checking out the address Daemon had given her. She found numerous rave reviews extolling the man's talents. Sarah felt real hope that things were about to change for the better.

She followed Daemon inside, where the smell of burning sage greeted them. Morning Star was seated cross-legged before a small fire. Sarah was struck by a feeling of ancient wisdom permeating the room, its sense emanating from his lined face and penetrating eyes as he gazed at her. She felt safe here but knew much more was watching her from behind his eyes than she could ever perceive.

Sarah felt a surge of anticipation.

"Welcome, Sarah. Please sit," Morning Star said in an unhurried, rich voice. He studied Sarah closely. "I can already tell you have crossed paths with a dangerous entity; it still lingers in your energy."

Sarah instinctively clutched her concealed tooth necklace. "You know of the dogman?"

Morning Star nodded grimly. "Daemon and I have talked about these creatures many times since his encounter with one of them." Morning Star gave Daemon a nod before returning his gaze to Sarah. "They are not mere legends but omens of imbalance. Tell me of your encounter."

At first, Sarah battled with a strangulated, anxious sensation at the back of her throat. Still, it eased as she realized Morning Star was in no hurry and seemed quite at ease with Sarah taking her time. Sarah gradually recounted her hiking experience and the missing memories she now endured. Morning Star listened, his face alternating between grave concern and reflective compassion as he heard her speak of witnessing a sasquatch's battle with a dogman, the protective role the female sasquatch now seemed to hold over her, and Sarah's knowing of the death of the sasquatch infant.

"Sasquatch spoke to you?" Morning Star asked, an air of wonder in his voice as Sarah reached the end of her story.

"I heard her thoughts like a voice in my head, warning me, saying, repeating, *he is here*," Sarah said, tailing off.

She caught a glimpse of Daemon's reaction, his mouth open... fearfulness in his expression. Looking back at

Morning Star, Sarah saw the same fear enter the old shaman's eyes.

"Yes," said Morning Star. "He *is* still here... This creature, this dogman—for it is no skinwalker that we talk of here—it has marked you."

Sarah caught her breath, the unsettling hand of repressed horror beginning to grasp again at her soul.

"Marked me?" she gasped. "But what does that mean?"

Morning Star closed his eyes. "The dogman—him with the broken fang—has marked you."

Sarah looked at Daemon questioningly and then back at the old shaman.

"How did you—" Sarah looked back at Daemon, who shook his head.

"I didn't tell him about the tooth," he said. "Trust me, I didn't tell him."

Sarah turned back to Morning Star, whose eyes were still closed. "I told Daemon that all I want is to somehow stop this nightmare, stop this dogman from being a part of my life!" Sarah bowed her head, emotions threatening to well up. "I just want to make peace with it and be left alone... I was hoping you could help me."

The old shaman's eyes opened.

"That is only half the truth," he said, those piercing eyes now fixed on Sarah. "You also need answers to questions, answers that I cannot give."

Morning Star slowly stood up, his bone necklace lightly rustling about his neck.

"But you have asked for peace between you and the creature... and that is a good thing." Morning Star motioned for Sarah to stand. "Are you open to receiving cleansing from his influence?"

Sarah stood up. It was as if she didn't need to answer, but she said: "Yes."

Morning Star led Sarah and Daemon outside, where he had prepared a ritual space ringed with stones. He lit herbs in a clay bowl, filling the air with pungent, purifying smoke. Chanting rhythmically, he moved around Sarah, waving an eagle feather to dispel dark remnants.

Sarah coughed as the pungent smoke wafted around her. But as Morning Star began chanting and circling with his eagle feather, her senses heightened. The scent of sage and cedar surrounded her with pleasant incense.

As the ritual progressed, Morning Star's rhythmic voice seemed to echo as if emanating from some cosmic void. Sarah found her perception was beginning to shift and blur. She no longer felt her physical body but a great expansiveness.

Strange visions then began swirling before her mind's eye; a star-filled sky over endless forests and mountains. Glowing animals—a white stag, red-eyed wolf, and raven—circled around her as if sizing her up.

As fear began to grip Sarah, the three creatures dispersed into a mist. She felt an unearthly chill wash over and through her as if some darkness that had clung to her spirit was now being released.

The last thing Sarah sensed was the white stag bowing its head as if approving of the complete cleansing. As the vision faded, she thought she glimpsed a large, hairy bipedal shape lurking at the edge of the trees, watching over her.

Then, the expansive feeling receded, and she became aware of her surroundings and Morning Star's voice again. The glimpse of a guardian-like sasquatch left her with a renewed sense of protection and purpose.

Morning Star spoke: "The ritual has purified you to a small degree, but true protection requires deeper understanding. You must come to see these forces, not as monster's but as manifestations of spirit."

He then spoke to Sarah about the art of gifting, the leaving of offerings to appease unknown powers in nature. He told her that these were old traditions amongst his people and that she, too, could discover the peace that came with a giving heart.

"Can gifts restore balance with the one that attacked me?" Sarah asked hopefully.

"Balance is never so simple," Morning Star cautioned. "But your role in all this remains unclear."

He then offered her a drink of pure mountain spring water and told her to remain silent for a while to let the cleansing energies finish their work.

Sarah stayed longer, helping clean up the ritual space and asking more questions. But Morning Star now seemed elusive, as if more profound mysteries concerning Sarah and the creature were yet to unravel. However, he did point out that such things would only come after time. But Sarah found this hard to hear, her impatience at finding an ending the nightmare tugging at her nerves.

As Sarah finally made to leave, an impulse struck her. "May I ask you something in private?" she said.

Morning Star thought for a while and then quietly assented. Sarah told Daemon she would meet him at her car. Now alone with the elder, Sarah fretfully brought up the issue of her missing memories, her aborted regression therapy session with Dr. Cooper, and asked if he could help recover them through a deeper ritual.

Morning Star nodded, an intrigued look in his eyes, and brought her to another room set up for spiritual work. Burning more medicinal herbs, he began chanting and invoking unseen forces. Suddenly, he stopped, eyes flying open. "A darkness guards your lost days. There is grave danger probing further."

He hastily brought the ritual to a close. "Do not seek those memories unprepared. Return only when the tooth's purpose is restored," he urged cryptically, turning away from her to go through another doorway into a different room.

Left alone, Sarah knew better than to press on with more questions. The old shaman had already told her he didn't have the answers she sought. But an overwhelming sense of helplessness now surged through her as Morning Star brought a curtain over the door he had just passed through. It was a straightforward yet silent indication that it was time for her to leave.

Unnerved by Morning Star's abrupt reaction, Sarah made her way out to her car, even more troubled than before.

"How did it go?" Daemon asked her as she approached, though he could clearly see she was upset.

"I'm not sure... I'm really not sure," Sarah said, shaking her head. "He said something about a darkness guarding my lost memories or something."

"What, those lost memories you told me about back in the coffee shop?"

Sarah looked at Daemon, her vulnerability clear to see. "He told me to only return when the tooth's purpose is restored, whatever that means."

Sarah realized that she was clutching hard at the tooth through her sweater as it dangled at her throat. The hard, jagged sharpness of its edges had cut into her finger, and blood began to pour out over her hand as she yanked it back in pain.

"Oh my god!" Daemon said, alarmed. "It's cut you."

Sarah stared at the blood flowing between her fingers and bunched her hand into a fist.

"It's just like what happened with Dr. Cooper," she wailed. "It's like something is making sure that I'm never going to find out what happened to me!"

She turned back to Daemon, but he was just standing there, as if struck by a bolt out of the blue. He looked at her hard, his eyes questioning.

"Did you say 'Dr. Cooper'?" he asked, his eyes squinting but never leaving hers.

Sarah started at Daemon's intensity. She had once caught a glimpse of that intensity when she had seen him wrestle a large dog into his animal-control van. His eyes had held a latent but suppressed violence on that day, and she could sense the same latency in the way he was looking at her now. It scared her.

"Yes, she was the shrink the hospital set me up with," Sarah said. "What about it? In any case, she's gone, left town..."

Daemon's face softened. He seemed to be somewhere else for a moment but then returned his attention to Sarah. The darkness in his eyes had evaporated, leaving in its place some moment of realization that had taken hold of him.

"Yeah," he breathed. "I know Dr. Cooper... I know her well."

Sarah blinked hard. "Daemon? How do you know Dr. Cooper?"

Daemon smiled as if to himself, and it wasn't a pleasant smile.

"It was after my radio interview on Oregon Night Talk, when I told them I had seen a werewolf." He regarded Sarah as if a part of a gigantic puzzle had just dropped into place. "My boss at animal-control told me that if I wanted to keep my job, I had to get some therapy—they sent me to Dr. Cooper."

Sarah looked away from Daemon, dumbfounded, now oblivious to the blood flow oozing out between her fingers. But something had taken hold of her.

"Daemon, we have to leave," she said hoarsely. "We have to leave now!"

The direction of Sarah's sudden panic drew Daemon's eyes out to the dirt road that had brought them to their meeting with Morning Star. Parked in the distance, about a quarter mile away, was a stationary black SUV... with tinted windows.

Sarah found herself turning back towards Morning Star's rustic cabin. The old shaman was standing there, watching her. Fear infused the distance between them, and Sarah began to hear a voice... a familiar voice... *He is here...*

16

"Sarah, you leave now," Daemon said, pointing to the road where the black SUV was parked like some predator waiting to ambush its prey. "I'm going to stay back and talk with Morning Star; whoever that is out there on the road, they won't do anything while we're watching, especially if they're government."

"It's like it's happening all over again," Sarah said as she climbed into her car and put it in gear. "I'm not like you, Daemon, seeing conspiracies around every corner, but I'm starting to think something or someone is really taking an interest."

"Go!" said Daemon, not in the least bit hurt by Sarah's conspiracy aspersions. "Drive carefully and slowly; don't give them a reason to pull you over."

Sarah pulled out onto the road. In her rear-view mirror, she could see Daemon joining Morning Star to stand vigil. Ahead of her, the black SUV loomed, its shaded windows hiding whatever new threat sat inside.

But before Sarah had even reached halfway to the SUV, a sheriff's police cruiser came up from behind the SUV at speed, skidding to a dusty stop just behind it. Before the police cruiser had come to a complete stop, a man got out of it from the passenger side. Sarah inhaled; it was Detective Mike Lee, and he looked angry.

Sarah continued driving slowly forward. As she neared the black SUV, she could see Detective Lee angrily confronting its driver. She strained to see who was in the vehicle, but the driver's side window was only down a crack and too heavily tinted.

Detective Lee noticed Sarah's car approaching. His eyes locked with hers, his expression livid. Sarah's mind raced under his fiery gaze. She had not believed that the normally reserved detective could appear so incensed.

Carefully passing the cruiser, Sarah was shocked to also recognize Deputy Rogers behind the wheel, stone-faced and avoiding looking at her. What was going on?

Sarah drove on in growing confusion. Glancing back, she saw Detective Lee turning his tirade back to the shadowy SUV occupant. She wondered if Rogers had brought Lee out because of her and Daemon's meeting with Morning Star. It made her wonder whose side Rogers was really on...

Lost in a fog of conflicting thoughts, combined with Morning Star's adverse reaction to her missing memories, and the sight of Lee and Rogers accosting the black SUV, Sarah drove on for several miles before a movement up ahead made her gasp. A vast, hairy bipedal creature was crossing the road. Sarah slowed, her heart in her throat, and she immediately recognized what it was.

It was a sasquatch and it turned to look directly at her before continuing into the dense forest. It was not the female sasquatch she had encountered before but a male of immense size and stature. Its eyes held a sadness about them, yet Sarah felt comforted by the presence of the great shaggy being after the morning's tumultuous events.

Then Sarah began sensing a vague invitation echoing in her mind—to return to the woods without fear. A gentle voice from inside assured her she would be protected. With relief flooding through her, Sarah clung to the feeling as she continued homeward, letting the message of the forest spirit temper her swirling doubts and anxieties.

17

Over the next couple of days, Sarah resolved to act on gifting the dogman's tooth back into the wilderness. However, she had no idea exactly how to do this.

She had called Daemon, who told her it was simply a matter of intent and not technique when it came to gifting, a bit like feeding ducks, but with a much more focused mindset.

"And what was that you were saying about Dr. Cooper?" Sarah had reminded Daemon, herself only vaguely remembering Daemon's claims of having also been referred to the vanished psychologist.

"I was sent to her," he had said. "But I hadn't thought about it until you mentioned that you'd been seeing her, too."

"Did you do any regression stuff with her?" Sarah had pressed.

"Nah!" Daemon had laughed. "She said I was too schizoid for any of that, whatever that meant."

Sarah had been a bit fazed over Daemon's casual use of the 'schizoid' word, but she had let it ride at the time.

A week later, Sarah was taking a deep breath as she, Daemon, and a reluctant Deputy Rogers hiked into the shadowy depths of the Mount Hood forest. She had insisted Rogers be a part of the expedition, hoping the experience would mend her doubts over him and his involvement in Detective Lee's tense confrontation with the person, or persons, in the black SUV.

Rogers had been non-committal in explaining to Sarah why he had been with Detective Lee that day. He claimed Lee had been riding shotgun with him while asking more questions about the Homeland Security agents' case when a call had come in on the detective's mobile. Rogers had told Sarah that something about the call had provoked Lee to react angrily. Lee had immediately ordered Rogers to drive out to Morning Star's place, where the grizzled detective had then confronted someone in a black SUV.

"Probably government people," Rogers had semi-confirmed, but he still maintained that Lee had not made him privy to the full details.

"Why didn't you look at me as I drove past you?" Sarah had asked Rogers.

But Rogers had just shrugged it off, claiming he was concentrating on Lee at the time and hadn't noticed Sarah. But Rogers' explanations had done little to assuage Sarah's reservations. Still, she was pleased when he grudgingly agreed to go camping with her and Daemon.

"Remind me again why we're trudging through sasquatch territory?" Rogers said, eyeing the dense woods nervously. He clutched a serious-looking hunting rifle.

"I told you we're going to try gifting the tooth necklace to promote peace," Sarah replied.

Rogers shook his head. "Let's just camp quick and get this over with."

Daemon, who was following up behind, chuckled. "Not keen on another dogman run-in, deputy?"

Rogers prickled. He had never been that sweet on the 'crazy guy' from animal-control, and he even less liked the idea that his deputy colleagues might find out he had been camping out in the woods with the notorious Daemon

Skinner. "You said yourself there are multiple types of those things out here, right?"

"Don't worry; the gift is for the one who's been stalking Sarah specifically," Daemon said. You might be the law dog keeping the peace on the county's streets, but out here, this is how things are done."

The two men glared at each other, and Sarah thought they might eventually come to blows before the trip was done. But both men seemed to back down at the last second, their shared knowledge of the dogman's existence sensibly quashing any petty ego contests they might harbor.

Reaching the campsite, Sarah quickly placed the necklace on a ritual cloth. An old battered stump made for a convenient plinth on which the tooth gleamed dully in the diminishing light. Daemon had advised channeling positive intentions into the gift. However, he noted that Sarah's dried blood remained evident on the tooth's serrated edges.

"I just didn't think about cleaning it," Sarah said apologetically.

"We should discuss Sarah's plan," Daemon said to both of them. "I spoke more with Morning Star about gifting. He said motivation is key—you must be truly seeking peace and balance in your heart... and that includes the people around you." He specifically looked at Rogers. "The elder also warned us not to have expectations. When it comes to these things, we have no way of controlling the forces we might end up dealing with."

Rogers scoffed. "Sounds like mystical mumbo-jumbo mixed with woo-woo to me." He looked back at Daemon hard, lifting his rifle up. "This is what I expect will control any animal situation that comes our way—Remington's

Model 700 .375 three hundred grain bullet at nearly three thousand feet per second!"

Rogers shot the bolt of his rifle. The sound echoed through the woods as a live round slammed into the chamber.

"Loaded for bear, huh?" Daemon reached into his side bag and pulled out a powerful-looking revolver. "357 Taurus Tracker... Good for tight situations when things go bad."

The two stood there, sizing each other up like it was the gunfight at the OK Corral.

"Two little boys having a pissing contest," Sarah interjected angrily. "This is supposed to be about making peace, you idiots!"

Rogers and Daemon looked at Sarah, then back at each other, glowering.

"Mine's bigger than yours," Rogers muttered, eyeing Daemon with a surly look.

"What?" hissed Sarah—and then both men broke out laughing.

"Oh, come on, Sarah," laughed Daemon. "We can't totally lose our sense of humor."

It was now Sarah's turn to glower at them both.

"You've both seen the thing," she shot back, unamused. "Bullets are no good against a creature like that; it's an act of faith that will get us through all this!"

"Okay, Sarah," said Rogers, with no condescension in his voice though his nervousness edged through. "But you can't blame us for wanting to be prepared." He waved the barrel of his rifle in a wide circle. "It's not just dogmen we have to be worried about out here. There are bears, big cats, and wolves, too, you know?"

"Whoa there, deputy," Daemon said, holding up his hand to calm things down. "We both know Sarah's heart is in the right place—not that I'd expect you to understand the whole of it—so let's just remember why we're all up here, shall we?"

Rogers's antagonism towards Skinner flared again, but Sarah stepped in to diffuse tension. "Look, guys, however this thing turns out, we have to try. My life feels like it's at the mercy of this thing—I need to take back some control, and I know both of you get that. Please, no more arguing tonight."

The two men fell quiet.

Lightning flashed.

"Sure, Sarah. Sorry," Rogers mumbled. He looked skyward. "We'd better get pitched for the night before it closes in on us."

Sarah cast her eyes out over the horizon, where an angry bank of clouds was gathering. The towering peak of Mount Hood, a spectacular volcanic cone known as *Wy'east* by the local indigenous peoples, was gradually succumbing under the dark shroud. Sarah had checked the weather forecast before setting out that day, and there had been no mention of bad weather on the way. She prayed the darkening skies would not doom their attempt at reconciliation. Still, she was confident that their collective camp craft would see them ride out any nasty weather that Mother Nature might unexpectedly throw their way.

It took little time to set up. As dusk turned to night, Sarah checked that the necklace with the dogman tooth was securely settled on a tree stump they had found. She said a short prayer into the dusky light, asking for peace and safety, and then listened. She had not heard the comforting inner voice since crossing paths with a sasquatch on the road back from Morning Star's cabin, and she heard nothing now. Pensively satisfied, Sarah retired to her tent, the men to theirs. The wind kicked up as the unexpected storm approached...

18

The storm descended startlingly, lashing Sarah's tent with howling wind and rain. Thunder boomed deafeningly as lightning lit up the canvas walls in hellish flashes.

Fighting claustrophobia, Sarah finally stumbled outside, buffeted by the gale. In a lightning burst, she glimpsed canine eyes glowing red, watching from the trees—Sarah froze.

As she stood there the wind and rain lashed against her face. More lightning revealed other eyes as dull amber this time, sad and weary like those of the two sasquatch Sarah had already encountered. It frightened her but also told her she might have friends out there. Even so, Sarah picked up ominous shapes lurking in the darkness between flashes. For some strange reason, Sarah connected her sightings and the arrival of bad weather, like there was some link whenever a dogman was around—Sarah called out to her sasquatch protectors but heard nothing; no voice came to her.

"Sarah!" Daemon shouted through the storm. He and Rogers bundled themselves out of their tent and came running over.

"Something's out there, in the trees!" Sarah yelled.

Rogers raised his rifle and fired two shots into the air. "Get back, you hear! Get outta here!"

An eerie keening cut through the tempest, but the lightning only illuminated an empty forest. The keening stopped—whatever had been watching was now gone.

Daemon swept his flashlight beam around, pointing it to the ground. He was searching for tracks.

"Here," he said grimly, illuminating a huge canine-like print near Sarah's tent. More surrounded the campsite.

"Oh my god!" Sarah whispered. "He was right here!"

The enormous dog-like footprint and its close proximity to her tent was a severe fright for Sarah. It was like it had been standing right behind her while she had been looking at the tree line.

"The necklace?" she called out, spinning round as Rogers made to cover her with his rifle.

All three hurried over to check on the stump altar. The necklace lay undisturbed.

"Why didn't it take the gift?" Sarah despaired.

"These things don't happen instantly," Daemon offered. But doubt, even fear, tinged his voice.

"Let's get the hell out of here come daylight," Rogers said through chattering teeth. "Group camping is *SO OVER*!"

Shaken, the three chose to huddle in Sarah's tent. Outside, unseen eyes watched from the darkness, as if awaiting the right time.

19

The day after they returned from Mount Hood Forest, Sarah sat at home, obsessively turning the tooth necklace over in her hands. She still couldn't understand why it had not been taken as a gift, and she hoped Daemon would soon call with guidance from Morning Star about their failed gifting attempt.

A knock at the door made her jump. She opened it to a stern-looking man holding up an FBI badge. "Agent John Smith. Mind if I come in to ask you a few follow-up questions concerning the Homeland Security case?"

The man was tall and extremely fit looking, more like someone you would expect from the military than from the FBI. Sarah hesitated, noting that he was without a partner. There was also something oddly familiar about him, but she couldn’t put her finger on it. And even so, shouldn't the FBI call first to arrange a meeting?

"Oh, we're just tying up some loose ends; it won't take but a minute of your time," he said breezily, letting himself in.

Sarah bristled as he pushed past her and looked around. She sauntered back into her cabin and took a seat on her couch. She watched him as he casually settled himself uncomfortably close to her on the same sofa instead of taking the armchair she had left open for him.

Sarah caught a look at Agent John Smith’s eyes. There was a cruelty to them, and she realised where she had seen this guy before: the day she and Rogers had revisited Agent

Murphy's murder scene for more questioning by Detective Lee.

"You're one of those FBI guys that were watching the crime scene the other week, aren't you?"

Sarah pulled away from the man to face him more head on. His face was creased with a condescending smile, and she remembered the deep dearth of empathy she had seen in his eyes that dreadful day.

"Indeed Ms. Shaw, so let's talk a bit more about the day you discovered Agent Murphy's body," he began, his eyes drifting disturbingly to the necklace that was hanging outside of her blouse. "Quite the interesting pendant you have there."

Sarah clasped at the tooth as he leaned in to examine it, his proximity making Sarah's skin crawl. "That tooth must've come from one big doggy, eh?" He chuckled.

A noise from outside pulled the agent up. He was suddenly alert as he rose to look out Sarah's kitchen window. Sarah stood up, too, and looked outside too. A large sedan had pulled up, and Detective Lee was getting out. He had the same look of thunder on his face that Sarah had seen on the road back from Morning Star's place. He stormed over and burst through the front door.

"You people obviously didn't get the memo from our last chat! I told you any interviews go through me first," Lee fumed at Agent Smith.

Looking uneasy, the agent moved past Lee to the open door as if to check for anything else that might be outside. "Hey now," he said, turning to Lee, all friendly and collegial. "Just following orders to tie up some loose ends on this case."

Lee seemed unimpressed.

"Let's see some identification then," he demanded.

Sarah saw the agent's eyes shift nervously. He made a quick excuse about leaving his ID in the car and quickly jogged lightly over to a parked black SUV.

Sarah hadn't noticed the SUV up till this point. Still, its shiny black exterior and tinted windows threw her mind back to Agent Murphy's dead body and the mutilated remains of Agent Meyer. It had to be the same SUV she had seen Detective Lee confront a little over a week ago.

Sarah looked at Lee as he watched the man get into the SUV and drive away. This visibly troubled Lee. "I'm not sure that guy is actually the FBI. What name did he give you?"

When Sarah told him, Lee shook his head. "'Agent John Smith', huh? I don't like this one bit. It's time to pack a bag; you should lay low for a while. I'll call Rogers, too."

"Why, what's wrong?" Sarah asked, surprised at the abruptness of Lee's demand.

Lee rounded on her, but the anger he had arrived with was turning to concern.

"I'll tell you what's wrong," Lee said to her forcefully but quietly. "I've got two dead Homeland Security agents on my territory, an FBI investigation that wants my help but gives me no help... And now there's these serious FBI guys—probably not real FBI—crawling all over the county interfering in my investigation!" He fixed Sarah with a firm look. "And for some reason, you're the one getting a lot of attention from these guys, even though I've conclusively cleared you as a suspect."

Sarah let Lee's words sink in.

"I'm not a suspect? But that's been kind of obvious hasn't it?"

The anger returned to Lee's eyes.

"Then why are you a subject of interest for the FBI, or whoever they are?" He turned to look back outside as if he expected to see the black SUV returning. "Something's not right, I tell you. Something's definitely not right!"

Lee took out his phone and speed dialed a number.

"Rogers! Lee here!"

Sarah strained to hear what Rogers was saying but couldn't make out the words.

"Listen, Rogers, this is real 'signal thirteen' stuff I'm giving you." Lee almost shouted into his phone. "You need to get your bug-out kit, or whatever you have stashed for unexpected travel, and get your ass out to that place we discussed the other day, pronto!" Lee listened for a few seconds and then cut whatever Rogers said off. "Go now! Don't worry, I've got Sarah Shaw covered."

Lee hung up and looked at Sarah, who was looking at him, trance-like.

"So where's your bag?" he barked at her.

Sarah's trance broke, and she rushed urgently to pack. Even so, as things seemed to be imploding around her, Sarah thought about how the bogus FBI agent knew her pendant was a canine tooth, and not some larger animal tooth. As she hurriedly through stuff into a bag she hoped Daemon would call back soon. Right now, she needed all the help she could get in understanding why the damned tooth, much less herself, seemed to now be at the center of everyone's interest.

Then Detective Lee called out to her. "Lose your phone!"

His order completely sideswiped her.

“You can't make contact with or be contacted by anyone until I get to the bottom of what's going on, savvy?" Lee said tersely but firmly.

Sarah left her phone on her kitchen table... It was like she was saying goodbye to her life.

20

The drive to Lee's cabin was tense and hushed. Sarah gazed out the window as the detective's car wound along narrow back roads into a deeply wooded area. Lee kept checking his rearview mirror, which only added to the tension.

When they arrived, Rogers was waiting, still in full working uniform. Sarah thought he looked uncharacteristically rattled, his deputy badge and gun usually giving him a self-confident air of authority. Lee told Rogers to park his pickup under a nearby grove of shady trees.

Lee had brought them to a rundown holiday cabin near a small lake known for its fishing. It had an old generator for lighting, which Lee fired up, and a crude gas stove for boiling water and cooking food. Water came from a barrel that collected rain off the cabin's roof. Lee told them to boil the water before drinking it if they knew what was good for them.

Sarah and Rogers looked around at their newly acquired hideout. Sarah was only now coming to terms with the gravity of the situation, the strain was showing on her face.

“Make yourselves comfy, but quickly,” Lee said as he took a furtive look out the cabin’s dusty front window.

There was a double bed and a beaten-up old sofa for Sarah and Rogers to sleep on. Rogers offered to take the couch. An old-fashioned pitcher and basin served as the cabin's washing facility. At the same time, a wooden table with a collection of stools around it made up the rest of the dilapidated cabin's furnishings. Lee told them that a drop latrine was available by the clump of trees under which Rogers had parked his truck.

Once settled, Lee wasted no time.

"I want you both to know you're not suspects in my investigation," he said. "But someone is connecting you two to Agent Murphy's death. I don't know who or why yet, but I don’t like the way its happening."

Rogers shifted uncomfortably in his seat. "About that, sir, I hope you don't mind, but I told Daemon Skinner he could lay low here too."

"Daemon Skinner? Crazy Daemon Skinner, the *werewolf* guy?" Lee said, throwing up his arms in disbelief. "What does that loony have to do with all this?"

Seeing Rogers' discomfort at Lee's outburst, Sarah intervened.

"He's my friend, Detective Lee. He was out at the Morning Star Outfitters place when those guys turned up in the SUV that you were so angry with... remember?" She paused, knowing she was about to tell a lie. "Those black SUVs have been following him, too."

"Really?" Lee said, looking from Sarah to Rogers and back again. "I haven't got time for this right now," he said irritably. "But you two will have to let me in on whatever you're involved in." He rubbed his temples. "I don't like it, but fine! Better the crazy wolf-boy is in here than out there alone." He checked his gun grimly. "Stay inside, don't go anywhere. I'll be in touch in a couple of days."

As he made to leave, Lee turned to Rogers. "Remember, Deputy, you're on the job, so stay alert!"

After Lee left, an uneasy quiet descended on the cabin.

"He's gonna find out sooner or later," Rogers sighed. "And then that's my career gone."

Rogers walked up behind Sarah, who had moved to the cabin's front window.

"You heard the way he characterized Skinner, huh? That'll be me soon."

Sarah stared out the cabin's dirty window as Lee drove away. The night was beginning to fall, and she realized she was out in the middle of nowhere... prime dogman country.

"How long do you think this will last?" she asked broodingly.

"Until Lee says it's over," Rogers said, instinctively checking his sidearm. "I didn't even have time to get my rifle.

Sarah started as two figures emerged from behind some trees at the edge of the cabin's property line.

"What in hell..." Rogers said and started to rack his pistol.

The figures approached and soon resolved into the most welcome sight Sarah had seen in a long time—Daemon had arrived, and with him was the regal figure of Morning Star, a military-grade weapon cradled in his arms. The two of them cautiously negotiated the rough driveway to the cabin's door.

Sarah flung the door open, ran up to Daemon, and embraced him. Even Rogers looked pleased to see him.

"Thank god you're here," Sarah sputtered. "So much has happened!"

Daemon, unused to being enthused over, seemed lost for words. Morning Star spoke, first acknowledging Rogers and then Sarah, his voice kindly but strained. "You must attempt another offer of peace before the next full moon.

Daemon has told me of the events in the shadow of *Wy'east*... they mean great trouble is ahead."

Sarah heard Morning Star's words but seemed incapable of processing them. The disappointment on her face must have been palpable to the elder shaman. He looked at her, his eyes kindly, yet as strained as his voice.

"Take heart, Sarah Shaw, because the sasquatch people know you—you whom they call Mountain Daughter—and want you to know that you are protected... this is something I have seen."

Sarah felt the tears well up in her eyes. Warmth spread through her being like the coming of a peaceful sleep. She had no words, even as Morning Star turned to leave.

"Daemon has news for you," Morning Star said, looking back at them. "Be careful in how you respond. I wish you all well."

Morning Star faded back into the dusk, his soft feet barely disturbing the grass he walked over as he made his way back past the trees from which he and Daemon had emerged.

"You can let go of me, now," Daemon said huskily as they lost sight of the old shaman.

Sarah started and then hugged Daemon even closer, who gave Rogers a sly wink from behind her back.

"I would say get a room," said Rogers wryly. "But it seems we already have one."

Still reeling from Morning Star's words, Sarah took no notice, but eventually released Daemon and turned back into the house. She wiped away her tears.

"Okay, enough of that, then," she sniffed. "What's this news you have for us, Daemon?"

Daemon surveyed the cramped, dingy cabin with a suitably satisfied sweep of his eyes. "*Mmm*, just like home," he purred as he sat at the table, the wobbly stool he'd chosen creaking under his weight. "Make us a cup of coffee, would you, Rogers?"

Rogers snarled but went about gathering the cabin's assortment of cracked mugs and tin cups as he fired up the stove to boil some water. Like any good soldier, he had brought coffee as part of his bug-out kit.

Daemon turned solemn.

"Morning Star gave me the name and number of a person connected to some serious-sounding people in the cryptid world—people with knowledge," he said bluntly. "When he saw those government types out on the road watching us the other day, he got busy and put some feelers out for what's going down."

"What did he find out?" asked Rogers as he poured them coffee, his curiosity piqued.

Sarah looked at Daemon, a cool chill spreading over her where there had been warmth after hearing Morning Star's words. "It's bad, isn't it?" she said, coughing over the pungent mug of coffee Rogers had given her.

"Yeah," said Daemon. "It's bad... and it explains why those black government cars have been turning up all over the place."

"They're surveilling people who have had dogman encounters," said Rogers nervously.

"According to this new contact, it's mostly people who have had Bigfoot sightings that they're going after," said Daemon. He hadn't touched the coffee he had requested.

Sarah suddenly sat bolt upright as if struck by some elemental truth too terrible to believe.

"They're watching people who have had contact with the sasquatch," she said, her voice cracking. "Because it's the sasquatch they're really going after!"

Daemon looked up at Sarah, sharing her pain at what she had intuitively realized.

"According to this contact," Daemon said, his voice lowering to a whispered hush, "they're putting together some kind of death squad to take out what killed those Homeland Security agents everyone's been talking about."

"And they think the sasquatch did it." Rogers whistled. "How dumb can they be?"

Sarah sat there stone-faced, thinking.

"Daemon!" she eventually said. "We've got to meet this contact..."

Rogers looked up sharply, and it wasn't the bitterness of his coffee that had made his nose scrunch up.

"Lee will kill us if we go anywhere without telling him, and I doubt he's going to be cool with the idea of us paying social visits with some Bigfeet believers," he said, spilling his drink as he banged the cup down on the table.

"Are we being detained, Deputy Rogers?" Sarah said coolly. She had a determined look on her face.

"... No," Rogers said, mildly surprised by the firm turn in Sarah's bearing.

"Good," she said. If it makes the detective feel any better, we can inform him of our intentions once we're on the way." Sarah looked at Daemon. "We really need to meet this person!"

21

Sarah fidgeted anxiously as they waited in the cramped, concrete room. The room consisted of four walls with two opposing doors, one of which Sarah had entered through with Daemon and a highly dubious Deputy Rogers. There was an old lounge suit consisting of two sofas sitting opposite each other with a sparse coffee table in between. A wing-backed armchair was strategically placed in front of the bunker's other entrance, a big metal door with a industrial-like lock on it.

The small tourist town they had previously arrived in was picturesque, set in a valley surrounded by soaring pines and jagged mountain peaks. As they had passed through the quaint main street filled with log cabin galleries and rustic eateries, Sarah had thought she could happily retire in such a scenic place. Yet she had also felt uneasy being so far from other people, isolated in prime territory for the predatory cryptids she had encountered. It might have been her imagination, but the vacant wilderness had seemed to close in around their pickup as they had followed the winding back roads to the remote property.

Daemon had navigated them to an isolated property owned by his contact, an elderly woman whom he was told went by the name Katarina Kovacs. On arrival, they were met by a live-in nurse responsible for caring for Ms. Kovacs. She had shown them to an outer work shed on the property, where they had been informed they would meet Ms. Kovacs in a secure underground room.

Looking around, Sarah could see that the property had evidently once been an old workshop facility before being repurposed as a homestead-like residence for its current owner. They had descended below ground in an old freight elevator cleverly nestled in the back of the shed, Ms Kovacs' nurse leading them into what appeared to be a fallout shelter. It was the kind of bunker-like structure that had been built in the 1950s during the atomic scares of the Cold War era.

"This is some serious prepper stuff," Rogers had winced, eyeing the thick concrete walls and secure metal doors. "Are you sure this Kovacs lady isn't just some paranoid nutcase?"

Sarah had ignored him, but Daemon had informed them the bunker supposedly acted as a safe meeting space for the secretive cryptozoology society Morning Star had told him about. Though quite why these people needed something so literally *underground*, he had not told Daemon.

Heavy footsteps had signaled Ms. Kovacs's approach from behind the door leading further into the bunker. The nurse creaked the large, secure-looking metal door open, revealing an elderly woman leaning on a cane. The woman had extremely long and luscious reddish-grey hair; her piercing eyes belied her body's frailty. She wore an expensive darkly hued pantsuit, all business, all formality.

"Welcome," she said in a slight European-sounding inflection and added, upon seeing Sarah's curiosity, "I'm originally Hungarian, dear; hence the accent... Please, sit."

They sat, Sarah and Daemon on one sofa, Rogers gingerly at the end of the other. They all watched the old woman as she painfully dropped into the armchair but tried to avoid staring. After fussing over a blanket placed over the old woman's legs, the nurse left the room to arrange some refreshments.

"As you have no doubt guessed, my name is Katarina Kovacs," the woman introduced herself. "But you must call me Katarina." She smiled and looked directly at Sarah. "And you are Sarah Shaw, the one who has so interestingly seen both a sasquatch and one of these wretched *dogmen* simultaneously, no?"

"Yes," Sarah smiled back, feeling a bit sheepish. She turned and indicated Daemon and Rogers. "And these are my friends, Daemon and Tim... ah, Deputy Rogers, who has also seen the dogman and the sasquatch I encountered."

“Ah, yes,” said Katarina. "Morning Star has told me good things about you, Daemon," she said, looking at Daemon like a proud grandmother. She nodded in turn to Rogers. "And a Deputy Sheriff, no less, has joined the ranks of those that know..."

"Actually, Ms. Katarina, I don't know anything besides what I saw." Rogers looked at Sarah with a jaundiced eye. "We're just here trying to find out what's going on."

"Yes, yes, yes," Katarina shushed him with a kindly hand. "But first, you should know who and what I am; this person you have traveled to speak with..."

The nurse again interrupted with a selection of tea and coffee carried in on an expensive-looking silver tray. She poured them all a cup of their choice into delicately patterned china cups and then exited again through the big metal door.

Sarah, Daemon, and Rogers sat sipping their refreshments, the very picture of polite patience.

And then Katarina Kovacs began to tell her story... her life story.

"I was born *Katarína Kovács* in Budapest in 1944 at the height of the war between the Soviets and the Nazis on the Eastern Front," she began. "My family endured great hardship under the Nazis, but worse was to come when the Communists seized power in Hungary after the war. We escaped to America in 1946 when I was still an infant."

She went on to describe their impoverished early years as immigrants in New York, how her parents had passed away before her fifteenth birthday, leaving young Katarina alone in a foreign land. But she persevered, working menial jobs during the day while studying English at night.

Katarina then told her visitors how she had eventually found work as a translator and clerk at an immigration law office, helping other Hungarian immigrants navigate the complex American legal system. This exposed her to the entertainment world when she began assisting a troupe of Hungarian actors and musicians in securing work visas.

"As my English improved, I moved to Los Angeles and eventually started my own practice specializing in entertainment law," she continued. "I dealt with the debauched side of Hollywood in those days—the drugs, the decadence. But it made me a powerful broker in the negotiating of deals between studios, producers, and high-profile stars."

She gave more details on accumulating her wealth through corporate mergers of production companies and studios while also engaging in hushed political dealings. "I became a discreet 'fixer' for the rich and influential. But that world eventually shattered..."

As Katarina continued her life story, Sarah felt impatient for the elderly woman to get to the encounter Sarah wanted to know about. But she also understood that people from the older generations have a different sense of priorities when it comes to what is important, and she respected that. For his part, Daemon seemed rapt by it all, especially the Hollywood stuff. Rogers was beginning to look bored.

As if sensing the room's mood, Katarina paused, looked about at her guests with tired eyes, and then continued.

"You need to know these things because of what happened to me next..."

"Your dogman encounter?" Sarah said hopefully but also with a tinge of apprehension.

"Yes," Katarina confirmed, her eyes resting on Sarah as if she were now talking only to her. "At the time, in 2004, I thought it might have been the Bigfoot creature they all talk about. But what I saw was no Bigfoot. It was a creature of nightmares... and it destroyed my life!

"I was 60 years old and at the height of my success," she continued. "I had traveled to Vancouver for a discreet night-time meeting with a celebrity client on a movie set. We were handling a damaging scandal that could ruin powerful figures in both Hollywood and Washington."

She described having said goodnight to her client once their meeting had ended and then walking alone to her rental car on the shadowy fringes of the set. "That's when it appeared... a towering, wolf-like creature that moved on two legs. It had a vaguely human-shaped torso but with powerful clawed limbs and a monstrous head. But the worst part was its eyes—filled with a malign intellect I cannot properly describe."

Katarina recounted the blur of being attacked and her terror. "I have no memory after that. I lost three days before awakening, bloodied and confused. I was in some godforsaken industrial area miles away. My important legal files had vanished. I never learned what became of them."

Sarah shivered, reminded of her own trauma as Katarina emphasized the missing time and fragmented memories of her encounter.

"I knew this was no ordinary animal," she concluded, but with still so much more to add. "These things happened, just as you too have experienced... but the worst of it was yet to come..."

"No one believed you, did they," Sarah offered, knowing the answer.

"After the attack, everything changed," Katarina continued. "My colleagues doubted my fantastical story. Whispers followed me, about me having a mental breakdown or using hallucinogens for stress." She described how former friends and clients had come to shun her overnight, believing the elderly woman had lost her grip on reality. "I was accused of concocting a crazy Bigfoot hoax as some ill-advised publicity stunt."

"What happened then?" asked Daemon.

Katarina described how her client base had evaporated, how she had been forced to take early retirement in disgrace from the career she had worked so hard to build. "My reputation was destroyed over what I endured despite telling the truth—The truth! I swear this to you!"

"Ain't that the way of things," mumbled Rogers.

The cold dread of social exile pulled at Sarah's heart and she exchanged glances with Daemon.

Katarina then spoke of becoming obsessed with understanding what had attacked her and how to recover her memories.

"I spent years consulting every expert," she said. "Hypnotists, paranormal investigators, and even psychic mediums; always desperate for answers."

But she admitted no one had been able to provide definitive insights into what the creature was or her missing three days. "It became my life's mission to uncover the truth, although it has continued to elude me."

She gave Sarah a sympathetic look.

"Like you and your friend, I recently underwent regression hypnosis with the same doctor who treated both of you, Dr. Cooper."

"What did she find?" Sarah asked expectantly, sensing the moment she had hoped for that would cast some light on her own regression session with Dr. Cooper—but it was not to be...

"I had hoped to uncover repressed details with this Dr. Cooper—she came highly recommended," Katarina said with as much sensitivity as she could muster. "But the sessions raised more questions than answers, and I soon terminated my relationship with her."

"She did the same with me—more questions than answers," Sarah interjected, an urgency welling inside her. "But then she refused to tell me what she discovered while I was under!"

"And now it seems she's skipped town, and nobody knows where she has gone," Rogers added.

Katarina was silent for a while. They all were.

"This does not surprise me one bit," she scowled, then coughed.

"Are you okay, Ms... Katarina?" Rogers asked, the concern of the ever faithful public servant showing across his face.

"Yes, yes... I'm fine," Katarina replied as she stifled another cough. "My health suffered badly after the loss of my business; the stress of it all." She looked up, her complexion flushed. "But, in some ways, it has been good for me... I no longer have to worry about the filth of Hollywood and the politics that comes with it."

"What can you tell us about Dr. Cooper?" Daemon ventured, as keen as Sarah was on finding out anything of value concerning the doctor. "I know that Sarah and I would really like to get your opinions on her."

Katarina smiled to herself, then took a deep breath.

"I have come to believe the good doctor works for more than just her patients' interests," Kovacs replied darkly.

When Sarah asked further, Kovacs waved it off. "Another time. What matters is that you have endured and survived... the *Rake*!"

"The Rake?" asked Daemon.

"The term some in my circles use for this creature—this dogman, as you say." Katarina lowered her voice to a barely audible hiss. "After your own encounters, I fear its kind have turned their eyes on this region."

"What's a Rake?" Rogers asked, his hackles prickling across the back of his neck.

"It's another type of cryptid, similar in viciousness to a Type-Three dogman," said Daemon, trying to be helpful.

"Dogmen! Werewolves? Bigfoot? And now something called a Rake?" said Rogers, his voice swelling with incredulous alarm. "How many of these things are there?"

"My dear deputy," Katarina said after sipping some tea. "There is so much more to what is out there than you or I will ever comprehend."

"What do you mean?" Sarah asked, her own uneasiness now rising. “Tell us what you know!”

Katarina's piercing eyes took on a dead look, which frightened Sarah as they came to bear down on her. The woman's voice seemed to drop an octave to a harsher, less tolerant-sounding pitch; the Hungarian accent was somehow thicker.

"We today have forgotten so much of what happened in the past, but the past has not forgotten us..." Katarina's eyes closed. "Dogmen... Rakes... perverted science... Nazi experiments that the world still knows nothing of...” She swooned, but caught herself. “Of hybrid creations made out of creatures that people still refuse to accept exist... part man, part beast..." She tailed off...

Sarah looked at Daemon and Rogers as the old woman slumped wearily into the depths of her chair. "What is she talking about?" she whispered.

"There are those today who continue such work in the shadows," Katarina warned, as if in answer, as if from the edge of a deep and dangerous sleep. "These are those who are watching you now."

Sarah asked urgently, "Because they want to get at the sasquatch, right?"

"Isn't it clear? These Rakes—these dog creatures—are encroaching on the forests of the sasquatch, these people... for they are a people!” Katarina's eyes briefly opened, the piercing light of their intensity back again. "The killings blamed on your sasquatch friends are the work of these dogmen."

Sarah stood abruptly. "How do we stop what they are doing before they begin slaughtering these...” She struggled for the words, her previous intense and peaceful encounter with a mother sasquatch welling up within her. "These... innocent beings!"

But there was only an old woman's mirthless laughter, and then Kovacs was slumbering, her eyes shut again. "Trust no government agent who claims to be your all," she mumbled. "And beware of the Rake's curse. It haunts all who have seen its form... I've said too much..."

The nurse reappeared through the big steel door, her face anxious and concerned.

"Ms. Kovacs has overstrained herself... please understand," the nurse said, leaning over to check on her employer.

"Sure, of course," said Rogers, politely. He turned to the others. "I think it's time we skedaddled," he advised in a hoarse whisper.

Sarah was reluctant to leave, but a look from Daemon that said he agreed with Rogers for once had them all turning to go. "I've said... too much," were the last words they heard from the old, sickly woman as they thanked her exited the concrete bunker. Sarah got the chilling feeling that they were leaving a dank, grey concrete tomb as they ascended back to the surface.

They all clambered into Rogers' pickup, the drive starting off in silence as they began digesting what they had all heard.

"That thing Ms. Kovacs said about people watching you... watching us!" Rogers said after about twenty minutes of driving as a heavy dusk began to fall. "I think it's time we told Detective Lee what's really going on."

22

As they drove on, Sarah stared out the pickup's window at the passing darkness, the mountain roads no longer beautiful now that she knew the horrors they concealed. She couldn't help but wonder why Katarina Kovacs had mentioned things like Nazis and perverted science, why she had talked about hybrids, of things being part men and part beast. It only served to confuse Sarah more than ever.

Rogers drove in tense silence while Daemon sat motionless in the back, each lost in their thoughts after the disturbing meeting with Katarina Kovacs. They were almost back to the main highway when, without warning, blinding lights flooded the cab from behind. A vortex of blue flashing lights then silently erupted around them.

"What the hell?" Rogers shouted, squinting back at the vehicle tailgating them. He eased off the gas, hoping whoever they were would pass, then yelled as their truck was rammed from behind. The shock of the impact threw them all against their seatbelts.

"Hold on!" Rogers slammed down on the accelerator, but the aging pickup was no match for the heavily armored SUV in pursuit. After another jolting impact that nearly sent them into a skid, Rogers had no choice but to pull over, fuming. He went to reach inside the glove box but then cursed.

"Dammit! Forgot to bring my gun!"

Two more vehicles with blinking blue lights appeared, one being another black SUV and the other a blacked-out panel van. The panel van parked in front of Rogers' now stationary pickup, its doors being flung open as four heavily armed masked men leaped out, assault rifles pointed at Rogers' vehicle as they advanced. The other SUV positioned itself next to the pickup, still half on the road. All three vehicles had effectively boxed Sarah and her friends in; it all had the feel of a military operation.

Sarah's heart pounded as she marked out two people exiting the rear SUV, its grill lights still flashing. It could easily be the same vehicle she'd seen park up form Morning Star's place; or the one the rogue FBI agent John Smith had driven away in. Panic began to build in her.

But even more intimidating were the four armed men in tactical gear rapidly surrounding them, laser sights dancing across their chests. Sarah was struck by the unnerving silence of it all; no sirens, only the chilling strobes of blue light mingling with the bright headlights. Usually, scenes like this came with lots of shouting and barked-out orders, but these men were deadly quiet as they advanced.

One figure detached from the rest, lowering his mask. It revealed the harsh visage of Agent John Smith's, only this time, his facade of lawfulness was utterly absent. Sarah's heart dropped in recognition, the man's eyes hard and cold, devoid of any mercy. At that moment she knew he was a man capable of anything.

Sarah and her friends were ordered out, Daemon being virtually dragged out by the scruff of his neck as one of the thuggish men reached in with a pistol pointing menacingly. It was all too shocking and fast for any of them to respond.

"On the ground, now," Agent Smith ordered. When no one moved, several agents forced the three friends to their knees at gunpoint.

"Who are you people?" Rogers demanded, straining at the zip ties being cinched on his wrists. "I'm an off-duty Deputy Sheriff—you have no jurisdiction here!"

Smith chuckled, a chilling sound, his eyes still focusing on Sarah. "Let's just say we operate in realms beyond concepts like *jurisdiction*—your little tin badge carries no weight with us." He briefly looked down at the kneeling deputy. "And unless you want to end up like your friend Detective Lee, I suggest full cooperation."

Rogers paled. "What do you mean, 'end up like...'?"

"Poor bastard cornered the Sasquatch that's been on a killing spree," Smith replied. "He won't be a problem anymore—if only he had listened and minded his own business."

Rogers looked like he had just been eviscerated, unable to believe Lee was dead. Daemon and Sarah exchanged horrified looks. This couldn't be happening.

The agents hauled them to their feet, finished zip-tying them, and then forced them into separate vehicles, Sarah into the rear SUV, Rogers and Daemon into the car parked alongside the pickup. As the doors slammed shut, Rogers yelled to Sarah, "It'll be okay, just do what they say!" But his eyes flashed urgent doubt.

As she was forced into the rear seat of Agent John Smith's car, a hood was unceremoniously brought down over Sarah's head by another man who had remained in the SUV. Blindfolded and cuffed, Sarah pleaded to the silent agents. "Let us go, we've done nothing wrong! I don't know anything about any of these killings!"

No one answered, and Sarah became aware that they were now moving.

"Where are we going?" she demanded.

She recognized Smith's voice from the front passenger seat as he said: "Back to the scene of the crime—where all criminals eventually end up."

Sarah's throat tightened. "Back to where Agent Murphy was killed... Why?"

There was a tense pause, and then Agent Smith said: "Murphy was a friend of mine!"

He let the words sink in, but Sarah shook her head as if trying to free herself from the hooded blindfold.

"You're not FBI or Homeland Security! So, who are you?"

But it was fruitless, and they drove on in silence for the next forty minutes. Sarah was able to make out the change in the road from a sealed surface to a gravel road. And she realized they were heading into the forest where she had first encountered the beasts that had destroyed her life. Eventually, the SUV slowed down, its bump and roll indicating they had arrived at the parking lot where Agents Murphy and Meyers had been slaughtered.

Pulling her from the vehicle, Smith tore off Sarah's blindfold hood. Even in the dark she recognized the area instantly—they had indeed brought her back to where she'd first seen the Dogman and the mother sasquatch. Fear gripped her heart.

"Why are you doing this to me?" she whimpered, dreading the answer.

"It's time for a reckoning, and you're going to help us flush out the killers," Smith replied.

Helpless in their grip, Agent Smith's men strapped a GoPro-like camera to Sarah's head and a tracking device to her wrist. A communications mike and earpiece were rigged to the camera—Sarah could make out Agent Smith's excited breathing in her earpiece.

"We know the sasquatch has been tracking you," Smith continued, his words exploding into her ear even though he was whispering. "We're going to use you as bait, send you on a little walk, to draw it out into the open. Then we eliminate the threat."

“What if I don’t do what you want?” Sarah panted.

There was a short silence, then Smith’s voice crackled into her ear.

“I’ve already taken out a full police detective today, Ms. Shaw... you sure you want to test me?”

“I thought you said the sasquatch killed him?” Sarah said, already dealing with the implications of the lie she had just caught Agent Smith in. “You’re a murderer...”

But the rogue agent didn’t reply.

Sarah counted five of them in total, including Agent Smith, all gathered around her in a tactical huddle. Their weapons were all military grade, their uniforms black as night. They looked like seasoned killers, people who had seen war and wanted to see more.

Sarah felt sick. "No! You don't understand! The sasquatch people aren't a threat; they're peaceful, intelligent—"

Agent Smith cut her off with a cruel laugh. "Sweetie, you have no idea what you're involved with." He eyed the bump caused by the broken tooth necklace that he knew Sarah wore under her sweater. Reaching rudely down through the neck of the sweater, he pulled it free.

"How dare you!" was all that Sarah could muster.

Holding the tooth in his hand, Smith gently lifted the necklace's leather thong over Sarah's head. "I think I'll take this now," he grinned at the others. "If this is what I think it is, then some people I know would pay their eye teeth for one of these," he laughed, looking around to see if anyone had picked up on the attempted pun.

But nobody laughed and Smith pulled the necklace over his own head and let it settle with the tooth resting against his chest. Sarah thought it seemed to gleam with a supernatural malevolence in the sparse light, its razor-sharp edges giving off a dull sparkle. The others seemed almost wary of it as it dangled from Smith's neck.

One of the men said he was receiving a message through his telecoms unit: "Drone is in position, detecting something large, two clicks out."

"Two clicks, huh?" Smith responded. "That was quick."

He grabbed Sarah by her arm and cut the zip tie still holding her wrists together with a glinting sharp blade.

"Looks like we've got company," he said harshly. "Now get moving before we really give you something to cry about." He shoved her toward the shadowy treeline, Agent Smith and his men fanning out in a flanking maneuver, guns being checked and readied for action.

Sarah stumbled towards the treeline, looking about her wildly as Agent Smith and his men blended into the background on her left flank.

"*I always knew you were connected, somehow... just like Murphy did,*" Sarah heard Agent Smith hiss through her earpiece. "*It's like you're some kind of magnet for these things. But don't worry... we've got enough firepower to take down a herd of these sasquatch things...*" He clicked off.

The silent loneliness that engulfed Sarah made her feel like she was standing on the edge of an abyss, an inky jungle of sinister intentions that she could not process. Agent Smith's soft, commanding voice re-entered her ear:

"*Keep moving forward, through the treeline—we've got you covered...*"

But then something else entered her head, something familiar. "*He is here...*"

"He's here..." Sarah repeated.

"Who's *here?*" returned Smith's edgy voice over the earpiece.

Sarah stayed quiet, focusing on the repetitious voice only meant for her, a warning of approaching doom.

"*Where?*" demanded Smith again through the coms unit. "*Where is it?*"

"Follow me..." Sarah said, and on an impulse from nowhere, she started forward into the trees ahead of her, her legs moving as if by another's will.

"*Incoming target,*" Sarah heard one of Agent Smith's men say, and her blood froze. "*Half a click out, and closing... fast!*"

"*Maintain equidistance!*" she could hear Agent Smith ordering his men, the blue blackness around her amplifying the static of his voice and their voices in her ear.

Time crawled as Sarah stumbled forward over fallen branches, silently calling out desperately to the sasquatch, her previous saviors, those who now called her Mountain Daughter. But deep down, she knew the true monster was tracking her every movement.

"*Sarah!*" the familiar voice suddenly called, beyond the earpiece and the hearing of the armed men surrounding her. "*Be still!*"

Ahead of her, Sarah saw the two glowing red eyes she knew to be the dogman, *he* with the *broken fang*. She instinctively clutched for the necklace. Feeling it not there, she watched as the eyes winked out, and everything became as silent as death.

A cold rage began to build in Sarah's heart.

"Remember, *Agent John Smith,*" said Sarah into her coms mic. "You wanted it this way..."

A bloodcurdling howl split the night before Agent Smith could respond, followed by panicked shouts and bursts of automatic gunfire. A flash-bang went off, coating the entire forest in a split second of slimy green light, enough for Sarah's rigid eyes to pick out an enormous dark wolf-like shape moving like black lightning through the trees.

"*Be still!*" came the voice again in Sarah's head as all communications died in the earpiece.

A series of sickening screams then echoed through the trees. Sarah heard the sounds of a desperate fight for life being mercilessly snuffed out as she crouched down into a ball, her head swiveling violently. She pressed her hands into the pit of her stomach, physically trying to suppress a fear more intense than anything she had yet endured, and yet she obeyed the voice, trusting it to the end. She became still.

The screams stopped almost as suddenly as they had erupted, an eerie silence falling on the black forest enveloping Sarah. Then Sarah's mind froze, like a deer in headlights, her body trembling as crashing footfalls approached from the darkness.

The enormous bipedal creature of Sarah's worst nightmares materialized from the shadows. Glowing red eyes bored into her. Sarah gasped—There, in its claws, those hand-like appendages from hell, was the ripped torso and head of Agent Smith, his lifeless eyes still screaming in an agony that no one could hear. Agent Smith's mangled body hung limply in the dogman's powerful grasp.

Sarah could barely process the mess of humanity that had once been Agent John Smith, even as the dogman advanced, holding out Agent Smith's gory remains like some kind of offering—or like a trophy! Sarah could not tell. As the hellish upright horror of the beast crept closer, Sarah was able to make out the jagged and broken tooth at the end of the necklace that Smith had taken from her. It was somehow still dangling from his torn neck. It jiggled loosely, gruesomely, as the creature approached.

And then the dogman did something hideous: It grinned. It grinned as if taking maximum pleasure... as if enjoying the growing revulsion spreading throughout Sarah's body and mind.

That's when Sarah saw it—a confirmation that this creature was the same that had assaulted her and stalked her over the past few weeks—she saw the jagged stump of a broken tooth that had once been one of its deadly upper fangs. The broken stump was clearly visible even in the sparse moonlight that filtered through into the thicket.

The dogman paused, its nostrils flaring as it scented her. It dropped Agent Smith's pathetic torso, a meaty slap resounding between them as it hit the forest floor. Sarah's hands shook violently as the creature snarled, baring its remaining bloody fang as it started toward her, a weird electrical popping sound seeming to emanate from its bony joints.

Sarah couldn't take it anymore; the carnage and mayhem threatening to overpower her. She spun and fled blindly, hearing the pursuing footfalls closing in, but she knew she was no match for its savage speed and power. As she felt it nearing for the kill, a bright light flashed, illuminating the forest.

"No further, beast!" a voice commanded. Sarah fell in relief and shock as the strident figure of Morning Star emerged from the blinding aura, walking steadily toward the snarling dogman. He seemed without fear, ancient-sounding words of power rolling off his tongue as if a thunderstorm had struck.

As Sarah watched Morning Star step past her towards the fearful wolf-thing, she detected two sets of eyes watching out at her from beyond the treeline. They were of a shine closer to amber, and their presence quelled the moment of insane panic that had threatened to overwhelm her.

The sasquatch is here, she thought, elated.

The dogman roared in fury but kept its distance from the imposing shaman. Sensing its prey had slipped away, and what else might lay in wait, the creature melted back into the shadows, dropped to all fours, and then was gone in a second, its bulk tearing a path through the forest's darkness.

Morning Star backed up towards Sarah and helped her to her feet. "We must go quickly," he urged.

"Daemon, Rogers?" Sarah managed between the frantic sobs that were now starting to well up inside of her.

"They are safe," Morning Star assured her. "My people have been watching the people that took you closely. Your friends are recovering at my compound."

Exhausted relief washed over Sarah as Morning Star gave her a confirming nod. Sarah desperately looked about her again, seeking out the amber glow of the eyes she had just seen, but they were gone.

"The sasquatch?" Sarah whimpered, imploring an answer from Morning Star.

"They watch over you, Sarah," Morning Star said, putting Sarah's arm across his shoulders to help her walk. He stopped momentarily, looked back to where the dogman had been, and then back to Sarah as if waiting.

Then something fell at their feet like some unseen hand had tossed it through the forest gloom.

Sarah looked down and saw the bloodied broken tooth necklace; its leather thong snapped, and the tooth's mount caked in gore.

"Take it; they want you to have it," Morning Star said, his eyes alert for any movement. "It is their gift to you."

Sarah bent down and retrieved the fearsome fang. She pulled out a handkerchief and wrapped the tooth in it.

"But why?" she implored Morning Star. Why do they want me to have this... especially after I tried to gift it back?"

Morning Star looked at Sarah forlornly. There was sadness in his eyes.

"That I do not know," he replied, and then jerked his head as if feeling something touch him. He returned his darkened eyes to Sarah. "But know this, Mountain Daughter," he said solemnly. "The Spirits of the Forest have spoken; you can now never go home... never!"

Part 3

The Ghost in the Beast

The Cryptid Dossier: Confidential Case File 3

They are *among us!*

****

23

INCIDENT REPORT

Date: [redacted]

Reporting Officer: Det. Mark Lee

Incident Classification: Suspicious Circumstance

At approximately 1400 hours, I conducted an interview with Ms Jane Wilkins regarding information she claimed to have about possible criminal activity. Ms. Wilkins arrived at the station asking to speak with an officer. She stated she is employed as a receptionist at the psychological practice of Dr. Andrea Cooper, located at 1432 Pine Street.

Ms. Wilkins reported that 2 days prior, she accidentally viewed a patient file left on Dr. Cooper's desk while cleaning the office after hours. She claimed the file contained information about experimental medical procedures and DNA tests being conducted on a female patient without proper consent. Ms. Wilkins stated she also saw unknown government department seals on the documents within the file.

Before Ms. Wilkins could read the entire file, she stated that Dr. Cooper returned to the office unexpectedly and quickly secured the documents, reprimanding Ms. Wilkins for looking through confidential information. Ms Wilkins informed me that Dr Cooper has since gone missing, having shut down her practice abruptly. All patient files are missing from the office.

Based on these circumstances, Ms. Wilkins became greatly concerned for the well-being of the patient named in the file. At the conclusion of the interview, Ms. Wilkins identified the patient as Ms. Sarah Shaw. Ms. Wilkins strongly urged this department to locate Ms. Shaw to assess her health and safety.

I assured Ms Wilkins that I would look further into the information provided. The interview was terminated at approximately 1600 hours. Once Dr. Cooper is located, a follow-up consult is expected pending an investigation into Ms. Wilkins's claims today.

Reporting Officer Signature:
Det. Mark Lee

They were aware that they were being followed. They expected it.

Winter was beginning to bite with the first flurries of snow brushing over Oregon's vast forested mountain slopes. It had the effect of delicate icing on a Christmas cake.

Overcast, and with the day's light starting to dwindle, the road on which a sheriff deputy's brand new cruiser traveled looked like a dark ribbon spooled out over a mottled landscape of peppered rocks and tough-looking bushes.

Outside, it was a chilly thirty-seven degrees, but inside the cruiser, there was an even more frigid wariness that cut the air between its two occupants; not for each other, but for the lone black SUV that had been following them since leaving the county Sheriff's Office over an hour ago.

Up ahead, the two of them could see their destination emerge out of the light snow that dampened their windscreen. It was one of those lonely roadside pit stop cafés, hoping to entice the occasional lost tourist in for some hot food and a few gallons of extra gas for the journey ahead.

The cruiser pulled in, and the passenger side door opened to let out a large man wrapped warmly in a dark woolen coat, his collars turned up, and a thick scarf stuffed in over his shirt and tie. He was unfashionably topped with a thick winter trilby, which framed a face shaded by aviator sunglasses; they helped reduce the snow glare of the day.

As the man made his way to the ramshackle building that served as both a café and a gas station convenience store, the deputy in charge of the cruiser got out and went about the formalities of topping up his gas tank. Both men paused momentarily and then looked back up the road to where the tailing black SUV had parked at a discreet distance. Almost as one, they nodded in the SUV's direction, like they were telling its occupants, 'We know you're following us.' The tough-looking utility vehicle just sat there, humming, predatory, hunching down like a black cat itching to snap up a rat.

The trilby-topped man looked at the deputy once more, gave him a last nod, and entered into the warm glow of the café's front shop, the establishment's windows already shuttered against the oncoming night.

Inside, he encountered a shop assistant, an ancient woman of Native American descent. She was the only one present. She looked up at him and took in his woolen coat, plain scarf, trilby hat, and aviator shades. She gave a slight nod of approval and then a sharp whistle towards the café section at the back of the shop. A large man appeared, as large as the one who had just entered; both wore identical woolen coats, the same scarf, and the same winter thick trilby hat. Both sported aviator sunglasses to lessen the glare of the day. Both large men looked at each other.

The shop assistant clicked her tongue in annoyance; something was wrong with the man who had just emerged from the café's back section. She shuffled around to him, grabbed his collars, and yanked them up around his ears. She stepped back, took a satisfied look at her handiwork, and said, "It's the little details that your friends will notice."

She was talking to the first man, who also gave a satisfied nod of agreement.

Both men then looked at each other again, studying the likeness between them, and then nodded their final approval. The second man was decidedly younger than the first, but this would be impossible to tell at a distance. He walked towards the shop's front door and slipped into the cold, leaving the shop assistant and the first man sheltering inside. Outside, he quickly made his way to the passenger side of the deputy's cruiser and gave a hasty look back at the surveilling black SUV as he got in. The deputy finished gassing his car and did the same. Once both had settled in, the deputy's flash new cruiser pulled back onto the road and continued on its way. Back inside the shop, the elderly woman took a surreptitious look past the shop's window blinds, confirming that the black SUV had resumed its tailing of the cruiser.

She then turned to the man, now standing at the back of the shop, out of sight of the road. "Seems to have worked," she said grimly.

The man nodded back.

"My appreciation to your son for agreeing to meet me," he said.

The woman jerked her head back towards the café section.

"He's in there, waiting for you."

Taking his hat and sunglasses off, the man looked apprehensively in the direction she had indicated, towards a wide door that opened into another room. An amber glow radiated from an old potbelly stove. It was the only light in a room furnished with four wooden tables and chairs. Rustic was the term that some people might give to a place like this; cheap and practical was the real spirit behind the café's décor.

Another man in his late sixties sat at the table closest to the potbelly stove. His hair was grey and long, tied back from his face. He wore the clothes of an outdoorsman. He was armed, a revolver packed to his side. The first man had not noticed him when he entered the shop—He approached the table.

"I'm Detective Mark Lee, Sheriff's Office," he said as he walked up. He did not hold out his hand for the customary handshake; Lee knew men like this didn't follow the norms of American society when on home turf.

"I know," the man at the table confirmed guardedly. "Where will Deputy Rogers be taking my nephew?"

Lee shrugged lightly. "Oh, you know, a bit of a tour of Oregon's sights over the next couple of hours... and then wherever he wants to go."

The man observed Lee silently, a sense of alertness about him that belied his calm eyes. It unsettled Lee.

"I'm told by Deputy Rogers that you go by the name Morning Star?" Lee asked tentatively.

"My people and those who come to me for help know me as Morning Star," the man replied softly. "It is after the name *Kahtséhnho Wa'kíyxata*, which was given to me... but you can call me Kah."

Detective Lee smiled, and the warmth returned to the man's face. They were roughly the same generation, with Morning Star being the elder by about a decade.

Lee considered his next move. What little information he had been able to scrape up on this man called Morning Star, or Kah as he would have it, was primarily based on checking out his website, business records, and military service records. All were in perfect order and without a single blemish as far as Lee could tell. He smiled to himself. Digging into Morning Star's military background had been an interesting exercise, something Lee couldn't help but go over in his mind...

Lee had learned that the aged Native American before him had apparently enlisted in the US Army in 1972 at age seventeen. After displaying remarkable resilience and wilderness survival abilities, skills already learned at a young age as a tracker in his tribal homeland, the man his people called *Kahtséhnho 'Kah' Wa'kíyxata* had risen rapidly from Infantry to Airborne training by 1974. Elite

Ranger training followed soon after, with records showing Morning Star's tremendous physical stamina and leadership skills, which allowed him to quickly specialize in reconnaissance efforts.

Detective Lee took a chair opposite Morning Star and looked into the face of a man he knew had been part of three classified overseas tours of duty between 1975 and 1981. Morning Star looked back, expectant but seemingly unconcerned despite the coiled tension Lee knew lay beneath the surface.

The available official mission reports on Morning Star had listed regional operations and tactical objectives as either redacted or only providing sparse details on engagements with hostile forces across rugged terrain. But whatever had happened during those years, the man across from Detective Lee had sustained multiple injuries, receiving two Purple Hearts. He had also earned numerous commendations for courage under fire and for his proficiency in tribal tracking techniques applied in the field. He had obtained the rank of First Sergeant before his honorable discharge in 1982.

Lee knew the kind of man he had requested to meet with, a man with eight years of decorated service marked by several gaps hidden behind red tape, suggesting covert operations involvement. Though a senior detective with the Sheriff's Office, Lee had been unable to confirm any verified link between Morning Star—or 'Kah' as he liked to be called—to any classified units.

Lee decided the man opposite him was the type who would appreciate getting to the point.

“We need to talk,” Lee said. “We need to talk about Sarah Shaw.”

Morning Star looked at the veteran detective, his eyes placid, but the alert concentration of an old warrior suffusing his being like spring steel.

“Yes, we do,” Morning Star said quietly. “Yes, we do.”

24

The journey with Morning Star had been the toughest test of Sarah's will to live. He had told her she could not return home, insisting they trek across the cold forested mountains to a destination that Morning Star would not divulge.

"If the kinds of men that seek you actually succeed in taking you captive, you will tell them of this place," he had said when she protested. "I know this breed of man, and there is nothing you could do to deny them what they would know—but they can never know!"

Sarah had thought about the previous night, the terrifying destruction of a team of military-trained men by a dogman she now called in her mind Broken Fang. The men had been under the command of an FBI imposter called Agent John Smith, an operative for some unknown entity that seemed to be tracking people with connections to sasquatch sightings. They looked tough, experienced, and self-assured in their own martial prowess. Still, nothing could have prepared them for the annihilating force that had come upon them.

Smith had kidnapped Sarah with the express purpose of using her as bait in luring out a sasquatch clan marked for extermination. He had perceived a connection between her and the woodland giants, a connection that he had wanted to exploit. Smith had blamed the Sasquatch for the deaths of Agents Murphy and Meyer, supposed Homeland Security employees and personal friends of his.

Horrifyingly, though, Sarah had only served to attract the shockingly violent attention of a creature more than capable of making short and ferocious work of Agent Smith and his men. The carnage had been extreme, and at the moment that Sarah had thought all was lost, as the dogman's gory maw bore down on her, Morning Star had appeared... and the beast had retreated.

That night, the night of Broken Fang's attack, Morning Star took Sarah by the arm and led her through hours and hours of unending forest, the blackest forest that Sarah had ever known. All the while, as Morning Star carefully negotiated their way through the murky shades of shadow and night, she could feel the broken tooth of the dogman as a great heaviness in her pocket. It had inexplicably been thrown back to her by some unseen hand, ripped from the neck of the mangled corpse of Agent Smith who had taken it as a trophy from Sarah. She dared not even touch it with her bare hand, its presence a sharp and bloody reminder of the frightening menace that seemingly stalked her no matter what attempts at appeasement she made.

"But why can't I go home?" Sarah had cried as Morning Star led her deeper into the dark expanse of Oregon's silently towering pines.

Morning Star had stopped and rounded on her, looking at her as if he had only now seen her for the first time. He pulled her towards him and reached into her pocket. He pulled out the fanged tooth and held it up to her.

"Because of this!" he had hissed, his eyes uncharacteristically hard. "This is now a part of you, Mountain Daughter, more than you or I, or nature itself can ever understand."

Sarah had blanched at Morning Star calling her by her sasquatch name.

"But I don't want it!" she wailed. "I only want to give it back, to gift it like we discussed."

"None will now take it!" Morning Star had said unkindly. "It is now a part of who you are... something they have seen—something I have seen..." He had struggled to find his words. "They cannot commune with you as they have done in the past!"

Sarah had been devastated by what Morning Star had said. She had not even registered him placing the tooth necklace back in her pocket, had not realized that they were moving again, and was not even aware of a distant and hollow howl that echoed off the mountainsides that rose above them. It was dark, but Sarah's mind was darker... she could see no future.

Later on, on that first night, icy rain had needled down as Sarah had struggled to put one boot in front of the other, the soggy forest floor sucking at her feet. The feeble pre-dawn light had come, barely illuminating the narrow deer trail that Morning Star followed effortlessly. Sarah had eventually lost track of how many bone-weary miles they had covered.

As they walked, and walked, each frigid gasp of air that Sarah pulled into her burning lungs smelled like decay—dead vegetation, rich soil, things best left buried. Or perhaps it was the cold sense of death upon her, emanating from the damned tooth that weighed ever more heavily in her pocket, a grim and frightening reminder. She had still been unable to touch it, but had felt its malignant presence all the same, leeching away her vigor.

The calls and skittering of unseen forest creatures in the brush seemed to mock their clumsy passage. Sarah's heart would pound at the crack of a branch, imagination conjuring a pursuing predator. Each time, Morning Star had maintained his steady pace ahead, either oblivious or indifferent to all threats beyond his occasional and cryptic reference to "eyes above us." For him, this endless press through tangled boughs and sinkholes had appeared as natural as breathing. In contrast, Sarah had found herself scraping by solely on the fumes of desperation.

When they finally collapsed each night, exhaustion overriding cold and hunger, Sarah's brief periods of restless unconsciousness had brought no relief. She endured only more distorted dreams wracked by canine shadows, the scent of carrion, whimpers, and snarls. Each glimpse into the abyss had left her less sure of who she was; she would awaken to Morning Star rousing her roughly to resume their slog through the lonely woods, a world not yet touched by dawn's grace.

"It's not the creature with the broken tooth that we need to take heed of now," he had told Sarah as they shivered together on their third night outdoors. "Those men who died back there... there will be consequences." He had looked out high into the skies above them. "The people those men worked for, they have eyes above us. And they will be looking."

"What do they want?" Sarah had asked fearfully.

Morning Star had seemed distant towards her, even though they had been huddled close for warmth.

"The answer is in that tooth you carry," he had said without looking at her. "It has changed your very essence, and for this reason, you can never go home."

"Changed? How?"

Only then had Morning Star turned to look at her in the dull light of the creeping dawn. A solemnity was weighing down on his voice, at other times so bright and clear.

"It is your spirit and its connection to this world," he said. "Something within you has fractured, broken away—I know not what this means—only that the spirits of this world no longer see you for who you once were."

"What are you talking about?" Sarah had implored of the old warrior shaman. "What do you see?"

But he had turned away from her as the clouds and morning mist broke. The shining sun of the dawn now illuminated a small mountain valley that had appeared ahead of them.

"We have arrived," Morning Star said, his hand shielding his eyes from the glare coming off a small, pristine mountain lake.

Sarah saw a stout mountain lodge emerge from the haze on the lake's far shore. It was large by most people's standards, imposing, and probably boasting as many as eight bedrooms. It seemed abandoned, its grandeur having seen better days.

"What is it?" Sarah asked, a shiver touching her heart.

Morning Star smiled back at her, his first trace of warmth towards Sarah since their escape from the bloodbath of Agent Smith and his team's massacre three nights ago.

"It is your new home, Mountain Daughter," he said before once more turning somber. "It is your new home, at least for now."

25

Angola, one week earlier...

An anguished trumpeting sound split the reddened skies of a cloudless African sunset; everything fell silent.

Massive and dominant, it was as if the source of that tormented primal screech had walked the planet for a thousand years—yet it was but five years old. A decaying behemoth of flesh and blood, its sounded fury was the distress of a creature enraged by its own foul existence; the reality was that it was the product of filth-driven dreams in a fallen world engulfed by an outer darkness. Here, wandering alone in the primordial landscape of Africa, was a sentient life form that only those whose thoughts were conceived in madness could ever comprehend.

The sparse border region between Angola and Namibia was where it had ranged since its release. No one knew its name. It had no name, at least not in the official sense. But there it stood, seemingly at the center of Africa itself... ill in its evil, erect one last time on the raw, red-baked soil of the oldest land on earth.

Dust was now silently swirling around it, floating on waves of ebbing heat stirred by a slow-moving yet wary gathering of elephants. This hard-pressed native herd was cautiously parting its ranks to make way for this living thing of colossal bulk. And there it was, an animal being that had lived briefly in their midst but always as something unnatural and separate. Only the herd's mighty bull elephant now attempted to stand its ground as the brutish apparition emerged from out of the shallows of a small watering hole. A one-sided battle would now ensue between two giants for the right to rule the one source of life-giving sustenance that every creature within a ten-mile radius relied upon.

Balanced on the dry grassy lip of the shallow oasis, a man sucked in the dry African air as he slowly blinked away the glare of the day. Sweat from his top lip flavored the atmosphere's acidity with its salty moisture.

The sweat of fear...

The man lay prone on the hot rocky escarpment and observed the enormity of what stood below. It stood a third larger than the elephants gathered to water their parched throats. He peered through a scope mounted on a heavy-duty anti-materiel rifle. It was a military-grade weapon designed to take out armored vehicles; it was the right amount of gun for the job that he was there to do.

"That's the biggest one yet," murmured a young woman perched low to the man's left just ahead of him. Her moistened eyes scanned the frightful scene below them. "Its tusks are bigger than any I've seen so far... it has four of them!"

The man grunted. By human standards, he was almost as freakishly big compared to other men as this creature was to the surrounding elephant herd. He lined the thing up in his sights, the enormous gun almost looking like a regular firearm in his hands. His heavy, unkempt beard padded his cheek as he rested it against the gun's stock; the man's wild red hair was caked in the sandy grim earned from over four days of hard driving and grubby tracking. He sighed; the job was almost done; a life would be taken... and he would be paid.

“These things have been designed that way,” the man said. “It’s a male variant. It was originally intended that producing these things would provide an alternative to the black market in ivory.”

He adjusted his scope and reassessed his sighting. No creature like the one that filled its view had ever existed before, and it should not exist. The beast was a singular entity of physical vastness, its muscled mass appearing acutely unnatural. Yet there it stood, a hulking monstrosity forcing its presence onto the African landscape, a rampaging killer roaming amongst the noblest giants in all Creation.

The elephant herd that had arranged itself around the beast was a mere seven in number. They stood mournfully apart from it, cautious in their own silent way. Only the herd’s bull seemed ready to confront this unprecedented threat to his authority. But it was a futile gesture, the herd’s collective bulk being dwarfed by the crude parody of their species that challenged their right of way.

The man had a thought: If there is a name for this thing, then let it be *Abomination*!

The abomination standing below them in the shallow water hole, its vast bulk swaying under a final African sunset, was an unfinished, grey-skinned facsimile of an African elephant. But it could not be called an elephant, its uncanny shape being a curious blend of pachyderm dominated by the discordant hairless features of the ancient and now extinct Siberian mammoth. It did not have the majestic wide ears of the African elephant but the minor flaps of the long-lost mammoth species of Asia. And instead of two tusks, the thing sported four; two enormous curling main tusks with two shorter and sharper tusks protruding from its lower jaw. It was, the man already knew, a manufactured *hybrid,* the essence of humanity's belief that it had an inherent right to play God.

Double the payload in ivory and double your profit, the man thought. Clever!

The lower tusks gave the beast a distinctly murderous advantage in overcoming any rival male African elephants it came upon in the arid wilds of Angola's Kunene region. Such encounters usually occurred as contests over herd dominance and territory, which was an instinctual part of the creature's nature; to seek out such conflicts. Easily a third larger than any known bull elephant, the beast had displayed an aggressiveness that made it almost predatory by nature, something that it unleashed upon virtually any annoyance or frustration that dared cross its wide-ranging path.

Three days ago, the man, and the woman with him, had tracked the animal down to an area a few miles south of where they were currently observing it. There, they had witnessed the monster stamp a rhino to pulp over a dispute involving access to a fruiting copse of bushes. It had been an awesome display of ferocious and extreme power, the beast's fury sending it on a subsequent rampage across the dry and cracked country in search of water. They had followed it to where it now wallowed below them.

"How much would those tusks get on the Chinese market?" the woman wondered. She glanced sharply at the man behind his rifle as he slid an armor-piercing round into its chamber. She quickly realized that she might have asked something indiscreet. "Just a thought," she smiled apologetically.

"They will never make it to market... to any market," the man said quietly. "The genetics that make up that thing are proprietary." He adjusted the focus on his scope. "As soon as we're finished here, the whole place will be napalmed and then finished off with a load of thermobaric ordinance."

"Including that elephant herd down there?" she asked pensively.

"Yes," said the man. "And everything else down there with that monstrosity."

He estimated one hundred and sixty yards between them and the target and adjusted his scope.

"It's a small price, ecologically speaking, to pay for the greater ecological good," he muttered. "At least that's what I'm told."

"How is killing this thing, and then everything else around it with napalm, solving an ecological problem?" she queried.

She did not expect an answer. She got one anyway.

"The thing is sterile," the man said. "But it's killing any male elephant it comes across." He made another tiny final adjustment to the scope. "That was an unexpected side effect they hadn't taken into account when they let it loose."

"So, no fertile male elephants left for the fertile female elephants wherever this thing turns up," she nodded.

"Plus, it would be irresponsible to allow its carcass to be consumed by scavengers," the man added. "Hence the napalm—too much of a risk on the *mutational* side of the equation."

The woman nodded again, somewhat forlornly, as if a great opportunity was going begging. She made a final range calculation through a set of dirt-encrusted binoculars.

"My estimate is about one-fifty hundred meters," she called out.

The man grunted in agreement, even though the estimate was given in the pesky metric system he hated so much. He blinked slowly, deliberately, like a big hairy cat, and then flicked a tense eye toward the woman's young profile. He knew her well, as well as any man like him could know a former refugee in a world of refugees. He had not seen her for about five years, but he knew she would now be about twenty-seven. It was, however, impossible to tell with her kind.

Her kind, he thought, catching himself with the term...

She was a special breed, a peculiar kind of person that had seen so much in her short life that it often made her appear older than she probably was. Yet, *her kind* knew so little.

"It's time you were blooded," the man said quietly, even emphatically. "You will take the shot!"

She didn't budge but continued gazing through her binoculars at the bewitching sight unfolding in the water hole. The man couldn't help but notice the small, damp red lesions that pimpled her hairline, her dark Serbian locks now wet with the strain of the day's end. He raised himself to a low kneeling crouch.

"You will take the shot," he repeated.

Maybe, the man thought, she might have one day come to know what it might be to be alive—*really* alive. But he doubted that she and all the other ones like her knew anything about *why* they were alive.

The man had known the young woman with him for about ten years, a useful stray the *Organisation* had picked up during the savage Balkans conflicts. He had first met her when she only looked about sixteen or seventeen. Still, she had already established herself as part of the human trafficking operations that proliferated in the region at that time.

At the time he had been working as a procurement specialist for private interests but had soon found himself partnering with the young woman for a few jobs over the next several years. She had been good at what she did; she spoke a number of languages and could play the helpful niece or daughter whenever required—such was the nature of their work.

"Maybe we should get closer," the woman suggested, "just in case we only wing it and it takes off."

The man snorted, which told her he had no intention of taking up her suggestion.

"Its physical state, while imposing, is inferior and diseased," he said. "It is getting weaker—like all of *its kind* eventually do." He took one last look at the young woman's blood-dappled hairline and then glanced down the scope. "From this distance, two shots at the most."

Almost sadly, the man looked over at the woman and told her, "It's an easy target. Its size may have once been to its advantage, but this one is now too far gone for it to give us a chase—you will take the shot!"

The woman dipped her binoculars but still peered over them across the silent desert-like depression. The elephant herd stood by, eerily, oscillating gently as the bull now moved to confront the colossus before them, a monstrosity even to their eyes.

"But you are the hunter!" she said, a slight edge to her voice. "You always tell me it's my time to take the shot, but then you always change your mind." She looked back at him, her eyes piqued with a questioning air.

It was true. Some did call the man the Hunter. But those who did really knew nothing about him. Others knew better, that he was more of a ghost than a hunter. In truth, he was an executioner! Indeed, the only trophy the man had ever sought in making a kill was in the knowledge that he had been responsible for there being one less abomination in a vile and contaminated world–human or animal. In his mind, it had become a spiritual thing, a spiritual form of killing. After all, something had to be done in the name of Creation, if not in the name of God...

The man sighed. "Not today." He moved away from the extreme-caliber weapon and motioned for her to take his place. "This time, you will take the shot." He held out his hand to take the woman's binoculars.

"Look after those as if your life depended on it," the woman said half-jokingly, reluctantly handing them to him. "They are my only connection–"

She didn't finish.

"Of course," he replied solemnly.

He took a closer look at the sand-colored binoculars as he held them. Interestingly, this was the first time he had ever held them. They were a pair of antique yet highly functional German U-boat glasses of Second World War vintage. He realized that she seemed to have carried them everywhere in all the years he had known her. He looked back at her. "For once, Nastassja, a righteous thing will be done here."

At first, the woman flinched ever so slightly. Not because he had brought some moral abstraction into their exchange but because this had been the first time during this particular job—any job for that matter—that the man had used her actual name; *Nastassja.*

She nodded, a half-smile tugging at the corners of her mouth. Over the years, she had come to appreciate one fact; that whenever this man used her name, or anyone else's real name, there was an inherent seriousness to the situation. For her, it was a strangely comforting development, proof that he still considered her part of his rarefied inner circle. But she also knew it was a circle that could be one of the most dangerous places for anyone to be. But it had always paid well.

Nastassja thought again of how much money those gigantic tusks could bring on the Asian market...

"Okay," she said hesitantly, moving into position behind the rifle where the man had been. "So, I guess I'll be able to tell my grandkids about taking out some diseased experiment that saved the elephants of Africa."

If she had been trying to ease the tenseness that had developed between them, it was not working.

"First time for everything, I guess," she added, and then settled into position to steady her hand and eye.

The man had instructed Nastassja several times in the use of large-caliber weapons, so he knew she could squeeze off a competent shot. He remembered how this woman had already been a seasoned child soldier when he first encountered her all those years ago.

He had first run into Nastassja when his Albanian employers had sent him to Serbia to make contact with a bunch of fifteen or so trafficked kids. When he found them, they were all holed up in some abandoned warehouse, a prearranged pickup point near the Kosovo border. Nastassja, then a dark-haired teen armed with an oversized Kalashnikov, was the hapless group's guide and captor. She had already shot one of the children dead to keep the rest of them in line. But she had also been quick to ruthlessly assert that she still expected to be paid in total for all the kids, including the kid she had so callously dispatched.

She had been paid.

Upon reporting the situation to the Albanians, the man remembered how they had insisted that this slight yet vicious child, this Nastassja, be quickly recruited into their organization—the *Organisation*. She was precisely the kind of kid they could put to work. And so Nastassja rapidly became a crucial and profitable cog in the engine that drove their organization's trade in human misery.

"You don't know my true name, do you?" the man gently said, repositioning himself behind her, still maintaining his low crouch.

Nastassja raised her head, her right eyebrow cocked in puzzlement at the question. She took her eye off the target.

"No," she said quietly. "I doubt that real names are ever used in our world." She returned her eye to the scope, an uneasy alertness stiffening her grip on the gun. "I know your call sign is the Hunter... or Mr. Hunter, which is all I need to know, I'm told."

The man paused a beat, realizing he had inadvertently introduced an element of suspicion between them with the question. It was a dynamic that had no place in the greater scheme of things regarding their professional relationship. Yes, he knew *her* name because he had effectively recruited her. But he had always withheld his true name from the people he worked with, and she had learned from him that knowing someone's real name brought the risk of betrayal when it came to their world. Senior to her that he was, she had always accepted that she would probably never know the name he had been born with.

But why would he talk about it now?

The man could sense Nastassja's mind asking the question; it was a rare mistake on his part.

Since first meeting her, the man had always been aware that children like Nastassja were cursed with no memory of having parents or even knowledge of their family names. He had, in the beginning, accepted this as a natural consequence of her being a traumatized orphan, one of many created by a vicious war that had produced thousands of orphans. But he had also noticed something else behind her clear steel-blue eyes. Strangely, this 'something' had piqued his interest. As world-weary as he had become, he had often wondered if this interest in her was some form of misplaced paternalistic empathy on his part... or worse.

She was much younger than him, but that accounted for nothing in their world. Yet it had troubled him that he had eventually come to care for her. But to fall in love with someone in their business would have been the most stupid and dangerous thing to do, so he had ensured nothing came of it. However, over time, he realized that what he had been feeling was an baffling form of like-mindedness with her. Both were born survivors in a world where survival meant possessing a willingness to kill if need be. Theirs was not the mechanics of hate in a world full of hate; they both shared a deep fear of botching the job... something that had kept them both alert and alive over the years.

"So, I was right," Nastassja chortled. "One hundred and fifty meters or one hundred and sixty yards in old man speak."

"Yeah," he acknowledged. "*Old-man speak* is what I talk."

As he scanned the watering hole one more time, the man wondered if, in another world, he and Nastassja might have been father and daughter or brother and sister. They often displayed an uncanny affinity throughout their time together. It had been a priceless asset during their time together working for the main international human trafficking network that dominated the Adriatic region. Together they had cultivated a well-earned reputation for taking out the competition and removing obstacles. They would fix things, and the Albanians would pay them; eventually the Albanians had become too afraid not to pay them...

But now, the Abomination must die...

He considered the young woman, who was now lining up the shot that would signal the end of one of the most challenging jobs the man had ever undertaken. He knew her and *her* kind. She was someone who had picked up all the dubious tricks and nasty habits that came with forging a criminal career in service to some of the most ruthless organized criminals in existence. She had shown a talent for turning such an education to her own advantage, the exploitation of vulnerable people being all she had ever known. And yet, the man thought, he had been instrumental in molding such a creature...

Her kind were, after all, created for such things.

"Remember to breathe," he whispered to her in Russian. He saw her smile.

Nastassja's native tongue was Serbian, but somehow, she had picked up Albanian, Italian, Greek, and Spanish during a childhood she claimed she could barely remember. Her English was fluent. Russian, which also seemed to have come naturally to her, was the man's native tongue.

The man reflected on Nastassja's highly intelligent and resourceful, if dark, personality. He remembered how quickly she had demonstrated the temperament required for success in criminal enterprises. He thought about her natural aptitude for exploitation, her ability to manipulate a chosen victim without remorse, and her talent for playing the victim to seduce. He knew Nastassja had always been the type who was quietly ruthless when required and shockingly violent when needed. She had even added a commercial pilot's license to her list of achievements in the years after they had gone their separate ways... which had been about five years ago.

How many children, young Nastassja, have you delivered into the lairs and torture chambers of the international elite?

Probably as many as I have, the man thought to himself darkly.

Nastassja was currently employed in her capacity as a corporate jet pilot. Interestingly, her employer was the woman who had seen fit to reunite them in their current assignment. Nastassja's employer was an American blessed with substantial wealth and connections to some of the most decadent people on earth... an elderly woman with ties to the old continent of Europe...

"My name... my true name," said the man tentatively, an unexpected struggle welling up in his throat...

He never finished.

26

Present day, Oregon, USA.

She had slept, and slept.

There had been a small medic team, two muscular-looking men and a woman, to meet them at the imposing but dilapidated wood-framed lodge. Sarah had been made comfortable on a wide leather couch, assured by Morning Star that she was amongst friends. No names were exchanged. They gave her sedatives, and she slept.

Two days passed.

"They combed the area but found nothing," Morning Star told her when she awoke.

He had prepared a hearty breakfast, but Sarah's appetite was pitiful, even if the dry mouth aftereffects of the sedative had given her a sore thirst. She drank a cold glass of juice like it was the last drink on earth. The dogman's broken tooth bobbled on the end of its chain, its presence now back to nestling against her chest... It's still there, she thought.

"Tim and Daemon?" she gasped as the final drop of juice slid down her throat.

Morning Star took a sip of his black coffee.

"They're good," he said. "Deputy Rogers is a bit shook up. Daemon's taking time out back at my place." Morning Star turned his attention to the room's front window as if expecting something. "The men who took him and Daemon drove them into town and let them go, and then he got through to Detective Lee and alerted him to what was going on."

“Detective Lee is still alive?” Sarah almost shouted. “That bastard Smith said he had been killed.”

“A psychological ruse designed to put the fear of death into you,” Morning Star answered. “I would have probably done the same thing in his place,” he added quietly.

Sarah paused for a moment, Morning Star’s coldly analytical comment glancing off her frayed nerves. She decided it was best not to ask what he meant.

“But they’re all okay?” she asked.

“Yes,” said Morning Star. “They’re okay, but this Detective Lee launched a huge manhunt for you and the people who took you—they found nothing.”

“What? All those dead men? They didn’t find any of them?”

“Someone cleaned up.” Morning Star got up and moved over to the living room’s large window, which seemed to be the focus of his attention. It overlooked the small lake they had seen upon their arrival. The window was thick—not just bulletproof thick, but rocket-proof thick. “Someone, with a lot of money and pull, cleaned up back there after we got away.”

“What is this place?” Sarah said, looking up from her couch at the shaman’s silhouetted figure in the window. “You said I couldn’t go home... and that this is my new home?”

Morning Star was staring out the window, the expectation that something was coming still radiating off him like a dark glow. Sarah got up and made her way over to stand by him. They were on the lodge’s top floor, looking down onto the stretch of ground between the lodge and the lake.

“What’s really happening, Morning Star?” she whispered. “People are getting killed...”

He half-turned to her, still keeping his attention on the forested expanse that encircled the lonely mountain lodge and its small lake. The clouds looked thick with snow, the first sign of winter making its mark. Morning Star knew it would snow later that day.

"Scientists find it difficult to explain," Morning Star murmured. "But it is known that the creatures of the natural world have powers of perception beyond the average human being." He looked directly at her. "A pack of wolves will know when a rival pack has crossed into their territory, even though both packs may be separated by one or two mountain chains... How much more would a creature not of this world perceive where we cannot see?"

"What are you talking about?" Sarah said. "You're scaring me."

"That is not my intention," Morning Star said, a rueful smile cracking his lips. "You are here, Sarah"—he motioned his hand in an inclusive gesture—"because this creature... this Broken Fang as you think of it has a connection to you that none of us can fully understand." He closed his eyes. "At least not yet... And so it has been decided that you need protection and sanctuary until we know better."

"Decided?" Sarah said, taken aback. "Decided by *who*?"

Morning Star opened his eyes. The hardness Sarah had seen in them during their march through the forest was there again. The shaman was gone; a warrior looked back at her.

"Consider it protective custody until we all know what we are dealing with here," he said quietly, but finally. "Many people are now involved, and their lives—not just yours—may depend on what happens to you... and what happens to this Broken Fang creature."

Sarah drew a deep breath. Emotion welled up in her.

"That Smith guy, the fake FBI agent, he wanted to use me as bait for the Sasquatch people..." Sarah felt tears of fear form in her eyes. "Is that what is going on here? You're going to use me as bait for the dogman?"

Morning Star looked stunned.

"No... no, Sarah!" He shook his head slowly, his eyes fixed on hers. "This is about breaking the connection this creature has with you... That is why it was decided to bring you here."

"But what is this place?" Sarah demanded.

Morning Star's attention drifted towards the great outside again as if he were picking up something Sarah could not hear or see.

"They are arriving," he said to Sarah.

She asked, "Who are arriving?" Her eyes followed Morning Stars into the great expanse of overcast sky above them.

"Friends, Sarah," said Morning Star. "Friends who will help you and tell you what you need to know."

Sarah then followed Morning Star's eye line to a clump of trees by the near shore of the lake. There was no sound, but the trees gently bent and shook like a great wind had caught them. Sarah strained to hear what was happening but realized the room was soundproofed to the outside world. And then she saw the locust-like shape of a helicopter descending out of the snow-laden sky onto a landing area between the lodge and the mountain lake, its rotor blades now whipping up a tempest of pine needles and wet grass as it made to land.

The stormy silence of the helicopter's arrival produced a slither of apprehension deep within Sarah, as if something sinister, something new, was making itself known. It was a large helicopter, as large as the rescue choppers used by the park services and hospitals for medical evacuations. It was painted red with white markings and tinted windows, giving it an insect-like aura.

"Please excuse me, Sarah, but I have some business to attend to that will take me away for a couple of days," Morning Star said, turning to leave the room. "Please, stay here. You have nothing to fear."

27

Angola, one week earlier...

The huge bearded man shifted his attention to their quarry. The beast was now showing signs of agitation. The man looked down at Nastassja, her right eye now fully concentrating on the colossal thing they had marked for death. She suddenly seemed frail and fragile to him, far too delicate and innocent to be readying a high-caliber death machine to deliver its destructive payload. Oblivious to him now, she was doing what he had taught her, merging her mind into that special place of focused intent, the place one needed to be when making a kill shot. She would not have heard him had he finished what he had been trying to tell her.

As if in slow motion, he watched Nastassja rest her cheek lightly against the gun's carbon stock, her right eye sighting the target through the high-powered scope he had been looking through a few moments before. He was sad to notice more of the tiny lesions that had broken the skin around her hairline, something he had first noticed about a month ago when they had met to begin prepping for their current assignment.

She doesn't have long, the man thought.

"It looks even bigger and uglier through this than through the binoculars," he heard her comment, her brow concentrating on the task.

The man raised Nastassja's binoculars to his own eyes with his left hand while silently shifting his crouch to a position just behind her so he could look over her head at the target.

"It's moved head-on to us, as if it knows we're here," Nastassja said hesitantly. "Isn't the head the worst part to aim at?"

It was true that the average elephant skull, when facing head-on, was a hard nut to crack for most big game hunting rifles. But the rifle Nastassja aimed was several magnitudes more powerful than even the biggest elephant gun on the civilian market.

"We've got *enough gun* to deal with it," the man reaffirmed. "Hit it between the eyes... when you're ready."

He took a moment to look at the entire scene before them. It was quiet, the man thought, *really quiet.* He blinked against the African sun, slowly and deliberately.

Nastassja, the woman who had never known her family or even her own family name, squeezed the trigger and felt the enormous recoil of the military weapon kick back against her padded shoulder. Despite the padding, it was still a painful experience, as it always was when firing such guns. She struggled briefly to bring the rifle back into position for a second shot, but saw that it was not needed.

Behind her, the man watched the almost instantaneous result of the shot through Nastassja's German binoculars. It was a near-perfect shot, only slightly over the beast's left eye. There, a dark hole the size of a man's thumb appeared in the creature's forehead. Its knees then buckled, and the enormous bulk of the thing began to sink. Its entire being then crashed headfirst into the life-giving ripples of the African watering hole. It died almost instantly, the elephant herd already starting to gather around the fallen colossus having been only briefly startled by the metallic report of the anti-materiel rifle.

"Good shot, Nastassja," the man rasped, reaching into a side pocket, his throat sticky-dry with the afternoon dust.

"My first big game kill," she whispered proudly, looking back down the scope at her handiwork.

It was the last thing the woman called Nastassja ever said. A pistol shot rang out, and the back of her head exploded!

Forty minutes later, under the faux pretext of conducting a military training exercise, two Angolan Super *Tucano* light-attack aircraft released a cluster of napalm bombs over a small watering hole. The same watering hole would now be the executed creature's funeral pyre. They were followed up by a CASA C-212 transport plane tricked out to deliver a small payload of thermobaric bombs, their concussive fuel-air destructive force obliterating whatever remained at the watering hole; seven precious African elephants, countless birds and insects, and one genetically-modified monstrosity... and a young woman called Nastassja...

About twenty miles away, dusty and sick of his life, the man who had shot a pistol round into the back of Nastassja's head was making a call on a high-end satellite phone. An elderly woman with a noticeable Hungarian accent answered.

"Is it done?" she rasped, a sickly cough muffled as she spoke.

"Yes," said the man, "the Chinese connection has been terminated."

"How were you able to confirm it was her?" the woman on the other end of the connection demanded tensely.

"An account with a Laotian bank had been opened in her name. It included a safe deposit box with over four hundred thousand in gold and a new identity that had been deposited for her," the man said. "She betrayed us; she was planning on selling the genetically engineered ivory with enough DNA for the Chinese to get the jump on the market."

There was a long pause before the woman spoke again.

"You're a monster... a real monster!"

He winced, closed his eyes, and then breathed.

"I told you," he said calmly but firmly, "To catch a monster, you have to set a monster..."

Again, there was a pause.

"We need you in America as soon as possible," the woman said.

"But there are at least two more of these rogue beasts at large here in Africa," the man countered.

"This takes precedence," the woman said back down the connection. "There's been an unacceptable increase in dogman activity in the Oregon region. Our friends from the other side are most likely behind it. Your travel arrangements have been made through the usual channels."

"Of course," said the man. "Forty-eight hours at the maximum. See you there."

And then the line went dead, and he clicked his handset off.

"Yes, I am a monster," he said to himself. "But one that is, at least, still human..."

He blinked his slow feline blink.

28

Present day, Oregon, USA

Morning Star had left Sarah as if he had dematerialized out of the room, Sarah's mind now fully concentrated on focusing on the mesmerizing whirl of the arriving helicopter's blades.

The craft settled onto the ground, its blades starting their weary wind-down. Sarah saw Morning Star emerge from below her window and make his way over the short distance to the helicopter. He came to a stop and stood there, ready to receive whoever was inside.

The front passenger door of the helicopter popped open, and Sarah saw a huge and heavily bearded man with reddish hair and the fatigues of a hunter getting out and moving towards Morning Star. There was something unhurried about him, predacious and silent... and then the man looked up and briefly caught Sarah looking down at him. She had seen those eyes before, mainly in the feral cats brought to the animal shelter she had worked at over the last few years. The man's appearance was provoking an intensely unsettling reaction within Sarah; the word 'killer' seemed to well up in her mind.

They held each other's gaze.

The man then slowly blinked and then turned to Morning Star, embracing him like they were brothers. Sarah shuddered, but her near repulsion was quickly replaced by a sudden and incomprehensible need to know who this new man could be. She watched as the large man led Morning

Star towards the helicopter, where the rear doors had now slid open. Their parting revealed that the aircraft was indeed a medical-appointed vehicle.

Two brawny men dressed in the attire of rescue workers, probably the same men who had attended Sarah upon her arrival at the mountain lodge (she could not remember), hopped out of the helicopter's rear and began to wrestle a wheelchair-like contraption to the ground. Once it was secure, one of the men stepped back up to the helicopter's open door and reached up to take the frail figure of an elderly and warmly wrapped woman into his arms. He placed her into the chair, its back to Sarah's watchful eyes. Then he returned to the helicopter to help a second younger woman down out of the helicopter's cabin. Sarah immediately recognized the younger woman, and her attention shot back to the fragile figure in the chair.

Morning Star was now moving towards the woman as the men tending her began to turn the chair towards the lodge. His body momentarily blocked Sarah's view of the woman. But Sarah already understood who it was.

The woman and Morning Star conversed briefly, and then Morning Star turned and looked up towards Sarah standing in the top floor window. He waved a friendly smile towards her before joining the large man in the hunter's fatigues who was already getting back into the helicopter. The insectoid-like machine began revving its engine again. Sarah had waved back to Morning Star, but her mind was clouding with questions, even as she was transfixed by the tightly wrapped woman sitting in the wheelchair. Like needles, Katrina Kovacs' piercing eyes looked back up at her.

29

Detective Lee had just become aware of a third man in the café's back room.

The man was huge.

The beard was huge.

"Who's the big guy?" Detective Lee asked Morning Star from across the table that separated them.

Morning Star maintained his gaze on Lee. The big man had become as still as granite.

"He is the one man who probably knows more about what might have happened to Sarah Shaw than anyone else." The old shaman had spoken without even acknowledging the man's presence. "But please, no names need be exchanged beyond you and me."

Lee inclined his head to look more directly at the man. He wore drab outdoor clothing, probably suited to camping and hunting, but with none of the superfluous pockets and sewn-in ammo belts favored by the dilettante woodsman. He wore a warm weather cap with flaps to cover a close-cropped shading of red hair and his ears, though these were currently tied up over the head. Narrowed blue eyes regarded Lee from above the bushy beard that covered the man's weathered face.

"Is he Government?" Lee asked Morning Star without taking his focus off the big man.

Lee supposed the man was also most likely armed, even though he saw no apparent bulges or swellings from a concealed weapon. From years of experience dealing with the real thing, Lee knew that men like this moved through life with the acute situational awareness and readiness of the combat soldier; so, of course he would be armed. It was only a matter of whether it was a blade or firearm as to what weapon the man carried—most likely some form of both.

"No," the big man answered, his voice rumbling off the café's wooden walls. "I'm not even American. But I can be helpful in cases like this."

Lee detected a European flavor in the man's accent, but he was no expert on the different cadences of the Old World. However, Lee deduced there was something Scandinavian about the man, a whiff of the Viking.

"Cases like Sarah Shaw?" Lee said, directly addressing the man. "So, what do you know about Sarah Shaw?"

"Same as you, Detective Lee," the man replied.

"...And what might that be?" Lee pressed.

"That Sarah Shaw may be the victim of medical malpractice," the man said flatly. "The kind of medical malpractice that could be classed as experimental—and therefore dangerous, and even criminal."

Lee nodded slowly. The night was closing in outside, and the flames in the potbelly were dying down to an amber glow. It was cozy, but Lee only felt the chill of the big man's words.

"And how would you know that?" he asked guardedly.

It was Morning Star who answered.

"You are not the only one who has spoken with Ms. Jane Wilkins," he said.

Lee had been in the game long enough to know that asking men like these how they would know anything would be fruitless. He accepted that they knew as much about Sarah Shaw as he did and probably even more. It was time to cut to the chase.

"I'm about to open an investigation into a certain Dr. Andrea Cooper based on a statement given to me by Jane Wilkins," Lee said. "It concerns missing medical records pertaining to treatments and therapy received by Sarah Shaw."

"Missing persons or medical malpractice?" the big man asked.

Lee looked back and forth between both men. Though very different in person, their expressions were identical; placid yet alert. Lee had to remind himself that these men were likely former government operatives—maybe even current; both familiar with operating at a pay grade way above his own.

"That all depends on what Sarah Shaw has to say," Lee said. "Is Sarah Shaw a missing person at this time, or a victim in hiding?"

For the first time, Lee saw the two men exchange glances. It was Morning Star who gave the nod, and Lee realized he was the senior of the two—at least in the current context of the meeting.

"Sarah Shaw is currently a victim in hiding, a victim who needs to become a missing person," the big man said. "Let's just say that it is in her interests that her family is discreetly advised that Sarah is in protective custody but that, in the official sense, she has become a missing person."

Lee took on a doubtful look but understood exactly what he was being said.

"I can't facilitate that kind of status unless I know Sarah Shaw's exact status for myself," he said.

"We know," said Morning Star. "And that is why we are willing to take you to her." He blinked slowly, and when his eyes opened again, Lee could see the flinted edge behind his words. "But this will only be sanctioned on the understanding that you accept that Sarah Shaw needs *our* protection."

Lee looked back into the shaman's weathered face and felt the heightened awareness that accompanies a critical development.

"You need me to place Sarah Shaw on a missing person list," Lee said, confirming the gist of Morning Star's words. "Even though I would know she is alive and well?"

"Yes," said Morning Star. "Because the knowledge of Sarah Shaw being held in official protective custody would only serve to highlight that she remains a threat... a threat to the people that she most needs to be protected from."

The big man spoke: "When it comes to the people we are dealing with, it is better they think Sarah Shaw is out of the picture... and maybe dead."

Lee looked skeptical. He was himself, a man who dealt with facts and disliked not being told directly what he was dealing with.

"And by 'they,' you mean those guys who ran Sarah off the road along with my deputy and her friend Daemon Skinner?" Lee suggested doubtfully. His face had taken on a troubled frown. "We put out a massive search op for these people, and the only reason I signed off on the operation was because Deputy Rogers made a sworn statement that a kidnapping had taken place." Lee regarded both men thoughtfully. "We found nothing–including no sign of Sarah Shaw!"

Lee gave them time to digest what he was saying.

He continued: "All we know at this time is that Sarah Shaw was seen by two witnesses—one highly credible—to have been abducted by persons unknown posing as federal agents."

Lee paused again to gauge the reactions of the two men—nothing. "Naturally, there's already a current investigation being conducted into these allegations, and if you two know anything that could help us, I would appreciate some cooperation—it might be legally prudent to do so."

Morning Star and the big man exchanged glances, with Morning Star again okaying a response by the big man.

"The kidnappers were known to us, but they are now all dead," the big man said flatly. "It is my understanding that these men were simple yet highly trained contractors working for an interested party."

"Oh, really?" Lee said, raising a cynical eyebrow. "An interested party, you say?"

"The type of people who would take an intense interest in keeping quiet the truth behind Sarah Shaw's five-day disappearance while hiking the woods of Oregon," the man said.

"And what kind of people would these types be?"

"All in due course, Detective," was the big man's noncommittal answer.

Lee didn't like those kinds of answers, but he bit down on his natural inclination to push back.

"But you say Sarah Shaw is safe at this time?" Lee's skepticism remained in the slight smile that now pulled at the corners of his mouth.

"Sarah Shaw is safe... for now," Morning Star quietly confirmed.

"So you're telling me that people have been killed and that Sarah Shaw, who is alive and well, is somehow at the center of it all?" Lee's face hardened. "Gentlemen, if a crime has been committed, then I'm duty bound to investigate—I can tell you that even at this time, Sarah Shaw is already connected to an ongoing investigation, an investigation concerning the deaths of at least two federal agents." He looked at both men, alternating between them. "As an officer of the law, I'm telling you that you need to level with me on what you know."

Morning Star answered.

"As far as the kidnappers go, the ones that your deputy reported, we can confirm that there will be no bodies nor any witnesses other than Sarah Shaw as to what happened."

The words froze the air between the three men. An imperceptible glint had appeared in the old shaman's sharpened grey eyes.

He said, "But this is not important at this time. All that matters now is that the people who hired those men—those who would continue seeking to do harm to Sarah—that such people should be provided with a good reason to believe that she no longer poses a threat to them."

Lee's mind picked up on Morning Star's use of the phrase 'continue seeking to do harm,' but he thought better of pressing him.

The big man had now moved forward as Morning Star finished speaking and loomed over Lee. At any other time, Lee would have considered the move an act of intimidation and reacted accordingly. But something in the man's manner negated any sense of threat, only the sense of a man in control of the situation.

"All we can tell you at this time is that the men who took Sarah were ghosts—the kind of men who officially don't exist," the man said. He looked hard into Lee's eyes, no threat there, but no give either. "I can tell you this because I was once one of them."

Lee thought, so now I know; you're a *ghost*! He recalled reading through Morning Star's military records; the redacted indication of special ops and clandestine activities. Lee knew that he was being given as close to a confirmation of his own suspicions as he was ever likely to get, that this vast red-bearded man and the quiet native American sitting across from him were men cut from the same cloth—they were *ghosts* who moved in and within brutal and dark worlds, worlds beyond government and reason; disturbing and hidden worlds best left to monsters and madmen.

Lee said, "Okay, I get it. Please, go on."

The large man said, "The people that these men worked for are, we believe, the people responsible for Sarah Shaw's five-day memory loss. I know who they are, which means I know what Sarah Shaw is up against."

"You're referring to the unaccounted-for five days during Sarah Shaw's disappearance a few weeks ago?" Lee said, interested and feeling like he was now getting somewhere.

"Yes," confirmed Morning Star. He leaned in closer to Lee. "This is an important part of the picture, especially when it comes to your investigation into the deaths of those Homeland Security agents."

Lee listened as Morning Star tapped a finger on the table between them.

"It's important enough that we are willing to take you to Sarah, even though there is a significant risk to her life in doing so," Morning Star concluded,

It was not often that Lee experienced the sensation of losing control over an investigation. Still, ever since the case of Agent Murphy and Agent Meyer had been dumped in his lap, he had sensed forces at play way beyond anything he had ever had to deal with before. Sure, he had often butted heads with federal agencies over jurisdictional issues and suffered frustrations due to bureaucratic obstacles and red tape snaffles. But this case was something different, something beyond even the extraordinary—Sarah Shaw, her connections to agents Murphy and Meyer, her abduction, and everything about her now had its hooks in him.

"Okay," said Lee, focusing on Morning Star's offer. "All I want to do is ask her a few questions."

Morning Star nodded, but a hesitation crept into his voice. "You can ask her the questions you must... But we would request you also bring the woman named Jane Wilkins with you... so that Sarah may hear her testimony."

This surprised Lee, but he nodded anyway, feeling as if the desired compromise had been reached between them.

"I have no problem with that," Lee affirmed. "And in return—provided I'm satisfied with what I hear—I'll place Sarah Shaw on an official missing persons list for her own protection?"

The two men seemed satisfied, but Lee still found it hard to tell.

"I fear, Detective Lee, that your questions for Sarah Shaw will only lead to more questions," Morning Star said. "It has been the same for us—and we have been involved in these things for a long time." He leaned back, his posture conciliatory. "This is all we ask of you now, and I am happy you understand."

Lee hunched his shoulders and again attempted to study the faces of the two men before him. He found himself looking into the eyes of seasoned hunters, the calm perseverance of the patient predator. Lee felt the shiver of a man who has realized he might be way in over his head, but he reminded himself that he had a duty; Detective Lee had never shirked his duty in his entire career.

"Okay," Lee eventually said. "I'll arrange it."

"And Jane Wilkins?" queried the big man.

Lee looked over his shoulder towards the café's front door, the same one he had entered through little more than ten minutes before. It felt as if an age had passed since then, as if something imperceptible yet vitally significant had emerged, as if the craziness surrounding Sarah Shaw, the killings of two federal agents, and the disappearance of a prominent psychologist was only the beginning of something unprecedented.

"I'll arrange it," Lee confirmed.

30

"In the Old World, they are called *werewolves*," Katarina Kovacs said reflectively. "Here, in the Americas, they have the name dogman."

The living room in the timeworn mountain lodge was now well-warmed by a grand fire fed with pungent logs of cured pine. Outside, the air was rapidly cooling, and a slight sleeting of snow could be seen through the thick glass of the room's main window. A dusky blue had enveloped the forested slopes of the small mountain valley in which the darkly wooded mountain lodge rested.

It was now the day after Katarina Kovacs' arrival at the mountain lodge. She had first taken to her bed somewhere inside the log-encased building, too tired to speak with Sarah. Kovacs' nurse had informed Sarah they would talk the following day after her mistress had recovered from her journey. Sarah was actually thankful for the interlude.

The next day, Katarina had been seated into one of the living room's tall wing-backed chairs by her two burly helpers. She occupied a place near the fire's glowing warmth, with Kovacs' ever-present nurse now standing attentively at her shoulder. The fire's orange embers shed a light that seemed to dance silently across the woman's creased face.

Sarah noticed Katarina's threadbare skin and wondered what the older woman was thinking as she watched her peer into the fading flames. It was as if she were seeking some lost divination on their shared future.

Sarah huddled on the bed-like sofa across from Katarina, as if huddling against the older woman's disquieting presence. The two men who had arrived with Katarina had brought a welcome breakfast before leaving the room to attend to whatever chores awaited them elsewhere leaving the three women to eat together in silence.

Sarah now eyed the elderly woman as she sipped a black coffee. She had last spoken to this woman just before her abduction by Agent Smith and his team. That meeting had ended on a disturbing note, not unlike what Sarah felt now. Katarina's frailness seemed to accentuate Sarah's memory of the older woman's deep and evident fear upon hearing Sarah's accounts of her dogman encounters. Their previous parting had now seemed to Sarah like some harbinger of her abduction, the workings of unseen forces in the service of... what was the term Katarina had used? —*Perverted science...*

"In the last twenty years, the sightings have only increased," Katarina muttered as she stared into the warmth of the fire. "The encounters have only become more disconcerting, more aggressive... more violent."

Sarah did not interrupt, fearful in a way of what she might be hearing, despite it having become a compulsion to know of such things.

Katarina continued. "There are many, many people who have had their lives destroyed by such encounters—so many unfortunate meetings with something that nobody believes exists."

She rested her eyes on Sarah, blinking as she sought to focus on the younger woman.

"But we know better, don't we, my dear?"

Sarah felt the overwhelming need to scream. It was the eyes—those piercing eyes—that seemed to know things Sarah could never know, things that Sarah thought she *would* never know.

"They wanted to use me as bait to trap and kill the sasquatch," Sarah said. "But I brought in the dogman, didn't I?"

"So it would seem." Katarina stopped blinking, her eyes doleful in their intensity. "Our friend Morning Star says there is a connection?"

Sarah thought of Morning Star's words of warning to her and caught herself clutching once again at the bloodied tooth that hung from her neck. She saw that Katarina had noticed the involuntary action and she snatched her hand away from the infernal thing. She felt like a child who had been caught touching a taboo ornament in some austere aunt's house.

Katarina returned her gaze to the fire, again as if seeking out an elusive future.

"About four years ago, a woman in Wisconsin arrived at the dog kennel she worked at to find all twelve dogs in her care had been massacred, their throats torn out and their limbs separated from their bodies," Katarina said. "The cages had been broken into by some entity, some wild animal, during the night; the only survivor being a lone terrified pit bull that had to be put down soon after..."

She continued.

"Two months later, a farmer in Minnesota was out hunting with his dogs when he heard a howling from a nearby thicket of trees. He sent his dogs in, all three of them, to roust out what he thought might be a wolf or coyote—they never came back. A week after that, the mangled, half-eaten corpse of one of his dogs was deposited on his front porch. The farmer never saw what it was that did that to his dogs, but there was an overwhelmingly powerful stench of rotting meat that hung around his house for days after the unpleasant discovery, as if something was watching him from close by...

"The following year, we heard reports west of the Cheyenne River Reservation in South Dakota of at least five sightings of an upright sizeable black dog; one sighting in particular talking of this creature stalking a hunting party on a private ranch soon after they had bagged an elk. The hunters felt as if the beast had become enraged at their taking what might have been its prey. They tried filming the thing with their phones, but nothing conclusive could be seen in the footage. All three hunters were well-seasoned big game sportsmen; they all spoke of a crushing sense of dread whenever they became aware of the creature's presence...

"Seven months after that, on a road east of White Sulphur Springs, Montana, a holidaying family was menaced by a massive black dog they say ran alongside their car—upright on its back legs—for at least two hundred feet while trying to aggressively bite its way through the driver's side door window. The father said he was doing at least thirty-five miles per hour at the time! The beast only seemed to give up the chase when they accelerated away from it up to sixty miles an hour. When they got home, they found dents in the car doors on the driver's side. There were two young children in the car with their parents at the time; both are still receiving therapy for recurring nightmares, as are the parents..."

Katarina coughed, and her nurse began to fuss, but the older woman brushed her protestations aside.

Katarina swallowed before continuing. “Just west of the Red River Wildlife Management Area in Idaho, just over a year ago, a park ranger was taking some time out to do some fishing when he reported a series of unusual howls coming from near Sixtysix Creek. A massive dark dog-like creature then burst out of the trees, running on all fours but suddenly stopping when it seemed to become aware of the park ranger’s presence. The ranger swears that he saw it carrying in its mouth what looked like a human baby... And then the animal shot off again back into the forested area where the park ranger lost sight of it. The ranger quit his job shortly afterward and moved to Australia when nobody took his report as being serious...”

“Oh my god, it just gets worse,” Sarah said.

Katarina’s Hungarian accent was now coming through strongly as she spoke.

“And then about a year ago, a man working for animal-control in a small Oregon town reported an encounter in the Mount Hood National Forest with what he called a werewolf...”

“Daemon!” Sarah breathed, immediately recognizing the story that had brought so much ridicule and mockery down on her friend, including her own derision of him at the time.

“Yes, Daemon Skinner,” continued Katarina, looking back at Sarah. “And again, not long after his sighting, a young female hiker went missing for five days in the same general area, only to tell her rescuers that she had encountered not only a large dog-like creature, but also a mother sasquatch and its child as well...”

"Okay, okay," Sarah said. "I get it—loads of people have suffered the same thing as me!"

Katarina gave Sarah a calming smile. She again waved off her nurse, who seemed intent on taking the elderly woman's blood pressure.

"No, Sarah. That's not why I am telling you these things." Katarina's smile waned, giving her penetrating eyes a tired weariness. "I am telling you this because there is a pattern at work here."

Sarah looked up, an intense interest causing her brow to furrow.

"A pattern! What pattern?"

Katarina paused a beat before answering.

"We have been tracking these sightings and encounters, and we have come to the realization that all these sightings pertain to one single creature or dogman as people like to call these things."

Sarah closed her eyes as she saw what Katarina was suggesting.

"It's the same dogman that's been stalking me, isn't it?" she said apprehensively. "It's been moving west for the last two or three years..."

Sarah felt a panic take hold of her as she pictured the monstrous countenance of the beast that had turned her life upside down over the last several months.

"Are you saying this thing has been seeking me out from as far away as Wisconsin?" Sarah's voice was edged with hysteria, her eyes widening. "That this thing has been targeting me for more than three years?"

"Shush, Sarah!"

Katarina's stern rebuke brought Sarah back from the brink. Even so, tears began to roll down Sarah's cheeks, but

Katarina seemed unmoved. A sense of loneliness enveloped Sarah as she looked for hints of sympathy in the other woman's face.

Nothing.

"You must understand," the older woman said. "As bad as your story is, it is merely the latest part in the story of this particular dogman."

Sarah sniffed. "It wants to kill me!"

Katarina waved off Sarah's words harshly.

"That might be true, child. But your encounter with this dogman is simply the latest development in a series of developments that have been forcing it to leave its former habitat and seek out a new place to live... and hide."

Sarah wiped a tear away and stared defiantly back at Katarina. She didn't feel chastened, just angry at being caught up in something she believed she had no part in creating.

Katarina softened.

"It is tough for you, no doubt," Katarina continued. "But what I am saying is that something, or someone, is driving this dogman west–That this creature is trying to get away from something, and when an animal like this is cornered, they are at their most dangerous!"

Katarina slumped back into her chair, giving up the battle with her nurse to avoid yet another tiresome blood pressure test. The nurse duly wrapped the machine's cuff around Katarina's upper arm, and soon, its tight pressure elicited a painful grimace from her. Sarah waited respectfully for the test to be concluded before venturing into a question that had still not been answered.

"Why can't I go home?" she asked. "And why does Morning Star say this is my new home?"

Katarina gave one last grimace of pain as the blood pressure machine's cuff was removed from her. The nurse clucked over the machine's readings but seemed satisfied that all was as well as could be.

"I purchased this old house many years ago," Katarina said, waving her hand about her as she did. "I had the hope of turning it into a shelter for people like you and me... for the people who have endured and been destroyed by meetings with these creatures."

"Is that why the windows have four-inch thick glass—to keep the dogman out?" Sarah asked doubtfully. "Because I doubt even bulletproof glass can deter a dogman who wants to get you."

Katarina smiled, but it was a sad smile.

"The glass and bomb-proof walls are the legacy of the man who built this place in the 1960s," she said. "He was involved with the Mafia; had a lot of enemies—No, Sarah, four-inch thick glass could not stop a dogman from reaching you if it so chose."

"Then why this place, especially since it's in the mountains where these dogmen and things live?" Sarah felt an involuntary shiver go through her body. "Why not get a place in some city or somewhere where it's too hot for them?"

"Have you ever heard that rather quaint saying that 'opposites attract'?" Katarina said, her left eyebrow arching.

"Yeah," Sarah responded hesitantly.

"Well, humans are probably the least sensitive species when it comes to the Earth's natural magnetic fields," Katarina said, then paused. "We don't feel things the way other species do..."

Katarina took something out of her pocket and handed it to her nurse, her eyes locked on Sarah the whole time. It was a round object surrounded by a wide brass ring. Sarah thought it looked like an old pocket watch, but when Katarina's nurse crossed the space between Sarah and Katarina with it, she quickly realized it was an antique compass, its needle shimmering under a clear glass face.

Sarah fingered the solid piece of kit, its brass casing weighing heavy in her hand. She looked up with a questioning curl to her lips but saw that Katarina was squirming in her chair, struggling to turn her frail head enough to look back out at something through the room's thick, frosted glass window.

"This room looks out over the water in a westerly direction to catch the morning sun," Katarina said before the strain on her neck defeated her. She returned her cobalt eyes to the warmth of the dying flames. She raised a bony finger and pointed it through the fireplace, high up and through the smooth stone structure. "So north is in this direction..."

Sarah flicked her eyes as if she could see through the heavy wooden logs that made up the room's fireside wall.

"Look at the compass, Sarah, and tell me which way the needle is pointing."

Sarah did as she was told. She fully expected to see the needle pointing in the same direction as Katarina's finger, but the needle spun in slow but erratic circles. Sarah straightened the compass in her hand so that it was as level as she could, but the needle only seemed more agitated. It would not rest in a static position, even when Sarah got up and stepped away from the sofa.

"What's wrong with it?" she asked, confused at the compass' irregular readings.

"There is nothing wrong with it," Katarina answered. It tells you the truth about this place that we have brought you to."

Sarah said, "What truth?"

"That this house was built over a powerful magnetic anomaly, powerful enough to disrupt the natural senses of most magnetically sensitive animals," Katarina said.

Sarah pulled her eyes up from the compass and caught the fiery glint in Katarina's look.

"Including a dogman," Sarah said, a relieved smile breaking out on her face. "There's a magnetic anomaly here that will stop Broken Fang from finding me... like some kind of force field or something... yeah?"

"That is our hope," nodded Katarina. "But there is so much we do not understand about these creatures, so we have taken added precautions that we think your case merits."

Sarah found herself again clutching at the tooth necklace. Her mouth tightened pensively, and she said, "Added precautions... and who is 'we'?"

Katarina Kovacs' face seemed to toughen, but before she could answer Sarah, one of Katarina's male helpers knocked and entered the room.

"Two minutes out," he said to Katarina. "They have the detective and the receptionist."

"Ah, that is good," Katarina said, turning back to Sarah. "Today will be a significant day for all of us, but especially for you, my dear."

Sarah barely heard her. She looked out the window and saw the tops of the trees beginning to stir, a sign that the helicopter that had taken Morning Star away had returned.

As Sarah moved towards the window's cool pane to get a better view, Katarina's male helper and her nurse fetched the foldaway wheelchair and gently eased the elderly woman into it. They brought her up next to Sarah, where both women could take in the view. Again, the darkly red-painted chopper made its silent yet tempestuous descent. Sarah felt as if a cold shadow was gradually passing over them all.

"It takes a specially trained pilot to land a machine like that here—because of the anomaly," Katarina said. "Even so, night landings are still too dangerous to attempt."

"Who's in it?" Sarah asked, maintaining her focus on the helicopter's floating arrival.

"Someone who I believe can answer the question that troubles you the most," Katarina said.

Sarah turned to her, anxious expectancy lighting up her face. The effects of the sedatives she had been given still left a lingering dryness in her mouth, but the thought of finally receiving some long-awaited answers had made it extra arid and sticky.

"Who?" she demanded.

But Katarina motioned her silence with a restraining hand and pointed Sarah back to the helicopter. It had come to rest, its rear doors now opening.

For the second time in as many days, Sarah watched people step down out of the helicopter's rear cabin. This time, however, Morning Star was the first to exit, followed closely by a man in a thick winter coat and battered trilby. The man kept one hand clamped down on his hat to stop it from flying away as the chopper's rotor blades beat out their last revolutions. Sarah recognized him; it was Detective Lee. It brought a slight gasp to her throat.

"It is okay," said Katarina beside her. "He is here to help."

Sarah said nothing but felt even more alarmed when she saw a middle-aged woman following Lee out of the cabin. It was the receptionist from Dr. Cooper's offices.

Sarah glanced at Katarina, who said, "Her name is Jane Wilkins, and she has seen some of what was in the files that disappeared with Dr Cooper—the files relating to your missing five days..."

Sarah began to shake internally as if some kind of delayed shock was starting to set in. She had once held those files in her own hands as the savaged body of a Homeland Security agent had laid dead in the back of a government car, while another agent, mutilated and naked, lay undiscovered only a hundred yards away. And then the unearthly howls had come, and suddenly she no longer had those files in her hands; only the thought of survival as she and Deputy Rogers had fled for their lives.

"Does she know what Dr. Cooper found out when she put me through regression therapy?" Sarah asked expectantly.

"Not all of it, as far as we know," Katarina confessed. "But Ms Wilkins appears to have seen enough in Dr. Cooper's files to give us some clues as to what might have been revealed while undergoing your regression."

The jagged dogman tooth on the end of its chain seemed to radiate cold heat against Sarah's skin. But this time, she resisted the urge to grab it. Bile was rising in her throat, and she fought for control over deep emotions that lurked beneath. The fear of what the future might bring was completely subsumed by her essential need to know.

Then Sarah saw another man exiting the passenger side of the helicopter. She recognized him as the same huge red-bearded man she had seen embracing Morning Star the day before, the same man who had hugged the old shaman like some long-lost brother.

"He was here before… Who is he?" Sarah quietly asked.

Katarina paused for a moment, her eyes also studying the man.

"By now, Sarah, you must now know that we live in a world of monsters," she said darkly.

Sarah felt compelled to turn her head and look down closely at the wizened woman, her nurse hovering protectively close by.

Katarina did not return Sarah's questioning gaze but let her eyes follow the bearded man as he made to join the other three disembarked passengers. They all then began to make their way as a group towards the mountain lodge's lower entrance. But then the big man briefly stopped. He looked up and fleetingly caught Katarina staring back down at him. Again, thought Sarah, as she witnessed the exchange, he with the cat-like slow blink. Sarah saw a ghostly blue distance of the unknown in those eyes as she realized that he was offering up to her a slight but highly disconcerting smile. But then he turned, like a frosty breeze, and disappeared with the others below the window's lower ledge.

"I tell you, Sarah, this is truly a world of monsters." Katarina murmured as she turned her head towards Sarah and saw the younger woman visibly shaking. "And some of the worst monsters are human."

Sarah breathed deeply. She knew things had gone bad when Morning Star told her she could no longer go home.

However, it was only at this moment that she genuinely comprehended what she had always known since her first encounter with the dogman: the inevitable reality that her life had changed forever. Those indistinct eyes that the man had turned on her had somehow confirmed this...

"There's no going back, for sure," Sarah moaned, more to herself than to Katarina.

Katarina's face looked worried as she surveyed the younger woman's reaction.

"But you have friends, Sarah," she said reassuringly.

Sarah looked directly into Katarina's eyes, the older woman's face reflecting the concern that Sarah could feel eating at the life-force within her.

The time has come, Sarah thought.

"Take me to him first!" Sarah suddenly said, meaning the large red-bearded man. "I will speak to your human monster, the beast with the ghost in his eyes; I will speak with him first before I speak to the others!"

As soon as she said it, Sarah felt a change come over her. She hardly recognized her voice as the words spilled out from her.

"I, too, have questions!" she said.

31

Katarina had said nothing at first. Then, she had ordered her nurse to summon Morning Star.

"Sarah wishes to speak to your friend," she had told the old shaman.

"Are you sure?" Morning Star had asked Sarah, and when she affirmed her wish, she was led through a series of stifled passageways and staircases into the building's central depths. It was as if Morning Star had been expecting that Sarah would make the demand.

To Sarah, the mountain lodge appeared to be a gloomy affair, as much on the inside as on its outside. There were too many sparse and cold rooms, heavy wooden walls and roughly planked floors; so many floors and sub-floors that Sarah had wondered if she could have ever found her way back.

As they had dropped ever deeper into the mountain lodge's depths, Morning Star had found it prudent to apprise Sarah of the type of man she was demanding to speak to.

"This man you want to talk to is not like me; he is a man who lives by his own code," Morning Star had said. "He and his code are not of this world... and he will accept or reject you according to that code."

The old shaman had stopped Sarah for a moment, intent on emphasizing the nature of who she would be dealing with: "Men like this man wander this world like restless spirits. They are dangerous and lethal in ways the ordinary civilian has no understanding," he had said. "But this man... He is the Ghost that other ghosts fear!"

For the first time ever, Sarah had seen what she thought was fear in the eyes of this seemingly indestructible elder. It had triggered a feeling of terror within her, the horror of suddenly being lost, of being forgotten, as if by insisting she speak with this man had affected her connection with Morning Star, that their bond was fading into the blackness of the old shaman's own fears.

Who is this man... this Ghost, Sarah had thought... *And what is this place?*

She found herself longing for the intimate warmth of her cabin, where she had made a home for herself, a house according to her own needs and sense of self. She now desperately missed the functional simplicity of her old life and felt distantly out of place as they wound through the mountain lodge's web of austere rooms and darkened levels.

And then she stood before a solid, faceless metal door at the end of a short, dark hall.

"He is in there," Morning Star said without looking at her.

It was a similar door to the one that she, Daemon, and Deputy Rogers had previously passed through into the presence of Katarina Kovacs in her underground sanctuary. That had been a mere few days before, before their abduction by the rogue Agent Smith and his team, before Agent Smith's annihilation by the dogman.

Morning Star motioned for Sarah to wait and knocked on the metallic surface, his knuckles producing a dull, pinging sound. Without waiting for an answer, Morning Star opened the heavy door and stepped in. He left the door open behind him so Sarah could hear, but not enough that she could see who or what was in the room.

Sarah listened.

"Ms Shaw would like to speak with you first," Morning Star said, presumably to the large bearded man.

There was a slight pause, and a deep, throaty voice answered.

"Suits me," the voice said. "But I don't think that will sit well with the detective. He wanted first dibs on her."

Morning Star answered, "Sarah Shaw will decide whom she speaks to while under our protection!"

Morning Star had sounded emphatic. There was a silence, and then the voice said, "Very good, send her in... but then bring Detective Lee and his witness here in about fifteen minutes."

Morning Star seemed to hesitate.

"You're going to do it here?" he asked, his voice taking on a questioning tone.

Again, there was a pause before the rumbling voice answered.

"Sometimes it is better to *show* than to tell," Sarah heard the man say.

Morning Star returned to the door and gave Sarah a sad nod before gesturing for her to step inside. He moved past Sarah, barely looking at her on his way out before closing the door as he left the room.

Sarah had detected a heightened tenseness in Morning Star's bearing as he had passed by her. But she quickly found herself staring at the massive bearded man, whose almost monolithic bulk was more startling in person than Sarah had expected. He quite filled up one end of the windowless, bunker-like chamber.

In Sarah's increasingly traumatized experience, only the alpha male Sasquatch she had once encountered could have surpassed the effect of this man's sheer size and presence. He must have been close to, or even over, eight feet high, his intimidatingly large head hunched forward to avoid contact with the room's low ceiling. But the it was the breadth of the man's fatigues-clad body that threatened to overwhelm Sarah, as if she were standing before a human mountain. He seemed even larger to her than the dogman... at least as tall and potentially as violent, given the noticeable scarring on his massive hands and knuckles.

Sarah looked about herself. The combination of the enormous man and the stark room cramped in on her.

The room was completely bare. There were no chairs to sit on or creature comforts that Sarah could see other than a naked light bulb hanging starkly from a roughly finished wood ceiling. Its amber light illuminated the room's log-encased walls and naked planked floor. A kind of trapdoor lid lay closed shut at the feet of the large man.

The word 'trapped' forced itself into her mind, and Sarah felt even smaller and more alone in the moment, like a mouse trapped inside a room with a huge and curious cat-like being; his eyes slow-blinking in feral anticipation.

"I am Sarah Shaw," she said, her voice bouncing dryly off the sparse room's deadened walls.

He acknowledged her with a slight incline of his heavy head. He wore an impossibly large winter cap with its earflaps turned up. His untidy sideburns blended into his enormous, dark-red-hued mountain man's beard while his giant's eyes played passively upon her as he lightly shifted his bulk onto his left leg.

As the silence persisted, the man's slight movement allowed Sarah to pick up on the frightening shape of a massive, long-barreled gun that was propped up against the wall behind him. She was singularly uninterested in firearms, but even she could tell this was more than some hunting firearm—nothing like the high-caliber rifle Tim Rogers had recently taken to carry around everywhere. Sarah was looking at a military-level killing device... a war machine!

"We're not dealing with coyotes here," the man noted sardonically. He had been watching as Sarah's eyes had apprehensively taken in the oversized weapon.

Sarah thought the man's deep voice had a foreign tinge, an accent that eluded Sarah. It reminded her of Katarina Kovacs' dulcet inflections—maybe Eastern European.

Sarah stood assessing him, a human monster according to what Katarina Kovacs had intimated. His ghostly eyes assessed her in return. He stood at the casual attention of a military man awaiting orders.

So Sarah obliged.

"I'm told you are a monster and a ghost. But can you tell me who you actually are and what you know about why this dog-thing from hell that is stalking me?"

Again, Sarah barely recognized her own voice. It was intense, unafraid, even defiant, and all too unfamiliar to her. But her words were like a wave crashing against a granite cliff, the backwash merely confirming the immovability of the man's disturbingly intransigent gaze, a gaze they held for a long and heavy moment, his misty light blue eyes seemingly glinting with secrets.

"Are you sure you want to know what this monster can tell you... what *this* Ghost can *show* you?" the man eventually said.

Sarah said nothing, her mind processing the meaning and intent of his words.

The man broke into Sarah's thoughts, saying: "Because it's all very well that you make these demands, Ms. Sarah Shaw, but there are revelations to be had here that cannot be undone once revealed—which I'm sure Ms. Kovacs and my friend Morning Star have warned you about, eh?"

Sarah snapped her head up, forcefully projecting her determination into the man's eyes as he towered across from her.

"How can a man like Morning Star be a friend of *yours*?" she blurted out. "Everything about you—eyes like a predator; the aura of violence that anyone can see you carry with you—it all makes me believe you are part of the horror that has destroyed my life!"

Sarah tensely waited to see what affect her outburst might provoke in the paradox of this *Ghost's* rock-like appearance.

"Morning Star tells me you wear some kind of necklace made from the creature's broken tooth," he said calmly. "And that you now give this creature a name: Broken Fang?"

Sarah said nothing but inadvertently again found herself clutching the tooth under her sweater... something he noted. Then she saw him begin that menacing slow blink of his, the same cat-like blink he had given her while she had watched him during his arrival. It unnerved her even more this time.

"So let me tell you what I think has been happening," he said as his eyelids lifted. Sarah felt a foreboding chill as he did so. "Since it is most likely that it will be *me* who has to kill this poor creature... on account of *you*!"

Sarah's mouth dropped open. "On account of—"

"—I have hunted and killed multiple individuals of these species," he said, cutting her off, "...These creatures you and others call a dogman."

He stood motionless, implacable, and Sarah stood rooted to the spot as his profoundly resonant voice washed through the deadened room.

"The first four I killed in service of an organization that is dedicated to the harvesting of such creatures... and to the profitable exploitation of *their material*!"

Sarah fixed on the emphasis he made on the word *material.*

"What do you mean by *their material*?" she asked uneasily.

The man slowly nodded as if satisfied that a connection he had sought had been made.

"I will tell you a truth, Sarah Shaw," he said, quieter now. "A truth that you may find difficult to accept, but one that is vital if you are to understand the world that you have been dragged into..." He paused. "But it will be your choice to know."

Sarah felt like a frozen lump of emotion was passing down her throat and settling in her gut. *Was this actually it? The moment of truth?*

"Tell me," she said.

32

The man's eyes slow-blinked again; this giant of a man that Morning Star called the *Ghost*, that Katarina Kovacs had named a monster... The Ghost spoke: "This is what I know:

"There are people in this world connected to a past too bizarre for most minds to comprehend."

He paused for a beat... as if remembering...

"I work for an *organization* that has become a powerful entity within a hidden international system... a system that has thrived for over seven decades on the warped ideologies and the filth of a perverted science..."

Perverted science—Sarah remembered Katarina Kovacs had used of the same term.

"The people behind this organization believe their science can elevate them to the status of gods, gods made in their own image," he continued.

"Are you suggesting that these people created this dogman that's been coming after me?" Sarah interrupted, eager to get to the point.

"No, I'm not," the man said flatly. "The dogman you came into contact with is a creature as natural as you and I. But the men behind this organization simply want to *own* these unknown cryptid species."

Sarah was growing impatient.

"Look! All I want is to get rid of it!" Sarah exclaimed. "I don't care who owns it or who created it; I just want to rid myself of the thing that's been chasing me and get back to my life!"

"Then you will misunderstand the importance of knowing who these people are and what they want!" the man said curtly. "These people want to *change* all that is natural—and that includes this dogman species... and you!" His eyes narrowed dangerously. "They want to alter these dogmen into something they can *own*... and you have somehow become a part of that equation."

He had emphasized the word *own* as if this was an important distinction, but Sarah seemed confused, his words eluding her.

"You are a woman of science, are you not?" the Ghost said, trying to steer Sarah towards a conclusion. "You trained as a veterinary assistant, I believe?"

"Yes," she said.

"Then you will be familiar with genetics and DNA at some level?"

"I know a little about the subject, but I'm no expert," Sarah hedged, unsure where he was going with the subject.

The man nodded again, ready to continue with his story.

"Many years ago, I was recruited into a clandestine cryptozoology program, a special project that hunted strange and seemingly supernatural creatures that nobody believed existed, but that many have been unfortunate to encounter."

"Like the dogman," Sarah murmured.

"Yes, particularly these dogmen," he said, stroking his beard thoughtfully. "At first, I thought it my job to eliminate these things, as if to help protect humanity from their predatory ways... But this was a lie."

Sarah said, "A lie? How so?"

"They were conducting experiments, fusing human DNA with the DNA of the cryptids I killed."

The man stopped to let Sarah digest what he had said. She breathed incredulously. And then it hit Sarah directly between her eyes, the clarity of vision that comes with sudden and total realization.

“I see you understand now,” the man said.

"So, they’ve put my DNA in that creature, right?" she breathed. “That’s the connection?”

Sarah saw the man's eyes soften for the first time.

"It's so rare to catch a live one," he said, reluctance impregnating each word. "It’s my professional opinion that you happened to be in the wrong place at the wrong time, but were highly convenient to their immediate needs.”

Sarah closed her eyes and felt herself swoon in the room’s start light.

“What do you mean, *convenient to their immediate needs*?”

When she opened her eyes, the man seemed to have moved closer towards her.

“I’m speculating that at the time they came across this particular dogman they had to work fast, taking advantage of whatever resources where at hand... and so a part of you became a part of it."

Sarah felt like retching, like something fundamental and deep down in her core had been violated, like her sense of self had just been torn out.

"Why?" Sarah said, her voice barely above a whisper.

"I will tell you," he said softly. "I will tell you because you asked me to."

Sarah listened:

"Over eighty years ago, a brilliant geneticist engineered synthetic humans—not clones, but living beings capable of learning and adapting. Initially primitive and short-lived, these synthetic humans were later improved by splicing genes from natural humans into them. This resulted in the synthetic beings taking on the physical characteristics and even the personality of the human donor.

"Now, these synthetic beings can live up to forty years, although they suffer from adverse effects like spontaneous scalp bleeding when stressed. When infused with a real human's DNA, they become nearly indistinguishable from the donor, to the point of effectively replacing them."

Sarah listened, transfixed.

"And if they are infused with a real human's DNA, then they can hardly be told apart from the human donor... even to the point that they can effectively replace them..."

"Let me guess," Sarah interrupted, "if you can mix a normal human's DNA into one of these fake humans and get a reaction, then why not try crossing them with some other species and see what happens?"

"Precisely," the man said. "But when the doctor first discovered how to create synthetic humans, DNA was still a mystery. It was only later, after acquiring the remains of a so-called 'dogman' creature, that the doctor's understanding of genetics advanced significantly."

"They got a dogman, like the one that's after me?" Sarah asked, a quizzical tone entering her voice.

"A dead one," the man said. "The doctor experimented and produced results that caught the attention of influential men who could finance and protect him, nurturing his brilliance in creating hybrid creatures and chimeras."

Sarah interjected, "Protect him from what?"

"From the prying eyes and interference of all that is decent and natural," said a voice from behind Sarah.

Sarah turned, startled by Morning Star's silent reappearance, his grim expression frightening her. Before she could speak, the Ghost continued, "What you need to know from all this is that the doctor successfully created unnatural humans and animals over eighty years ago. Using genetic material from a dogman corpse, he developed a terrifying hybrid he called his 'werewolves'!"

"You're kidding me," Sarah said, her eyes now locked back on the giant's faded blue gaze.

"Type-Three dogman," Sarah heard Morning Star say from behind her. "The type of dogman that our friend Daemon encountered—and the same type that Katarina encountered."

"So Daemon saw a different dog-creature during his encounter," Sarah said cautiously.

"Most likely," said Morning Star. "An unnatural beast unlike the one you call Broken Fang."

Sarah turned to the big man at the other end of the room.

"But why?" she asked.

"All we really know is that the doctor's creation led to an organization dedicated to hunting and capturing the natural version of this dogmen species," the Ghost explained. "They exploited the times, working with Nazis, Soviets, and intelligence agencies, as long as they were free to pursue their true desires."

"Oh no, you don't!" Sarah cried suddenly, her fists banging against her ears. She looked up, angry. "OH, PLEASE! Don't you dare tell me this is all some world domination conspiracy crap. Like out of some bad sci-fi movie full of Nazi werewolves and mad scientists!"

Sarah actually advanced on the huge man, a man she had expected would give her some real answers to what had happened to her, and not some fantasy about evil Nazis and rogue secret agents! She stabbed her finger into the man's enormous rock-solid chest and shouted, "Just tell me what's with this dogman thing and why it's coming after me!"

"Sarah!"

Sarah whirled at the sound of Morning Star's raised voice. He stared at her hard, his head slowly but forcefully shaking in displeasure at her outburst.

"What we can do is can tell you that it's out there, outside now!" Morning Star said.

Sarah flinched.

"Broken Fang?" she rasped. "He's found me?"

"It seems so," said Morning Star, but he was already turning his attention to the man he called the *Ghost*. "We are also detecting the presence of a stealth craft in the area."

The giant brushed past Sarah to speak closer with Morning Star. It was as if he had passed her on air, his effortless movement belying the weight of his enormous bulk.

"Is it the *Beast*?" he asked Morning Star urgently.

"I think so," replied Morning Star, his face tense with concern. "You have to stay in here, where the anomaly is strongest, to avoid them discovering you are with us."

"What's the *Beast*?" insisted Sarah, inserting herself between the two men. "Another dogman?"

"No," said Morning Star. "The *Beast* is the organization you are being told about—the people who have taken your DNA and injected it into this Broken Fang creature without your consent."

"Why... what do they want?" Sarah stammered.

"I told you!" said the bearded giant, facing Sarah impatiently. His height dwarfed her as he fixed his eyes on hers. "They have used your DNA—your living essence—to see if they can re-engineer and change the living essence of this dogman. They want to make it into something else... something *new... something* they can *own...*"

"And in doing so," said Morning Star, "they have criminally tampered with both your soul and spirit, and that of the dogman's spirit being. They have created an unnatural connection between its world and your world..."

"And they will now do anything they can to understand this connection and to exploit it," added the Ghost, his voice dropping an octave in intensity. "Because they want to *own* everything and anything. They want to recreate the natural world according to their technology ..."

The calm blue hue of his eyes now blazed as he looked at Sarah. Morning Star moved between them and looked carefully at Sarah as she struggled to absorb the human giant's words.

"Understand that the sasquatch beings and natural creatures like them—like Broken Fang—are a connection between this world and another," the shaman said.

He moved towards Sarah and raised his hand to her face. Sarah didn't pull back, and Morning Star brushed her hair away from her forehead as a father would with a daughter.

"Sarah, you too are now a connection between these two worlds... The Sasquatch have spoken to me of it." He studied her face and skin, avoiding her eyes. "And these men who work for this *Beast* will do anything to take hold of and exploit that connection."

He now looked into her tearful eyes.

"We are convinced that everything that has happened to you since your first encounter with the dogman and the mother Sasquatch, including your missing memories, has been an experiment in trying to harness these spirit beings' connection with this other world."

Morning Star closed his eyes and murmured something that Sarah couldn't catch. She felt his fingers lightly stroking her hairline as if he were searching for something.

"You are their gateway," he abruptly said, withdrawing his hand from Sarah's face. "And now the *Beast* is coming for you... and for Broken Fang."

Sarah's mind reeled, but she saw that the Ghost was now too looking intently at her face and hair.

"Anything?" he said, his words obviously meant for Morning Star.

"No," Morning Star answered, relief in his voice. "She is not one of them."

"Good," breathed the giant.

Their exchange had a sobering effect on Sarah as if she had been offensively appraised somehow.

"Not one of *whom*?" she demanded, looking back and forth between the two men.

"Hush, Sarah!" Morning Star said. "Trust me when I say we have only your best interests at heart."

"I think I should be the judge of that!"

Sarah had thought the words, but had not said them, Instead, the voice came from the room's door, and they all turned to see the sharply stoic figure of Detective Lee standing in its open frame. He was visibly angry, with a stern and confrontational edge.

"Our agreement was that I would assess the state of Ms Sarah Shaw's condition before you engaged in any questions concerning her well-being!"

As Sarah and Morning Star took in Detective Lee's sudden announcement of his presence, the big man glided his bulk back to his first position, the very same spot that he had greeted Sarah upon her entry into the room. He looked up with a welcoming smile on his face.

"Of course, detective," he said. "But within these walls, Sarah Shaw will decide whom she speaks to and when she speaks."

Sarah felt the tension in the room ratchet up as the Ghost and Morning Star fully confronted the detective.

"It's alright, Detective Lee!" Sarah said, concerned that her demands may have led to an unfortunate misunderstanding between the three men.

"Ms. Sarah Shaw, is everything okay, and are you well?" Detective Lee said, his eyes still fixed on Morning Star and the enormous man he had first met in the highway café a couple of days earlier.

"Yes, yes," Sarah nodded emphatically. "I'm sorry if I've caused you any concern, but I wanted to speak to—" She stopped, realizing that she still did not fully know the name of the imposing man she had been speaking. "—I just needed to get some things worked out before I spoke with you... I'm sorry."

Lee shifted his attention directly to Sarah.

"That's okay, Ms. Shaw," he said, the tension draining from him. "I had an agreement with these two, but if you say you're doing well and everything is fine, then no harm done."

The grizzled detective moved further into the room and stood facing all three of them, his feet placed authoritatively apart. He seemed to be satisfied that Sarah was in no immediate danger.

"I need to ask Ms Shaw some questions, and I would prefer to do that with her alone," Lee said, his head inclined in a way that told the Ghost and Morning Star that this was not a request.

Sarah looked at Morning Star and realized that the old shaman retained an underlying tension in his stance. She watched as he bowed his head, directing his focus back towards the giant standing a small distance behind him.

"I would say incoming in about ten minutes," he said cryptically to him. "Can you deal with things here without me?"

The man seemed to shimmer in response, as if something had been activated in him.

"Detective Lee," the Ghost said, addressing the lawman directly. "Have you brought the woman Jane Wilkins with you to this room?"

The detective looked puzzled at first, and then severe.

"Yes, but I first want to discuss things with Ms. Shaw before I bring her in."

Sarah immediately realized they were talking about Dr. Cooper's receptionist, the woman she had recognized disembarking from the helicopter earlier. A surge of expectation gripped her at the thought of learning something new about Dr. Cooper's missing files.

"I saw Dr. Cooper's receptionist arrive with you," she eagerly told Lee. “Is she here to talk about those missing files that I told you about?"

Lee scratched his head and then remembered Sarah's claims about a bunch of missing files when he had first interviewed her at the scene of Homeland Security Agent Murphy's horrendous killing. It seemed like a lifetime ago to Lee, what with all the twists and developments that had come his way since being assigned by the FBI to follow up on the case at a local level.

"The missing files?" Lee said, his mind racing.

It was as if something had dropped, a crucial piece to a puzzle that Lee had failed to see until now—that the information brought by Jane Wilkins concerning evidence of some kind of medical malpractice might be the same missing files that Sarah Shaw had first claimed existed. Lee couldn't believe that he had not previously made the connection.

"Yeah," he said, distracted by his own thoughts. "She's just outside—"

"Bring her in," said the Ghost. "I'm sure Ms. Shaw would be most interested to hear what this Jane Wilkins has to say."

"No!" Lee said firmly, standing his ground. "First, I will speak with Ms. Shaw alone!"

Sarah was taken aback by Lee's determination to get things his way, and her hopes sagged at the thought of being delayed once more in getting to the more urgent answers that might await outside the room. But the atmosphere in the room had just become more dense, heavier with tension. She saw Morning Star take a measured step toward Lee, his focus keenly aimed at the detective's narrowing eyes.

"Bring the woman in, Detective Lee, because time is short," Morning Star said dangerously. "You will have all the answers you want."

It was as if a deadly stillness had suffused the air in the room creating a tension that Sarah was finding difficult to tap into. She saw Morning Star and Detective Lee seem to face off... and then something went off in Detective Lee's eyes, and Sarah heard him say: "It's your call, Ms. Shaw—do you want to speak to Ms. Wilkins?"

Sarah's reaction was instinctual, as much about getting to the truth as about diffusing a situation between the two men that seemed to have turned rancid.

"Please, I just want to ask her something..."

Nobody said anything, but Sarah became aware that Dr. Cooper's former receptionist was now in the room, her eyes nervously taking in the charged tension.

"Hello, Sarah," Jane Wilkins said, never taking her eyes off the three men. She saw Morning Star and Lee still glowering at each other, and the third, the enormous but silent man she had traveled with on the helicopter standing silently at the other end of the room, studying her intently.

"Hello," Sarah replied to her absently.

"Mountain Daughter! A word with you outside, please?"

Morning Star was now regarding Sarah, his hand motioning her towards the door, an imploring expression on his face.

"But—"

"It will only take a few seconds, and then you can return to speak with Detective Lee and this woman," Morning Star said, every fibre of each word urging her to comply.

"Okay," Sarah said, confused, more by Morning Star's insistence than by his request. She realized he had used her spirit name, and something within her responded to his underlying urgency.

Sarah started moving towards the door, but it was like she was moving in treacle. Morning Star slipped past Detective Lee to move closer to Sarah as he guided her past the stationary and perplexed figure of Jane Wilkins, whose eyes were now fixed on the giant man at the end of the room.

Jane Wilkins was bleeding.

As Sarah stepped past Jane Wilkins, Morning Star ushering her into the open corridor behind the door, something pricked at Sarah's subconscious; she knew it was something significant but did not know why.

"You're bleeding," Sarah said to Jane Wilkins, almost absently, her eyes seeing the signs of dappled pinpricks of blood breaking out along the woman's hairline.

Jane Wilkins gasped, her hand shooting up to her hair, the blood smearing over her fingertips... and then Sarah was outside, Morning Star deftly drawing her beyond the heavy steel door that he had slammed closed behind them, its weight causing it to bounce slightly leaving a tiny opening between the door and its frame.

"It had to be this way," Morning Star breathed into her ear as he folded her into a protective embrace, his full attention on the faceless metal door that now separated them from the three people still inside.

Sarah heard a scream and then a muffled crack, like a pistol shot! A ricocheting whine... She heard the voice of Detective Lee cry out—"What the hell!"

There was a thud and then silence. Only Morning Star's breathing filled Sarah's ears as he held her away from the closed door.

Then there was the sound of a desperate scuffle, the sound of violence; of Detective Lee grunting as if the air had been brutally squeezed out of him, followed by another heavy thud...

Silence.

Sarah felt Morning Star's embrace loosen, only one hand holding her as he moved back towards the door. She turned and saw him cautiously pulling it open, the room's single light bulb painfully glaring its light into her eyes.

"It had to be this way," she heard Morning Star say again. "They are among us... everywhere."

What Sarah saw seemed even more frightening to her than even Agent Smith's destruction at the dogman's hands in the darkened menace of a nocturne forest. The scene before her was not nearly as bloody, with no bodies having been torn apart or limbs dismembered, just the horror of the immediate violence of one human on another...

Jane Wilkins lay crumpled where she had stood, her head leaking a broad pool of pinkish viscous blood from a gaping exit wound in the back of her skull. Brain matter was spattered over the back of the room's door, but it had an alien-like anemic paleness to its color that Sarah didn't recognize. The woman's dead eyes looked up, open to the bobbing effect of the room's recently disturbed naked bulb, their unseeing stare taking in the dancing shadows it produced as it swayed on the end of its cord. Sarah saw a small pistol lying beside Jane Wilkins' body.

"That would have been for you, Sarah," Morning Star said quietly, pointing to the gun. "They are among us, everywhere; the real Jane Wilkins was probably murdered months ago... and replaced with this..."

More death... and more death, thought Sarah, her mind tightening in shock.

In the middle of the room, Sarah saw the unconscious figure of Detective Lee laying on the rough wooden floorboards, the giant and bestial-looking bearded man crouching over him, a large caliber revolver smoking in his right hand as his left hand checked the fallen man's vitals.

Sarah screamed!

"No, it's okay," Morning Star said, reaching out to calm Sarah as she reacted to what she thought was Detective Lee's dead body, a victim of the ogre squatting over his seemingly lifeless form. "He's okay, just unconscious. He was only neutralized, but he will be okay."

The Ghost, Sarah thought. *Is that this monster's actual name?*

The Ghost raised his head. He was calm, almost serene. The cool blue eyes slow-blinked.

"I can take care of the detective," he said, addressing Morning Star. "I'll fill him in with what he needs to know and what he needs to do; Ms Shaw will become a missing person, as discussed."

Morning Star took a moment to assess the situation.

"They'll be here within minutes. Ms. Kovacs has initiated the Budapest protocol, so we'll meet up in Seattle and proceed to the safe house from there," Morning Star said to the Ghost, who nodded his agreement. "But be careful, my friend; the *Beast* cannot know that you've betrayed them; that you walk with us."

Sarah barely processed what Morning Star was saying, and then it dawned on her.

"You still work for these people, don't you—this gang of Nazis, or whatever, this thing that you call the *Beast*?"

Sarah was dumbfounded and massively disappointed at her naivety, disappointed that she hadn't anticipated the dangerous intrigues that her cryptid encounters would provoke or the kind of person that would be drawn to her because of them. She thought of the brutal extinguishing of the Homeland Security agents, the extermination of Agent Smith and his team, and now the execution of Jane Wilkins, or whatever it was that had been posing as Jane Wilkins. *So much death... so much violence!*

A knowing smile broke out across the Ghost's face, entirely inappropriate... and Sarah hated him for it!

"Yes, I am Ms. Kovacs' spy in the organization," he said, "this *Beast* that you should remember is responsible for everything that has happened to you, Sarah Shaw."

"Who are you?" Sarah snarled, her hand angrily catching at the dogman's ragged and raw tooth that hung around her neck.

The giant lifted himself to his full height, and Sarah caught her breath. Gone was the knowing smirk; a cold blue fluorescence now seemed to be lancing out from behind his eyes as he first turned his attention to Morning Star.

"Take Ms. Shaw up top—use the M82," he said to the old shaman warrior, indicating the enormous gun behind him. "There are things that Ms. Shaw should see before we exfiltrate."

Morning Star silently acknowledged the Ghost's command and moved to collect the daunting weapon. The colossal man then shifted his eyes to Sarah.

"You ask who I am?" he said.

Sarah looked about her at the fearful finality of what had been Jane Wilkins, the unconscious form of Detective Lee sprawled on the floor before the great brute. White hot anger was replacing shock as she jutted her jaw in defiance.

"Tell me!" she hissed.

"I am the *Ghost* in the *Beast*!"

33

… … Sarah felt numb. She hardly felt Morning Star guiding her out, the giant rifle cradled in his sure arms as he led the way; she had hardly noticed the pitiless Ghost manhandling Detective Lee's limp body down through the open trap door she had guessed at before. She had no idea what she was feeling; an executed woman that she was supposed to believe was not even human? A hidden war between two worlds; cryptids versus hybrids versus humans versus synthetics?

Nothing could, or should ever make sense again... but Morning Star led Sarah onward, her feet dragging as they negotiated a dark maze of tunnels carved into the mountain beneath the lodge as if the structure had been built on some old mining complex. They entered a small cave behind some concealing snowbound bushes, its small entrance opening to a view of the clearing below. And somehow, it was now a white crystal night shining under a full moon.

Whether the cave acted as a defensive position or as a hunting hide, Sarah did not know or care. All she now knew was that beyond its open mouth was a new and infinitely more dangerous world; a world of dogmen, of werewolf hybrids... and human monsters like the Ghost and the people he worked with—or, more correctly, the people he worked against. And there was also Morning Star, who was now urging her to look through the cold glass scope of the huge weapon he had perched on the lip of the cave's open threshold.

Peering through the scope's icy lens, her heart pounding, Sarah gasped as she picked out a pack of five twisted, brutal-looking animals closing in on an isolated figure—it was the figure of Broken Fang! But these were not animals; Sarah was looking with shock at the terrifying shapes of *werewolf* hybrids. She watched as these dreadful and unnatural creatures formed a closing ring around the Dogman, these things that had been spawned by men and had only ever been poorly constructed images lurking in the darkest recesses of Sarah's mind. But their reality was magnitudes more horrifying.

An unfolding bloodbath was taking place as Broken Fang, raging with the primordial fury of one who is the last of his kind, stood surrounded by the snarling, misshapen Type-Three beasts—hulking bipedal mutants with the intelligence of men and the savagery of wild dogs.

But that was not the least of it. Leading the pack was a grey-furred horror dominating the others in size, a warped amalgam of wolf and man and machine. Its eyes smoldered with an infernal hunger exclusively directed at Broken Fang, and its lips bore back in snarling intent. A dark mechanized exoskeleton girded its torso, six-inch claws gleaming at the end of one metal arm, its body a towering horror that chilled the last vestige of warmth out of Sarah's blood—

"Now they have gone too far," Sarah heard Morning Star whisper in anger, and she knew he spoke of the organization that the Ghost called the *Beast*. Morning Star edged Sarah to the side of the gun and took her position as if to sight in the new monstrosity for elimination.

Sarah couldn't help but study the fearful new apparition. Its grey fur was rent by gruesomely fresh surgical scars, the metallic claws at the ends of its elongated arms and hands gleaming in the frigid light. And then she saw its eyes, or saw into them, the feral hunger that blazed as it forced its way forward onto Broken Fang. Sarah grasped the amulet at her neck, her skin crawling with the growing sense that this monster, this living machine from hell, wasn't just a random mutant.

As if hearing her thoughts, the beast raised its full face towards Sarah, and in the light of the pallid moon, she stifled a scream—she was looking into the mutilated visage of Agent Smith!

Oh my god, Sarah thought. The sociopath lived, after all, fused body and soul to some ghastly variation of the Type-Three abominations that raged around him. She saw his lips mouth something at her through blood-slathered fangs, "Revenge is sweet," it said—and Sarah's mind tore, everything becoming a staccato of blurred movement, a slow-motion frenzy in which the mind becomes encapsulated by a flood of emotional torment and physical agony.

She saw Broken Fang fight like a berserker, ripping the throat from one attacker, breaking the head of another... Saw the monstrous re-manifestation of Agent Smith and his venomous pack outmatching and steadily overwhelming the lone cryptid by sheer weight of numbers... And Sarah heard herself cry out as Broken Fang was hamstrung and forced down, set upon with ruthless and frightening fury... the feral eyes of the solitary dogman, once so maliciously focused in their predatory intent on her, now reaching out to Sarah as if it knew where to look for her... Its eyes were the eyes of fear, and then... the end... The pain Sarah felt was unbearable.

Then Sarah's senses caught the sound of Morning Star's wicked gun roar out along its destructive line of power, and Broken Fang's head disintegrated in a spray of bone and blood as the huge caliber round impacted with unimaginable force, taking at least two of the werewolf hybrids with it at the same time.

"Flesh and blood!" Sarah heard Morning Star mutter coolly as the rifle automatically re-chambered another round, the old shaman re-sighting his aim on the thwarted rage of the transformed Agent Smith. "And mercy in death..."

But now there was something else, something huge and black... Sarah's eyes were wrenched skywards as the moon's light disappeared behind the gargantuan emergence of dark and massive triangle-shaped craft. It hovered in uncanny silence as a broad beam of light lanced down menacingly from the center of the alien-looking vehicle, its glowing shaft an arm of ectoplasm-like traction reaching down to engulf the carnage-filled clearing. And then Sarah detected the arrival of more of the werewolf-things falling down through the light, their hideous bodies descending like limply grotesque floating ragdolls to join the fray.

"Pray now, Mountain Daughter," she heard Morning Star say quietly as he, too, caught sight of the fantastic craft and its slow-falling cargo of beasts. "They have our scent."

Sarah watched, a strange feeling of detachment seeming to separate her sense of self from the awesome sight. She became aware that Morning Star was lining up the new and terrifying incarnation of Agent Smith for a final kill shot.

"Kill him... kill him," she heard herself say as the animal-enhanced face of Agent Smith instinctually zeroed in on their presence, the discarded remnants of Broken Fang no longer the focus of his wrath.

Morning Star's fingers began to squeeze the trigger, the barrel of the .50 caliber Barrett projecting a clear line of white-hot fire to the center of Agent Smith's abominable head...

Click!

Misfire!

An unholy snarling smile of satisfaction broke across the former agent's corrupted features as if his keen ears had picked up the fatal clunk of Morning Star's failed attempt at his extermination. He began to move towards them.

Morning Star said, "We have no time—"

"Quiet!" Sarah said, her hand raised in urgent command.

Sarah looked at Morning Star, seemingly oblivious to the advancing horror of Agent Smith moving in for the kill.

"Don't you hear it?" she said.

"—No," replied the old shaman. But there was an understanding in his eyes... and hope.

Sarah closed her eyes, a sound like honey trickling into her mind...

"We are here," said the familiar voice, *"We are here!"*

As she opened her eyes, an ear-splitting roar shook the mountainside. The hybrid werewolf pack instantly abandoned its continuing violence on the remains of the slaughtered Broken Fang, a primitive terror overriding their engineered viciousness as they broke in panic. They dropped as one to all fours and sped into the surrounding forest, a flurry of snow dust masking their escape.

Agent Smith, or the beast that he now was, stood alone in the gore of Broken Fang's decapitated corpse. His moment of triumph and revenge exchanged with a curious mix of confusion... and fear. He looked up at the vast triangular craft above him and was almost immediately caught by the light beam's levitating force. It lifted him from the ground, his hugely grotesque animalistic form seemingly powerless to resist.

Morning Star began to urgently tear at his rifle, intent on freeing its jammed mechanism in an attempt at taking another shot at the monstrosity being retracted into the waiting craft. But it was a hopeless task, and both he and Sarah watched as Agent Smith's body disappeared into the depths of the massive black triangle—and then it was gone as if it had winked out of existence.

Sarah touched Morning Star's shoulder, directing his attention back to the scene of Broken Fang's torn carcass.

"They *are* here," the old shaman said wonderingly.

A series of glowing transparent orbs now circled and flitted about Broken Fang's fallen body, probing it for evidence of life and meaning. The effect was mesmerizing, and Sarah felt as if warmth had returned to her soul.

Then, from out of the forest, Sarah and Morning Star witnessed the breath-taking spectacle of an entire sasquatch clan, seven of them in number, striding out to lay claim to what was left of Broken Fang's ravaged body, the orbs of light fading out as they approached. Once again, Sarah was entranced by the sheer size of presence these *people of the forest* exert, like mythical gods come to reveal themselves to a tainted world...

"They lay claim to his spirit," Sarah heard Morning Star say and then heard him begin to offer his own prayers in the soft incantations of his own tongue.

Sarah saw—no felt—the lead elder of the sasquatch pause, his inner sight rising to meet communally with Sarah's, a melancholy understanding passing between them. She recognized him in spirit as the big alpha male she had encountered on a country road leading away from Morning Star's compound, which seemed like a lifetime ago. Through him, in an instant that lasted thousands of years, Sarah saw the eons of guardianship that he and his kind had exercised over the natural world, now disrupted by unnatural interlopers they did not understand and did not know how to resist.

"Help us," said the voice in Sarah's head one last time. *"Help us, Daughter of the Mountains."*

Then the Sasquatch collected the remains of Broken Fang and bore the dogman's body and spirit away with them, a silent retreat back into an impenetrable forest that had been their refuge since the beginning of time... then they were gone.

Sarah turned to Morning Star, the old shaman's eyes filled with a deep and comprehending awe.

He said, "Yes, I heard them too."

"I heard them give me a name," Sarah said.

Morning Star remained silent, but he nodded his understanding of what Sarah was referring to.

"Then you know that we must go, my friend," Sarah said. "The *Dogs of Budapest* await."

Morning Star's mouth dropped in surprise.

"How is it you know of this name?" he said, his former understanding turning to a look of misperception.

Sarah experienced a strange combination of confusion and clarity. She turned away from Morning Star and looked towards the East, as if that was where the answer lay. The sun was beginning to rise, its fingers of light arching out over the snowy horizon.

Sarah could not answer Morning Star...

Part 4
The Dogs of Budapest

The Cryptid Dossier: Confidential Case File 4

Origins of a Nightmare...

****

34

TOP SECRET
EYES ONLY

Date: May 15, 1945
To: Brigadier General Maxwell Taylor, Deputy Director of Military Intelligence
From: Lt. Col. Alexander Holmes, Military Intelligence Service
Subject: Translation and Analysis of Captured German Documents Regarding Pripet Marshes Incident

Sir,

Intelligence has uncovered and translated documents from the German military archives that shed light on a previously unknown incident in 1943 in the Pripet Marshes of Russia. The documents outline a secret investigation authorized by the German Secret Field Police (Geheime Feldpolizei, GFP) into the disappearance of a Waffen-SS unit in the marshes while combating Russian partisans along a railway.

According to the recovered documents, the area commander, Generalleutnant Otto Drescher of the 35th Infantry Division, suspected desertion, but the local SS commander, Sturmbannführer Schur, believed there was a more sinister explanation connected to the disappearance. Schur secretly instructed a Hungarian undercover operative codenamed "Johnny" Kovacs to investigate any links between the missing unit and the alleged biological weapons experiments of Dr. Alos Silasi, said to be taking place in the area.

A secondary element to Kovacs' mission seems to have been the acquiring of information concerning a potential British-run spy codenamed 'The Circassian.' Initial inquiries with our British allies have proved inconclusive as to any Allied asset operating in the region at that time.

The documents further indicate that Kovacs was provided authorization to access any Wehrmacht or SS facilities in the marshes. Accompanied by a three-man security escort, Kovacs appears to have traveled to a forward Wehrmacht resupply base commanded by Hauptmann Kluge, the last known stop of the missing Waffen-SS unit. Soldiers at Kluge's base referred to the single railway leading deep into the marshes as the "tracks to nowhere" due to its unfinished and frequent disruption by partisan attacks.

The recovered documents make no further mention of Kovacs or his investigation's findings. His mission seems to have been incomplete as far as German documents go. We will continue efforts to uncover additional documentation that may shed light on this incident and its implications. Please advise if you require any further analysis on this matter.

Respectfully,
Lt. Col. Alexander Holmes
Military Intelligence Service

TOP SECRET

Russia, Pripet Marshes, 1943.

"They were accused of helping the partisans," said one of the military escorts, his fingers nervously stroking the pistol grip of his submachine gun, his eyes flitting back and forth along the nearby treeline.

Kovacs grunted. He was looking at two wretched and rotting figures hanging from a dead solitary tree, one having been a young woman, her face a mutilated mess, the other being a badly beaten Russian partisan. The sight was horrific even for hardened veterans of the war like Kovacs. A murder of hungry crows swarmed over the tree's brittle and bleached limbs, taking turns pecking into what was left of the two corpses.

"My God!" Kovacs muttered contemplating the savaged remnants of the hanged woman's face. "Someone really didn't like you."

She gently swung in the breeze along with her Russian companion, the latest evidence of the Germans' brutal anti-partisan tactics. These tactics had sought to remedy the never-ending attacks and sabotage being inflicted on the *Wehrmacht's* overstretched supply lines.

Kovacs' two military escorts and the driver with his seconded *Typ G4* staff car were young—too young. The sheen of their once-fresh faces was now clearly stained by the haggard darkness of war. All three had a frightened tautness about them. Their eyes had been constantly scanning the edges of the swampy forests surrounding them as their lone military car had bumped along on its way to a small *Wehrmacht* outpost on a disused railway line.

Kovacs had asked them to stop for a while when the haunting sight of the hanging couple had emerged ahead of them. His escort detail had protested to a man, warning that loitering for any length of time could draw the attention of partisans.

"We wouldn't be doing our duty if we did not alert you to the fact that this area is under threat by the enemy, sir," Kovacs' second guard had said, armed and ready with a submachine gun.

"Noted," Kovacs had acknowledged.

But he was insistent they stop to take a look around. Kovacs had a gut feeling that this macabre vignette of horror might be necessary in some way to his investigation. The two swinging figures displayed all the hallmarks of the *Waffen-SS*, the ruthless signature of men who wore the death's head as part of their insignia. Kovacs considered the dreadful sight the first dot in a connecting series of movements left by a group of hardened combat veterans... men that had seemed to have vanished into thin air.

As he absorbed the barbaric essence of the scene, the resentful reticence shown by his security detail didn't surprise Kovacs. The toll suffered by the *Wehrmacht* at the hands of the determined Russian guerrilla fighters, the thousands that infested the nearby woods, had made the lives of German soldiers behind the front lines almost as dangerous as at the front itself. It was a brutal and dirty part of the larger conflict that few people back home had any conception of.

Kovacs listened to the three soldiers grumble to each other as he got out of the car to take a closer look at the hanging corpses. Though Hungarian was Kovacs' mother tongue, he spoke fluent German and several other languages, including Russian. His multilingual talents had been a deciding factor in landing him a job with the German army's feared policing arm, the GFP. But most Germans saw him as a foreigner, someone unable to fully grasp the nuances and intricacies of their language. Over the past two years, this assumption had gotten more than one surly soldier into trouble.

Kovacs decided to take a little more time to study the surrounding territory than was likely wise. His custom was to attempt to better understand the greater context of any point or detail that seemed pertinent to an investigation. So he let his eyes make a complete three-hundred-and-sixty-degree survey of the surrounding landscape... and that's when it caught his eye.

Close by, about half a kilometer away, Kovacs could pick out a decrepit-looking log cabin, maybe part of a small Russian farmstead. He decided on the spot—a gut reaction— that it was pertinent to investigate the structure before their planned arrival at the encampment commanded by the *Wehrmacht Hauptmann* Ernst A. Kluge.

"Has that place been cleared?" Kovacs asked, pointing to the cabin and its small collection of outbuildings.

"I don't think so," said the first soldier, his eyes still darting left and right even as he looked at where Kovacs' interest lay. "Some strange foreign woman had been living there, but no one has seen her for a while."

"A strange *foreign* woman, who is currently missing?" Kovacs' said, his interest spiking. "And no one has investigated why she is now missing?"

The two young men gave Kovacs the universal vacant look of the soldier, the kind of look given when something is discussed that is way above their rank—or concern.

"She came under suspicion of working with the partisans, and I assume she decided it was time to go," laughed the first soldier, nervously.

"Really?" said an incredulous Kovacs. "And no one has secured or searched that property since?"

The two of them looked at each other uncomfortably and went quiet. This happened a lot with soldiers when the likes of Kovacs started asking questions. Kovacs had long learned to attribute such behavior to a combination of not wanting to risk a possible encounter with hidden partisans, especially by poking around in some unimportant shithole. But the attitude was also due to his rank as an officer in the German army's secret field police. The ordinary German soldier dreaded the *GFP*, especially the almost total authority they were given in carrying out immediate justice against any soldier or officer suspected of defeatism or not doing their duty. Kovacs and men like him were feared and loathed in times of war.

"We have not been given orders," said one of the escorts weakly.

"Very well then," said Kovacs. "We shall do so now—and that is an order!"

Increasingly anxious at the unscheduled stop in hostile territory, and with the light of the day fading, Kovacs' two guards once again emphasized the wisdom of not hanging around. But despite their protests, Kovacs was equally insistent on taking a look at the deserted cabin.

As they approached the ramshackle cabin Kovacs wondered what a foreign woman would be doing living in a hovel in the middle of a Russian marshland. There was something about the unlikely scenario surrounding this deserted cabin that twinged a nerve within Kovacs. It was the kind of hunch that had kept Kovacs alive so far, something uncanny in a war that had already taken millions yet had left Kovacs relatively unscathed. But when he heard the driver mutter under his breath that there were more dangerous things out here than Russian partisans, it did give his gut some pause... But not enough to ask the soldier to explain himself. Kovacs had learned that idle grumblings from the ranks often held little worth when tracking down meaningful leads.

On closer inspection, as they neared the cabin along a rutted cart track, Kovacs determined it was part of a small homestead situated on a boggy piece of reclaimed swamp ground. He saw a rusty hand pump that seemed to be the only water source, while a small damaged barn showed signs of recent use. Parked behind the cabin, Kovacs could see a broken one-horse-covered wagon, its steel-shod wheels rusty with non-use.

They stopped about a hundred yards from the property, the two soldiers jumping from their car to scout out potential signs of the enemy. They found none, and once his escorts had secured the perimeter and outbuildings, Kovacs was cleared to take a look inside the cabin's shaded one-room interior. The sun's light was now quickly beginning its descent below the horizon.

The cabin's door had been left unlocked, and Kovacs could see evidence of recent occupation by what appeared to be a single resident. The cabin's interior had a rustic, bohemian quality, a clutter that suggested the lifestyle of an artist rather than that of a peasant farmer or homesteader. There was an interesting dichotomy in expectations to what Kovacs found inside this forlorn little Russian cottage.

Kovacs' eyes took some time to adjust to the interior gloom.

The feel of the place gave off a decidedly feminine quality. And yet Kovacs felt an air of lost melancholy lurking in the room's shadowed corners. To the rear of the cabin was a large and comfortable-looking bed with quilted blankets and a canopy. Two large paintings of contrasting styles were hung on the back wall and the windowless side wall, the first depicting a stylized study of the Eiffel Tower in Paris and the second a brooding landscape of the surrounding Pripet swamp lands.

Kovacs looked around. Elsewhere in the cabin, he came across a number of stacked painted canvasses, mostly with what looked like surrealist portraits and landscapes. They were racked against the side wall of the cabin that offered a solitary shuttered window onto the outside.

Upon closer inspection, the paintings had an aesthetic that gave Kovacs a sense of familiarity about them, but a familiarity he couldn't quite place. Yet, somehow, he was sure he had seen the style before. Even so, the name of the artist eluded him, even as Kovacs became keenly aware that the nature and style of the art was frowned upon in both Nazi Germany and Bolshevik Russia. It was the type of surreal-like art that Nazis and Bolsheviks alike referred to as decadent trash.

But Kovacs was curious about who would be painting in such a prohibitive style in the middle of a Russian wilderness—in the middle of a war. His instincts told him that something odd was going on in this little cabin stuck out alone in the Russian swamps of Pripet, but Kovacs could not yet tell exactly what it was that was giving him this feeling.

More importantly, Kovacs noticed a heavy typewriter sitting on a table by the shuttered solitary window. An unfinished loose-leaf manuscript was piled up next to it. He moved over to the table and gave the manuscript a cursory glance, expecting to see Cyrillic lettering, something he was unfamiliar with despite his adequate command of spoken Russian.

However, the manuscript was clearly written in English, and its title declared it to be *Memoirs of a Travelling Muse*. Kovacs looked closer at the title page, searching for the author's name, but he saw no name.

The fact that English was the manuscript's chosen language was intriguing to Kovacs and even alarming from a security perspective. The typewriter typed words using a Latin alphabet instead of Cyrillic script, which suggested to Kovacs that the cabin's missing occupant was indeed foreign. Also, given that a nearby messy bookcase was populated with some English language titles, Kovacs concluded the person had either a British background or had at least enjoyed an English education. Kovacs was aware that there had been many Cambridge and Oxford graduates whose sympathies had gravitated towards Communist Russia during the 1920s and 1930s. He speculated that the cabin's absent woman was most likely one of these *Champaign socialists*... well-to-do bourgeoisie choosing to live the Soviet dream before the inconvenient arrival of Hitler's Nazi hordes.

But something else of interest was tucked away among the English-titled books that haphazardly cluttered the bookcase's shelves. Kovacs spotted what looked like an expensive Rolliflex camera. Its casing was battered, but its body was otherwise in good condition.

As he picked it up and looked over it, Kovacs thought about the implications that the camera suggested. A civilian with a state-of-the-art camera in a war zone was never good, no matter what side they might be on. It made for all manner of suspicions on the part of the authorities, especially when the camera belonged to a citizen of a potentially foreign or hostile country. Whoever she is, Kovacs thought, this person who paints and writes is most assuredly foreign...

As Kovacs had already half-surmised, the cabin's missing occupant was most likely someone with a privileged and expensive English education; the camera's quality alone pointed to a person with possible links to the press—a former news correspondent, maybe?

Have we found you? Circassian?

Kovacs thought on the question: Was the enigmatic British operative—an elusive operative codenamed the *Circassian* that SS officer *Sturmbannführer* Shur had alluded to when briefing Kovacs for the mission—was this the very same woman who had previously occupied this non-descript shack in the middle of nowhere? For Kovacs, this meant only one thing; he now needed to find out everything he could when it came this intriguing but missing woman.

"Gentlemen," he said to the two loitering soldiers, now both grudgingly awaiting further instructions inside the cabin's door. "I am going to insist that this cabin is thoroughly searched... as a matter of the highest security!"

Kovacs marveled internally as the two soldiers snapped to attention and acknowledged the order with a harsh bark in the affirmative. One thing the German soldier could never be accused of was having a lax attitude to authority. Kovacs watched as the two began to systematically trash the place. Pulling out drawers, tumbling bed linen onto the floor, and rummaging through cabinets, they went about their work with the sullen determination to get things over with if only to be done with the wretched hut.

"Be on the lookout for any written materials, address books, etcetera," Kovacs reminded them.

He then pushed open the shutters of the cabin's solitary window to cast more light into the room, realizing it gave him a clear view of the distantly swaying corpses he had passed earlier.

"How long have those two been hanging there?" he asked one of his escorts, almost as an afterthought.

"About two or three weeks, maybe longer," one of the soldiers said, stopping briefly to look through the window over Kovacs' shoulder.

"They were executed for helping the partisans," the other soldier added again unnecessarily.

"And the woman who lived here? Was she also a part of why they were executed?" Kovacs asked.

Both soldiers had stopped their search activities to shrug at Kovacs' question, but they did not answer directly.

In the fresh light from the open window, Kovacs' eyes could now pick out a large photograph that had been placed face down next to the piled-up papers of the English manuscript. He turned it over with an inquisitive flick and saw it depicted an immediately recognizable scene. He looked at the Rolliflex camera still in his hands, like it was the most likely suspect in taking the shot, and then back at the photo.

Now, this is interesting...

Kovacs saw that the photo was a snapshot of the same hanged woman and partisan that he had seen earlier, the same victims that he could now see from the window of this small and depressing cabin. However, a German army officer was also present in the shot, his eyes looking up at the two corpses as he fired a pistol into the air. It looked to Kovacs like the gunshot had been made to frighten off the scavenging crows that had been feasting on the hanging bodies.

Kovacs took a moment to study the photo more closely. He felt there was an unnerving quality about its framing, the way the lens captured the subject matter. But the photo's unsettling effect was not because its context captured the barbarity of war—Kovacs had seen enough of that kind of barbarity to inure himself for a lifetime. It was because the image seemed to have captured a totally out of context act of kindness in the way German officer was attempting to scatter the crows feasting on two enemy combatants.

For Kovacs, the officer's conduct in the photo jarred with everything he understood about the German officer class. It jarred with the reality of a ruthless and cruel war that Kovacs had seen all too much of since being drafted into the GFP, the almost total loss of humanity that now governed actions on both sides of the conflict. Looking at that one pistol shot, the camera catching the muzzle flash perfectly in time, was for Kovacs, like feeling a pinprick in the skin of the unnatural savagery and extreme violence that the Eastern front had wrapped around him.

"Who is this?" Kovacs asked one of his escorts, pointing at the German officer in the picture.

"*Hauptmann* Kluge," the soldier confirmed with an uncomfortable look towards his fellow.

Hauptmann Kluge? The very man Kovacs was expecting to question over the last known movements of a unit of *SS* killers...

"And the girl hanging on the tree?" Kovacs prompted. "Exactly why was she executed?"

A silence made Kovacs turn his attention entirely onto the two soldiers.

"She was accused by *Waffen-SS* troops of helping the partisans," said one of the soldiers half-heartedly.

"I don't think she was guilty," mumbled the other soldier quietly.

The soldier's remark, bold in its own way, struck Kovacs as being almost sorrowful, even sympathetic.

"But sometimes an example must be made, eh?" suggested Kovacs.

Kovacs was not looking for an answer, however. The muffled disgust in the averted expressions of each of the men told Kovacs that these two German soldiers were not the types who reveled in the kind of warfare that increasingly counted women and children as legitimate targets.

But Kovacs wasn't there this time to scrutinize National Socialist fervor of the rank-and-file troops he encountered. He was there to find some answers, specific answers as to why a bunch of crack *Waffen-SS* soldiers had gone missing in the nearby forests of the Pripet marshes. Whatever misgivings these two conscripts felt about the course of the war—these two kids—this was not part of his immediate concern.

Kovacs put the photo down and picked up the thick manuscript. He was a man who boasted a good command of English, and it genuinely intrigued him what someone would be writing in that far-off language while in the middle of a Russian wilderness. More importantly, its presence suggested that it might cast some light on his task at hand; a further clue to the identity of some vague British operative that German intelligence claimed was operating in the area.

Kovacs licked the tip of his index finger and flicked the manuscript's cover page to the side, hoping to finally reveal the author's name on the next page. Again, no name presented itself. But as he was about to thumb his way further into the heavy document, something else caught his eye—a signature, or something like it. It was written onto the side of one of the canvasses stacked against the wall.

Kovacs pulled the painting out. It was a small-to-medium-sized canvas, twelve-by-sixteen inches or so. Upon turning it face up, he was confronted by an image of haunting feminine beauty, yet it was a visage both terrible and unparalleled in his experience. He heard the audible gasps of the two soldiers from behind him, and Kovacs could feel himself turning to stone and grasping the canvas harder.

"My God!" he muttered again for the second time that day.

Staring back at him was a pair of hypnotic Gorgon-like eyes, their color surreally glazed yet vibrantly amber; a set of manic eyes projecting a mad light that appeared to be shrouded within a woman's face... a young and beautiful face... and the massive jaws of a wolf-like beast consuming her head from behind as she stared out into the ether beyond...

Kovacs held the painting to the light to take in the woman's mesmerizing gaze. As he did so, he was reminded of a disturbing comment that Adolf Hitler had made upon first seeing Franz von Stuck's evocative portrait of the Medusa: '*Those are the eyes of my mother!*'

35

Present day, somewhere high above the North Sea...

"So, exactly how many of these dogman things have you killed?"

This was Sarah's first attempt at real conversation with the Ghost as their private jet lanced its way into European airspace. Four days earlier, the aged Native American shaman Morning Star had delivered her to a prearranged airstrip just outside Seattle, Washington. There, her journey as a fugitive from circumstances out of her control had begun. The jet's preliminary route had been circuitous, a necessary precaution to evade the surveillance efforts of the people who sought word or sight of Sarah Shaw at any cost.

"And how many of those Type-Three things have you killed?" Sarah added.

The Ghost was sitting up near the cockpit, his enormous bulk facing back down the aircraft's narrow cabin to where Sarah sat facing forward a short way back from him. Sarah could see that he had a ragged, sleepless bleakness to his eyes that matched her own.

"At least nine of the natural ones," he rumbled back, a knowing half-smirk tugging at the corners of his heavily whiskered mouth. "I've lost count of how many hybrids I've taken out."

"And how about those synthetic people you were talking about?" Sarah pressed, remembering the Ghost's clinical execution of the woman Sarah had assumed was Dr.

Cooper's former receptionist. "Killed a few of them, have you?"

The Ghost simply nodded.

"They're becoming more numerous than is healthy for the human species," he said. "If it's any comfort, it can be difficult even for someone like me to deal with." The Ghost thought back to a young Serbian synthetic woman he had dispatched a few days earlier on the plains of Angola. "They can be almost too human for my liking."

"It's no comfort at all," Sarah retorted. In her mind, taking a life was taking a life, even if it was some form of synthetic facsimile manufactured to masquerade as a human being.

They had stared at each other for the best part of the four hours since leaving Canadian airspace, the hum of the jet's air conditioning blending hypnotically with the cool whine of the engines. Sarah had occasionally glanced out the cabin window to look down onto the old continent of Europe, its dark territory silently slipping away beneath them. Her mind was still trying to shake off the trauma of witnessing the savage butchery of the dogman she had come to know as Broken Fang. The dogman's broken tooth still hung from her neck, a talisman of dubious worth... and the last physical connection to a creature she still found impossible to comprehend...

Sarah needed to know...

"So, do you also believe that this *Beast* outfit, this organization you mentioned, is using these hybrid werewolves to drive the dogman species out of their natural territories?"

Sarah's eyes scrutinized the Ghost for a reaction.

"What's that about?" she prodded.

The Ghost broke eye contact and looked behind himself as if to make sure the jet's pilots were minding their own business. He then returned his gaze to Sarah.

"Do I believe like... *who*?" he queried guardedly.

Sarah blanched, feeling as if she had betrayed a confidence. She stayed quiet.

"The hybrids are a manmade abomination!" The Ghost said flatly, his eyes fixing her with that cool blue stare of his. "But, as I told you, the dogman creature is something natural—because anything I can kill that has not been manufactured by humans has to be natural."

Sarah forced herself to maintain her own defiant stare back at him.

"But what are they?" she insisted.

The Ghost tapped his head as if he were about to impart an essential piece of knowledge.

"What are they?" he said, repeating her question. "They're dangerous, that's what they are."

Sarah said, "*Asshole!*"

The Ghost gave a short snort.

"The only way I know how to kill these dogmen is to put a big and very fast life cancelling bullet through their skull—hit anything else, and it's as if you haven't hit them at all."

Sarah thought about Morning Star's mercy shot that had taken off Broken Fang's head as she had witnessed a terrifying pack werewolf hybrids close in for the kill.

Morning Star knows, she thought.

The recollection of Broken Fang's violent demise was like an open wound.

"My own theory is that these natural dogman are part of the species called *Mustelidae*," The Ghost said. "It's a bad-tempered and highly aggressive family of mammals that includes weasels and badgers... and the extremely tough North American wolverine."

"I know what the *Mustelidae* species consists of," said Sarah dismissively, bristling at his presumption. "So, what? Are you saying that dogmen are some kind of giant wolverine?"

"Only in as much that I also know that the sasquatch species is some kind of humanoid," the Ghost responded.

Sarah took a moment to digest the Ghost's unexpected theorising on the nature of the two cryptid species that had turned her life upside down. She had experienced the uncanny human-like nature and appearance of the sasquatch for herself, probably on a level even this brute of a man would fail to appreciate. She had even found herself in some kind of ethereal communication with the great and hairy cryptids, and she knew them to be more than some ape-like creature; more like a people than animals.

36

Russia, Pripet Marshes, 1943.

"It's her," said one of the soldiers in a whisper.

"Who?" demanded Kovacs, ripping his gaze away from the painting and fixing it on the soldier who had spoken.

They stood there, all three of them in the ramshackle cabin, its air turning stale as they peered into the painted eyes of the portrait Kovacs was holding.

"The *Hauptmann's* woman," said the other soldier. "It is the *Hauptmann's* woman."

"*Hauptmann* Kluge's woman?" demanded Kovacs again. His mind raced to take in the unlikely coincidence of finding yet another connection to a man he would soon be questioning concerning a missing unit of crack *Waffen-SS* troops.

"Is this the woman who lived here?"

"No," said the first soldier. "It is not the woman who was in this cabin. I think the woman who lived here was the one who painted the picture." He pointed at the canvas in Kovacs's grasp. "Those eyes... everyone fell in love with them!"

"Really?"

Kovacs returned his gaze to the painting and let the surreal-like eyes stare back at him.

"You're telling me that the woman in this painting was the *Hauptmann's* whore?"

"She was a camp follower," the soldier clarified, seeming to be slightly offended. "She was one of the women Kluge kept to keep his bed warm at night."

"Is she a foreigner?" Kovacs barked, intent on establishing an identity.

"Yes," the soldier who had last spoken confirmed.

"Is she a *Britisher*?" Kovacs demanded. "Is this woman in this painting an *Englander*?"

Kovacs' two escorts looked at each other tensely, a bit confused. They might have been young, but they knew answers to questions from a *GFP* officer tended to lead to dire consequences.

"Tell me!" Kovacs shouted.

"No," said one of the soldiers hoarsely. "She was like you; Hungarian... a *Magyar*."

The other soldier said, "The *Hauptmann* called her his..." He seemed to be struggling to remember a word. "He called her his *Talos*, or *tiliss*, or something like that."

"You mean a *táltos*?" Kovacs said, immediately recognizing the Hungarian term. "As in like a witch, or a cunning woman?"

The first soldier grinned meekly and said: "The *Hauptmann* is a man with interesting and sometimes dark pursuits, if you know what I mean, sir?"

Kovacs looked fixedly at each soldier and then back at the painting. His mind clouded over for a moment as he took in the woman's beautiful features, his thoughts forming a new perspective on what he now saw confronting him.

What would a Hungarian táltos be doing sharing the bed of a humble Wehrmacht captain?

Then he remembered the first reason the painting had caught his attention: the hint of some kind of signature or wording along one of its sides. Kovacs turned the canvas in his hands, and there it was, in light cursive painted letters; the word *Circassian* in its clear English spelling!

Years of experience in the dark arts of espionage and national security had taught Kovacs that there is always that moment in any case, in any mission, where a chance discovery will set you on the right track. Be it a cryptic clue or moment of intellectual clarity the careful investigator will eventually stumble upon some clear-sighted direction in which to move—and Kovacs knew he was staring at precisely such a moment. He had found a direct reference to the suspected British operative alleged to be at large in the area, and had found it within this dark and dingy cabin; linked to a woman directly connected to one *Hauptmann* Kluge... Kovacs held hard evidence pointing to the suspected codename of a British operative.

Kovacs began excitedly stabbing a finger at the painted face before him. "You say this woman—depicted here in this painting—is a Hungarian *táltos*?"

He again focused on his two hapless escorts, who were cautiously nodding in response.

"Yes, Herr Lieutenant," said one of the soldiers. "That is, I think, the way he spoke of her—"

"—So, tell me, where is she now?" Kovacs commanded. "Is she at the *Hauptmann's* post, where we are going?"

"No," said one of the soldiers, his head shaking sadly.

The other soldier stepped forward and pointed the tip of his submachine gun's barrel at the painting that Kovacs held in his hand.

"The woman you see in this painting is the same woman now hanging out there on that tree!"

The soldier pointed to the tree away in the distance, its two hanging corpses still visible in the darkening end of the day. Kovacs was that a large grouping of crows had assembled in its branches, revoltingly intent on winkling out more morsels of rotting flesh to satisfy their hunger.

It took Kovacs a few seconds to digest what he had just learned, but now it all seemed to make sense. The photo of Kluge firing his pistol to scare away the crows had captured the pain of a man who had brutally suffered the loss of someone he loved to a bunch of *SS* fanatics. In Kovacs' investigative mind, this was tantamount to motive, a potential solution to what might have happened to a unit of hardened *Waffen-SS* butchers a few weeks before; thus a potential motive for why such men might have been designated for disappearance.

Kovacs looked sternly at his two military escorts, men who served under *Hauptmann* Kluge, who knew the woman in the painting and her relationship to their commanding officer. Kovacs let the canvas hang in his left hand as he used his right to unbutton the flap on his holster containing his service pistol. It was something that did not go unnoticed by his more heavily armed two escorts.

"About three weeks ago," said Kovacs, his voice thick with menace, "a unit of *Waffen-SS* came through this sector—"

Kovacs looked hard at the two young soldiers, standing alert and stressed before him. He drew his pistol slowly. Both men held their stances, showing no sign of countering Kovacs' action.

Disciplined to the last, Kovacs thought.

"I'm going to ask you two men a couple of questions... important questions," Kovacs said. "Consider your answers very carefully."

Both men nodded their understanding, their eyes fixed in subservient attention on Kovacs and not on the threat of his drawn weapon.

They are good, solid German soldiers, Kovacs thought. It would be a pity to have to kill them.

"Was it these *Waffen-SS* soldiers that hung *Hauptmann* Kluge's *táltos* woman when they came through this sector three weeks ago?"

One of the soldiers responded immediately: "Yes—"

"—They claimed she was aiding the partisans, that she was a spy," said the other soldier.

Kovacs nodded. It looked like an early conclusion to his mission's investigative objectives could be in the offing.

"And did *Hauptmann* Kluge take revenge on these *Waffen-SS* men for hanging his woman?

There was a silence as the two young men glanced at each other, each trying to assess what their answer should be... what the consequences would be in giving an answer.

"Answer the question," Kovacs said, his hand tensing on the trigger of his pistol.

Kovacs felt a deathly hue of silence grip the cabin, like nothing else existed at that moment; like fear and loathing was a thing hanging in the air...

But no answer came; there was no time.

The air outside the forlorn log cabin seemed to explode in a howling roar as Kovacs caught a movement in the corner of his eye, something dark and large that flashed past the cabin's open window... And then he heard an agonized and very human shriek pierced through the cabin's log walls!

"God in Heaven," moaned one of the soldiers as his comrade sank to his knees in fright. "They're here!" he cried and began trying to cock his submachine gun, his fingers fumbling at the weapon's stubborn mechanism.

Kovacs stood rooted to the spot.

"Partisans?" he croaked.

And then another searing animalistic screech shattered Kovacs' immobility into a mess of panic and terror. He leaped at the door and flung it wide open, hoping to understand the threat behind the ear-splitting howl...

What Kovacs saw beyond the door melted all reason and rhyme from his mind... In the grey twilight, Kovacs made out four giant wolves about thirty yards away, the ripped-apart remains of his driver scattered about before them... Kovacs could not process it, but the things were standing horrifyingly upright, with legs, arms, and torsos like a man, but with the heads of wolves... massive heads... And they were looking directly at Kovacs, a sneering grin splitting their maws and showing vile and vicious teeth and fangs... the killing tools of predators...

One of the soldiers fired off a volley of bullets at the creatures from behind Kovacs, but it seemed to have no effect. Even so, Kovacs had the presence of mind to empty his own pistol at the central beast—also to no effect; the muscled torsos of the lead creature taking the hits to its chest like they were no more than mosquito bites...

Kovacs slammed the cabin's door shut, its wooden slats a pitiful barrier to the powerful and huge beasts that were hovering threateningly on the outside, their sheer size testament to an evident ability to smash their way in any time they wanted. He lurched around, too late to stop one of his escorts, the one who had sunk to his knees, from blowing his own brains out.

Kovacs froze in shock, and then turned to the remaining man in his escort. The young soldier simply looked at Kovacs as his comrade's dead body slumped face down on the cabin's dusty floor, horror and recrimination galvanizing his face into a contorted mask of fear and anger.

"We should have never stopped!" he cried, his eyes welling with tears—and then he, too, blew his own brains out!

Kovacs was hardly aware of what he did next; fear and flight flooded his cortex in a rush of adrenal pain, and he flung himself towards the back of the cabin and under the bed, his empty pistol waving at the door uselessly as he fought to cover himself in some kind of protective cocoon of furniture and blankets—

—And then it was quiet... an emptiness like nothing Kovacs had felt before.

Kovacs seemed to become aware that he was moaning, a stifled groan coming from deep down in his gut—but the mad violence that had engulfed him before had now given way to silence, the blackness of night immersing the cabin's muted interior in the bloodbath that now wreathed its rough wooden floor...

It must have been hours before a group of German troops arrived at the lonely log cabin, a search party that had been sent out upon Kovacs' failure to arrive at *Hauptmann* Kluge's isolated post. Daylight was seeping into the cabin when a stunned and barely responsive Kovacs found himself being checked out by a couple of medics for wounds and injuries. He waved them off, stammering out in Hungarian that he was fine, and made for the table where the hefty manuscript still lay. He bypassed the carnage of the two bodies that had been his security detail, their heads shattered by the bullets of their own guns.

As he steadied himself, grasping the table for support, Kovacs saw the dropped painting of Kluge's Hungarian woman on the floor. The searing image of her mesmerizing head being engulfed by the jaws of some gigantic wolf was suddenly all too horrifically real for Kovacs's shattered mind. He picked up the canvas as if in a dream and put it into an artist's portfolio satchel resting against the wall. He was doing the same with the manuscript, its weight causing the bag to bulge untidily, when he turned to walk out the door. One of the medics insisted that more checks should be completed—and then Kovacs came face to face with *Hauptmann* Kluge!

Kovacs recognized him instantly from the harrowing photo he had found on the table, but the look of despair and horror in the other man's eyes seemed to have aged him beyond what Kovacs had seen in that awful and inhuman image; *Hauptmann* Kluge reflected the look of a man resigned to living in a world of monsters... the mien of imminent death well ingrained on his tired and worn face.

Hauptmann Kluge regarded Kovacs, noting the wide portfolio satchel in his hands with a resigned weariness. He closed his eyes.

"You saw them, didn't you?" the *Hauptmann* said, his voice weak and strained.

Kovacs nodded, an involuntary shiver icing his neck at a memory so recent it was like it was still happening.

"Yes," he said. "I saw them."

37

Present day, somewhere high over Northern Europe...

"So you don't believe the dogman is some kind of dog or wolf?" she said.

The Ghost looked down and studied some abrasion on his hand, his manner thoughtful, even doubtful.

"I really don't know," he said. "I've killed them, delivered their corpses to the client... but I've never seen an analysis of their DNA." He stroked his enormous beard with his huge, mitt-like left hand. "But I do listen to what people say about their encounters with these creatures."

"What do you mean you listen to people's encounters?" Sarah asked, her hand nervously clutching at the tooth necklace that still hung from her neck.

"Ever notice what most witnesses who have run into these things they say about their front paws?"

Sarah stopped short, her mind playing back over a myriad of dogman witness encounters she had heard. She thought of the ones that matched her own encounter while hiking in an Oregon forest park, an encounter with a frightening predator that had become the nemesis of her life... and then it came to her!

"They all say they look like they have *hands*," Sarah said almost inaudibly. "They say these creatures have claws, but that their front paws look like hands—"

"—What kind of hands?" the Ghost interjected impatiently. He held up his own hand for Sarah to see. "Hands like these, or hands like something else?"

Sarah gave the Ghost a baffled look. "Hands!" she said tersely.

The Ghost gave a sigh.

"Sarah," he said. "You are now a part of a very different world." He paused a beat. "In this world, details are important—it's how people like us stay alive."

Sarah blanched a second time, but something in her mind was activated as she looked at the Ghost's large raised hand...

"Many of them describe a dogman's hands as being raccoon-like," she said, her voice still soft, as if she dreaded where their conversation was leading them.

"And what family of mammals do raccoons belong to?" asked the Ghost just as quietly.

"*Mustelidae*," said Sarah.

"Yes," said the Ghost. "Probably the most territorially aggressive set of mammals on the planet."

Sarah's veterinarian-trained mind brooded on the concept. She knew that the Ghost spoke the truth about the mustelid species, that extreme aggression and territoriality was infused in their nature from the diminutive weasel to the dangerously hostile wolverines and honey badgers.

"So, you think dogmen are related because they have raccoon hands?" Sarah said, skepticism tinging her words. "I'm not buying it."

"There's also that chirping electronic-like sound that some people report when encountering a dogman," the Ghost offered in defense of his thinking. "When I've played back recorded raccoon chirps at a lower pitch to some witnesses, they tell me it sounds the same as what they heard from a dogman."

Sarah latched on to the Ghost having made contact with other victims of dogman encounters.

"So, you've spoken to other people about their dogman experiences?"

The Ghost actually smiled. It was a sympathetic smile, and it took Sarah aback.

"It's what we do, Sarah," he said. "And it's what we hope you will also become a part of if you decide to become one of us—you've got insights and so much more to offer than an old hack like me."

It was the first kind words from the Ghost she had heard him say, but Sarah didn't respond. The Ghost relaxed back into his seat seemingly pleased with himself. It was as if they had both temporarily exhausted the scope of their short conversation.

"I'm fully aware that you don't like me," he said to Sarah, his eyes catching hers. His look was intense but not confrontational. "But I think you will come to know the difference between what someone *has* to do... as opposed to *who* they really are."

Again, Sarah didn't respond. She looked out the window, the Ghost's theories chewing away at her mind.

The jet was now making its way into the heart of a country familiar to Sarah only through gothic novels and horror movies: Hungary. Its legendary capital, Budapest, was waiting for them like some dark, unvisited spot on the map of her mind. Sarah had been told by Morning Star that pronouncing the name 'Budapest' is ended correctly with a sibilant 'shhh'. Like, *Budapesh*.

"What happens now?" she had asked the old Native American shaman as she had boarded the compact jet at the beginning of the journey. "Will I ever see you again?"

Morning Star had looked at her with caring eyes, eyes that had then seemed to turn to stone.

"If not in this world, then in the one to come," he had said with a disturbing finality. It was hardly a reassuring goodbye as far as Sarah was concerned, and she had felt like a tearing in the fabric of their friendship had formed.

"And what about Detective Lee... and Tim... and Daemon?" she had asked Morning Star, realizing that she had hardly thought of her friends since the shock of Broken Fang's agonized destruction. Her mind was still plagued by the fresh memories of the grotesquely altered Agent Smith and his terrifying pack of hybrid werewolf dogmen.

"All is good with them," the old shaman had assured her. "You are the one they are interested in hunting down, not them—they will be fine." He had paused. “You will see them again, of that I am sure.”

Even so, Morning Star's words had done little to comfort her about her future and her friend’s future. She had taken one last look at the Pacific Northwest as she had boarded her secret flight, taken in the wide and beautiful mountains of her home she could no longer consider as home. On board, the colossal figure of the Ghost had silently greeted her, with neither she nor him initiating any conversation for most of the journey ahead.

Now, a continent and an ocean away, Sarah felt completely alone sitting in a pressurised cabin with only the gigantic presence of a seasoned killer for company.

She pulled out an envelope of documents Morning Star had handed her before the flight. A new identity and passport had been manufactured under the name Sarah Bergstrom. The new surname was like the Swedish name but without the accent over the 'o', as is common amongst the Swedes.

"It means 'mountain stream' among the Nordics," Morning Star had told Sarah. "It's best that you keep your first name—keeps things natural if someone calls you by your new first name, which is always the most difficult part of adapting to a new identity."

The passport retained Sarah's American citizenship, and it came with a pre-approved work visa for the European Union—Sarah apparently now being gainfully employed as some kind of consultant for an animal welfare NGO based in Romania, but with a brass-plaque office in Budapest. The NGO was obviously a no-show front in Katarina Kovacs' secret cryptid network, funded by her considerable wealth and facilitated by old family contacts in the landlocked country of her origin.

"It wasn't the dogman..." Sarah said as she watched the changing landscape below. "It wasn't even the werewolf hybrids that were so disturbing back at the mountain lodge... And it wasn't even you having murdered that woman you claim was some kind of *synthetic—"*

"—You're talking about the UFO that was hovering above?" the Ghost interjected, his head inclined in interest.

Sarah thought about the gigantic triangle of blackness that had mysteriously and alarmingly appeared above the mountain lodge, its spattering rows of lights illuminating the scene playing out below as she watched a pack of vicious Type-Three werewolves destroy Broken Fang. She remembered how the big black thing had made no noise, how some kind of powerful but eerie beam of light had seemed to be slowly dropping more and more of the awful werewolf creatures down to join in Broken Fang's slaughter, like it was some tractor-beam out of a bad sci-fi movie...

"That UFO thing you saw isn't alien," the Ghost said as if reading Sarah's mind. "It is part of an advanced terrestrial technology—probably built with some alien help—but part of what some call a breakaway civilization." He gave a small chuckle. "The *Beast* has friends in pretty high places; literally!"

He calls it the '*Beast*' thought Sarah; a hidden organization that he, and most likely Morning Star and Katrina Kovacs all believed was behind Sarah's missing memories; was behind the highly disturbing connection between herself and the now dead dogman she called Broken Fang. But that was not the beast that she was thinking about.

"No," Sarah said. "What I can't get out of my head is the image of a dead man come back to life as some robot-like wolf-monster..." She shivered. "I saw with my own eyes how that fake FBI agent John Smith was torn to pieces by Broken Fang, the same dogman that had been stalking me ever since that day out hiking."

Sarah slowly turned her head to look directly back at the Ghost.

"But Agent Smith came back!" She struggled with the memory. "It was him leading that pack of animals that brought down Broken Fang—and I'm sure he's still out there waiting... looking."

"Ah yes," said the Ghost. "Morning Star told me about that–"

"–And so I'm going to ask you the same thing I asked Morning Star–"

The Ghost waited.

"–What happens now?" Sarah demanded.

The Ghost waited a little more before answering.

"Simple. You have to now become Sarah Bergstrom," he said deliberately, emphasizing each word for maximum comprehension. "You have to become Sarah Bergstrom as if your life depended on it."

Sarah closed her eyes.

"How?" she asked. "How do I do that? I'm no method actor or seasoned convict on the lam!"

"What you are, Sarah," the Ghost said, "is a survivor!"

Sarah exhaled a deep and gloomy sigh.

"Only because Morning Star and Katarina helped me," she said. "Without them, I'm not sure what to do... I've never been outside America in my life."

"You start slowly," responded the Ghost. "You get established; you find a simple place to live; you stay offline; you observe the people around you..." He focused in on her. "You become a people watcher... And you keep to yourself–no boyfriends or girlfriends, whatever might be your thing."

The Ghost watched for a reaction, but none showed on Sarah's face. It was like she was somewhere else.

"It's kind of like what you were doing in your life before all of this," he continued. "It seems you were a loner by nature, a sigma female, and all you have to do now is adapt that same approach to your new life."

A sigma female?

Sarah said, "I don't even know the language down there."

The Ghost grunted.

"No one knows the language in Hungary, especially the Hungarians." He laughed dryly. “It's what makes Budapest so interesting; they're all making it up as they go along, both the locals and the expats. All you have to do is make up your own story and live it."

Sarah's lips thinned in frustration.

"You make it sound so easy."

The Ghost smiled.

"You have a new identity, enough cash in your pocket to get started," he said, trying to be cheerful about it. "Which is far more than most of us had when we got pulled into this world."

But Sarah was not smiling back... not in the least.

"You shouldn't worry," continued the Ghost. “Someone has already been assigned to help you... But you have to show that you can help yourself."

"Someone to help me?" Sarah exclaimed. "Why didn't you tell me that before, and how do I contact them?"

The Ghost shook his head and said, "They'll find you. But only when they're good and ready and when they think you're good and ready!"

Sarah's eyes narrowed. She was ready to make demands, but the Ghost cut her off.

"Surely now, you don't expect us to do all the work?"

38

It was a cheap way to enjoy the more salubrious aspects of city life—best enjoyed if you should ever find yourself on the run... or so Sarah had begun to believe...

They call them *ruin bars*, sublimely hidden drinking establishments snuggled away in the decrepit remains of some of Budapest's finest old buildings; some legal, some not; moldering carcasses of decaying masonry with some of the walls smashed out for extra space; everything looking like its held together by the exposed rusty plumbing leftover from a hateful era, the water in those iron veins having a metallic taste for those brave enough to try it unmixed. The mission: To party at the maximum in case the joint is gone tomorrow...

Sarah had never seen anything like them back in the States.

Sarah had never seen anyone like the tall, lithe young man sitting aloof from it all. She observed that he had the practiced vibe of disengagement about him, the same vibe she had been cultivating in herself since arriving in Budapest a month ago. She had seen him flitting around before, but this time he was standing around as if waiting for someone.

"That English cat you've been looking at is some kind of aristocrat," said one of the gallery of English-speaking expats that Sarah had loosely gravitated to. "He gets around Budapest's rooftops like a monkey with a can of paint, leaving his tags everywhere; they say he did the artwork in here for free."

The fellow pointed at the bar's stylized graffiti-like décor, knocking back his sixth shot of something green.

"He's been here a while," the man confided in Sarah. "Might know a place for you to crash; something for nothing if you know what I mean."

Sarah was happy to take up any suggestion on acquiring inexpensive accommodation. She had found a short-term lease on a small ground flat in Budapest's sixth district; one of the grittier parts of the central city area, but it all seemed remarkably safe for a woman living on her own. Her landlord was an absentee retired Irish woman whom Sarah had only spoken to over the phone, but keen to secure a rental agreement with an American expat.

The place was okay, but nothing like the charm of Sarah's cabin back in Oregon. Its ceilings were too high, and the dense, heavy wooden doors reminded her of castle porticos. The five-foot thick walls gave Sarah a sense of protection but also made her feel she was living inside a fortress; not a bad thing for someone in her situation, but it gave her a disheartening feeling of confinement. She felt like the proverbial pea rattling around in a concrete pod.

Sarah had bought a bed and slept for most of the first week, taking the advice of Morning Star. He had told her it would be a good way to deal with the post-stress disorder she would have undoubtedly suffered. The carnage she had witnessed back at Katarina Kovacs' mountain lodge had given her dreams a thickly suffocating aura, more about feelings rather than visuals, but nightmarish all the same. The Ghost had given her a bunch of sedatives to help, but only a few to make sure she didn't become dependent. "Essential to keep a clear mind," he had admonished her.

But Sarah was now quickly running out of money and needed to find something else on the cheap. She had taken the Ghost's suggestion of becoming a people watcher to heart and was soon patching into the unique pulse of the city. She liked the locals, especially their almost courtly grace and manners, and was able to strike up a few acquaintances amongst the expat community.

Much to Sarah's delight, she found that English was generally understood and spoken in most places in Budapest's central districts, especially since the kidults hailing out of the chilly British Isles were still intent on looking east for a good night out, ostensibly much safer in Budapest from suffering a good ol' English glassing.

Sarah had acquired a guidebook that had informed her it was wise to look out for the random spiked drink while sampling the town's nightlife. Otherwise, Budapest seemed a pretty safe city, the kind of place in which you really have to be looking for trouble to find it.

The city center seemed to lack the menace of random street violence that Sarah had been exposed to in some of the bigger American towns. Her past decision to live a more rural existence in small-town Oregon had partly been to avoid the threats that came with American city life; *but look how that had turned out, she thought*. Even so, here in Budapest, Sarah was not so naïve as to let her guard down when negotiating a city as large as the Hungarian capital.

Sarah had especially taken a liking to the charms of Budapest's famous ruin bars.

Looking over to where the 'English cat' stood with a full glass in his hand, Sarah picked up some courage and moved towards him. He saw her coming but remained still, seemingly interested in her approach, which encouraged Sarah. She thought he was like one of those curious stray cats that one meets on the backstreets of Budapest.

"I hear you know a few places that might be good to squat?" Sarah addressed him, deciding a direct approach would be the better part of presumption. This way she figured she would know quickly if he was amenable to her.

He looked at Sarah momentarily, as if processing her, and then beamed in what Sarah interpreted as a sign of approval. No names or introductions were given or expected; he just started to talk.

"A lot of places were simply put under tarps and left just as they were back in 1956—during the uprising," he said, his accent a rich Etonian burr. "Real *Marie Celeste* stuff, for sure."

Up close, Sarah could see that he was indeed young, maybe mid-twenties. He had agile eyes and an almost supernaturally supple elegance about him. She watched, amazed, as he calmly sprang back effortlessly levering himself onto a low window sill immediately behind him. In what seemed like one move, he settled into a regal, if eccentric, perch. His entire body seemed to deeply egress into the wall at about waist height. In doing so, he hadn't spilled a drop of his drink, and now he just crouched there comfortably, the light from the outside street lamps silhouetting him like some dark skinny owl on the watch.

"Who owns them?" Sarah asked, trying not to look impressed with the acrobatics.

"Old Hungarian nobility mostly—probably," he said. "The old money types, the ones that had to run when the communists took over."

“Why haven’t they come back now that the Iron Curtain’s gone?” asked Sarah, genuinely interested.

“Some *suicided* while in exile... Who knows?” A cheeky smile flashed across his face. “Who is it that wants to know?”

Sarah caught the fellow’s sassy question probing into her identity but wanted to know more before giving her name away.

“So why haven’t these apartments been claimed or sold?” she pushed on. “Surely the authorities can take possession if they’ve been abandoned that long?”

“Just doesn’t seem to happen,” he replied.

“Interesting,” was all Sarah could muster in response, and she raised her eyebrows as if expecting him to say more.

He gave her a wink and a smile in return, contriving a slight awkwardness for a beat or two.

“Actually, they’re quite spooky places in their own fashion,” he finally said, hunching his shoulders. “I once looked through a window on high, somewhere here in District Seven, and wondered why the interior hadn’t been ransacked; everything still under white sheets, all of it just begging to be checked out—”

“—But nobody ever has, eh?” Sarah butted in, suddenly hopeful that a claim might be in the offing.

“Yeah,” he said. “For some reason...”

Sarah was starting to feel tired. She wanted to get to the heart of the matter and decided to throw caution to the wind.

“I just need a place to crash for a few days or weeks.” She nodded at him, earnest in her intentions. “I’m no thief.”

“Then you’re a better *menschen* than I,” he chortled back at her, a teasingly sly look added to what now seemed to be a permanent winking in his eye. “They don’t call me the Black Cat for nothing!”

“Pleased to meet you, Black Cat,” Sarah said, offering a belated hand to shake on their newfound friendship. “My name is Sarah.”

“I know,” said the Black Cat, but Sarah had obviously already had one too many to grasp the significance of what he had just admitted. Her face flushed, her guard down. Was this what her life had come to? Bargaining with petty criminals for a stolen place to lay her head?

“Let me buy you another drink,” Sarah suggested.

Two drinks later and some small talk, Sarah’s patrician drinking buddy recommended they take their conversation and decamp to a little jazz club he knew. There, he assured her, they could better discuss Sarah’s situation.

Why not, Sarah thought. The night was still young, and she felt she was getting her second wind. This strangely charming English lad would either be her ticket to cheaper digs or just another chancer with a story to tell. She reasoned somewhere in the back of her mind that it was all part of becoming *Sarah Bergstrom*.

At this point, things had begun to make little difference to her. By now, Sarah had decided that her life was about waiting for the contact the Ghost had mentioned. Until then, Sarah thought she might try to enjoy life on a wilder side than she had ever experienced before in America—dogmen and Bigfoots notwithstanding. She had all but convinced herself that, in Budapest, no dogman or werewolf waited around the corner to spoil the party—at least that’s what she told herself...

39

Sarah and the Black Cat arrived at the jazz club a little after ten at night, a minor establishment with an intimate entertainment venue. A small audience was listening to a middle-aged female singer sigh through an after-midnight version of the AC/DC classic *Hells Bells.* A baby grand tinkled out the rhythms and a troupe of cabaret dancers could be seen warming up in the club's wings.

The Black Cat told Sarah that it was still early on the stroke of twelve and asked her if there was some kind of *usual* that she drank when listening to good music—it was his round, after all.

Sarah decided she would chug on a bottle of beer, making sure to see the barman flip the bottle cap... just to be sure.

"For sure, for sure," the Black Cat tittered as he handed Sarah her drink. "Looks like all the denizens of the night have come out to play, for sure."

Sarah looked around, trying to appear as nonchalant as possible while taking in the close-packed crowd.

"Who are they?" Sarah asked, trying not to be too obvious while indicating a prominent table with a number of well-dressed people sitting around it.

According to the Black Cat they were Hollywood types from Budapest's trendy porno set. Sarah could hear them cutting the air with their schmooze, and the Black Cat discreetly pointed out to Sarah who each of them was: a couple of big-time actors and their glam wives; a gay movie director; a hot-shot producer—who looked in his eighties—and his sycophantic studio intern.

Sarah saw that the group had prominence in the club, their table obviously being the joint's most exclusive social real estate. They were smoking fake Cahaba's, and a lonely plate of crapes at the center of the table waited on their attention. Sarah could hear them talking in English, talking about a long, cool woman in a black dress; they were talking about someone they called the *Love Goddess*...

Porno-types, Sarah thought... Charming.

The Black Cat turned his attention to a sallow Israeli drinking at the bar and introduced him to Sarah. He told her the guy was probably the best forger in town. Both men laughed at the comment and knocked back a set of Camden blue shots when some other dude, a heavy-set man wearing a red beret, roughly clapped one of his hands on the Black Cat's left shoulder.

"I *find* you!" the man said gruffly.

It seemed non-too friendly to Sarah, and she pushed back from the bar to give herself a little distance in case something kicked off. She sensed serious tension in the big man as he whispered something into the Black Cat's ear, the latter's face contorting at the man's sudden and unwelcome intrusion. On the other side of the Black Cat, his Israeli friend stared into an empty shot glass as if none of it was his business.

Sarah decided it was better if it was none of her business too, so she looked over her shoulder to see what was happening elsewhere, ready to jettison her new friend if necessary... And that's when she saw her...

It was a very brief moment, their eyes catching only by a fraction from across the room. But Sarah was transfixed as she saw the woman sway her way towards the Hollywood table. She was maybe a little older than herself, perhaps a little bit worse for wear, but she was a woman who could only be described as gorgeous!

Breathtakingly gorgeous! An otherworldly redhead right out of old Hollywood... and those eyes...

Sarah could see that the woman had been crying; she could immediately deduce that this was the so-called *Love Goddess* that she had previously overheard the Hollywood porno-types talking about; could see that the woman was hiding a tear as she made to sit down next to the decrepit old hot-shot film producer–

What! She's with him?

Jarringly, Sarah noticed that this woman was wearing what looked like a dog collar–like some rough leather chocker one would typically associate with the punk scene. It had a metal fastening ring dangling from its front, like where a leash or lead could be fastened. Sarah found it weird and unsettling.

But Sarah's ears were now picking up on what was happening behind her–the Black Cat and his friend were talking, and it sounded heavy.

"Yesterday, a gang of separatists started mass protests around the American naval base," the large fellow with the red beret was saying quietly, his hand still clamped down on the Black Cat's left shoulder. "I am sure you know of this..."

Sarah could detect an accent in the man's words that sounded like he came from somewhere in the Balkans. Only a month into her new life in Budapest, Sarah was already becoming proficient at sensing the differences between the myriad of inflections and accents that colored the city.

"Use the chaos as a distraction to get into the Dutchman's offices," the man continued conspiratorially. "For reasons that should already be obvious, we are sending the Belgian with you."

Sarah heard the Black Cat give a grunt and noted that his Israeli drinking buddy was still staying quiet. *Minding his business.*

"What's with the gun, Jozo?"

Sarah was startled to see that the big man was jabbing a rigid object from inside his jacket pocket into the Englishman's ribs. She stood rooted to the spot, danger sirens wailing in her head. This was definitely not her kind of scene.

"My name's not *Jozo*!" the man hissed, his sibilant lisp closer to the Black Cat's ear.

"You're all *Jozo the Bozo* to me," the Black Cat smiled, and Sarah saw that he was watching her in the bar's back wall mirror, and not the man in the beret. Both their reflections showed like grimy apparitions in the mirror's dirty surface—He winked at her, which only served to unnerve Sarah even more. She had a feeling that she was being sucked into some hard-boiled noir movie out of the 1950s.

Quickly, Sarah stole a glance back over her shoulder. It was as much to see if anyone else had picked up on the gunplay as to see if the Hollywood table was still shooting the breeze, now that the *Love Goddess* was back among them. She was disgusted to note that the movie producer had not even bothered to stand for the stunning redhead dame... *So much for living in an age of elegance...*

"I am warning *to* you, tough guy," Sarah heard the big guy's awkward syntax saying to the Black Cat. His words were being hissed through the side of his mouth. "Get the job done by tomorrow, or things will go *nuclear* blast!"

Well, things were definitely becoming more interesting as far as Sarah could tell, but for some inexplicable reason she found herself more fascinated with what was going on over in the Hollywood section of the club. She looked at the producer guy with the *Love Goddess* and realized that he was probably American, or at least Hungarian-American. He reeked of being the usual kind of arrogant hot-shot template that made for a woman's worst nightmare.

Get out while you can, whoever you are lady!

Sarah studied the movie producer's face and imagined it as a frozen pool of spite, the eyes like gravestones found by the side of a hard paved road, the kind of road that ends in a thirsty desert of drugs and alcoholic meanness. She could feel his mood, the deep crevasse of malice in its essence, and it made her think of an *insectoid... I bet this guy thinks he can face-rape movie stars for breakfast!*

And he was so, so old...

It made no sense to her...

Sarah caught herself... The anger she was feeling was not normal for her.

"Put away the gun, *Jozo,*" the Black Cat growled behind her. "And I'll tell you about how a bunch of neo-Nazis are behind those riots south of here, about how a new cartel is trying to muscle in on your thing."

Oh dear, Sarah thought.

"I told you, my name is not this *Jozo!*" repeated the big man, his stilted diction letting the Black Cat know he was skating hazardously close to something very unpleasant.

"But I would be remiss not to tell you—*Jozo*—that it's all a ruse." The Black Cat continued on coolly without missing a beat. "Those guys are really after a particular chemical, the kind that indicates the involvement of your enemies... the ones hailing out of Serbia."

"You call me *Jozo* one more time, and I'll—"

"—You'll what, *Jozo?*" the Black Cat shouted and then casually snorted away the threat with another shot of Camden that had magically appeared on the bar before him. He banged the empty shot glass down on the bar—and it sounded like a gunshot!

Sarah's heart started at the sharp report. Even the Hollywood porno-type swells cut their chit-chat briefly as the room went tense... And then the nightclub singer soothed it all over with a smooth-as-whisky 'Oh yeah!' and Sarah could have sworn she saw the Black Cat exchange winks with her. The singer curled her acid-hot lips around a retro silver microphone and stroked it suggestively with her hands. "Now, now, boys," she breathed. "This is a nice establishment."

She began crooning Motorhead's *The Ace of Spades*, a beautiful thing to behold if you're in the mood. But Sarah's mood was shifting to grave concern, feeling as if she was getting lost in a heady mix of dangerous adrenaline and a surreal sense of sexual tension... She looked back at the Black Cat's reflection in the bar mirror and saw that he was still eyeing her, scrutinizing her, but she also became aware that the *Love Goddess* was also observing her.

Those eyes... they are the eyes of...

The woman's dim reflection from across the room showed a distinct interest in Sarah, her incandescent eyes emanating out from under the shadows of her Hollywood mane. She wore deep red tresses brushed forward across her painfully beautiful face.

Like an old Hollywood movie star...

Sarah turned from the mirror, but the connection broke, and she could see that the woman was now attempting some small talk with one of the glam wives. Both women were trying to smile, but something was stirring in Sarah. She turned back to the Black Cat to look past him and continue her watch of this fascinating female from the relative anonymity of the mirror.

"Play it cool, buddy," Sarah heard the big man with the gun drawl into the Black Cat's ear. He was pulling his gun back to a less threatening distance. "Just call me *Julio* . . . and we *are to be* cool."

Sarah seemed to snap out of a dream. *WTF!* am I doing in a foreign bar with a guy that's got a gun pulled on him, Sarah thought urgently. The Black Cat seemed to pick up on her growing consternation.

"Please don't be alarmed," he said to Sarah over his shoulder, the same shoulder the big man's hand still clamped down on. "*Julio* is an old friend; he thinks the beret gives him the *Ché* look... The man makes his money as only an old-fashioned Marxist drug dealer can—by redistributing other people's income to pay himself."

"Enough!" *Julio* snapped. "We just want you to do the Dutchman job," he said, frustration starting to get the better of him. "Do the job, and then proceed to the rendezvous at the old airstrip before it becomes part of the news cycle." Julio looked about him suspiciously. "We are to be partnering with the Iranians on this, so it is must for us to communicate with them through the Belgian."

The Black Cat turned to look out into the room, past Sarah, and Sarah realized her mouth was tasting like a piece of carpet. She took a nervous swig from her warm beer.

"I don't need a babysitter," The Black Cat said to Julio. "The job will get done—"

Sarah flinched as she saw the *Love Goddess'* reflection in the bar mirror suddenly go rigid, a mortifying look reaching out into the club's hazy cigarette-filled space as the hot-shot movie producer whispered something nasty into her ear. Sarah saw the woman's tear-swollen eyes start flitting about... and then come to rest on Sarah, like a brief flash of alarm... then it was gone like gossamer caught on the wind—But Sarah knew something was wrong. She turned to the Black Cat, her eyes directing him to where the Hollywood types were sitting.

But *Julio* also picked up on their line of sight. "*Mmm*, a tasty dish," he smirked. "The siren call of *la femme Circassian*—they say her face has destroyed a thousand marriages."

"—And your point?" Sarah found herself saying, annoyed at letting this clown's opinion sully the focus of her growing concern.

"Business before *the pleasure*, buddy," stated *Julio*, though entirely for the Black Cat's benefit, as if Sarah was not even present. "Time enough to sing that baby your lullaby when the job is *kaput*... if it gets *kaput*."

The Black Cat turned on the big man.

"Just for the record, *Julio*, I'm a dancing man," he said looking him straight in the eye. "And whatever you think you've heard—I'm no singer!"

Julio blinked at the Black Cat's tone... but Sarah was staring hard past both of their reflections—back at *la femme Circassian*—focusing on a set of wounded glowing amber eyes, eyes that seemed to be searching for a way out.

"Pay attention," hissed Julio at the Black Cat, still wholly ignoring Sarah's intensifying presence. "I hear you are a piece *of the work*, but I never think you to be playing the stupid boy!" He gave a great leery sneer that matched his heavy Balkan accent. "So this is how the picture is to be for the wise guy: Just do the shit, and you get the money!"

But Sarah was now utterly indifferent in whatever heaviness was going down between her English aristocrat and his Balkans associate. At the most exclusive table in the joint, there was a scene in the making: words were being said, abusive words—words that stab through the air like knives. Sarah could make out that some movie project was failing and that a has-been washed-up talent was apparently to blame. The finger was being pointed—

"—You're nothing!" barked the movie producer into *la femme Circassian's* shocked face. "They told me you had talent! But I see no talent! All I see is a piece of ass well past its sell-by date! You're getting old, and you've got nothing left to give! You've ruined everything!"

Sarah lurched an inch forward...

"I am telling you a truth, for you to keep your eye on the ball," rasped Julio from behind Sarah, seemingly oblivious to the drama unfolding elsewhere in the club. "Do you *touch* me?"

Sarah rounded on Julio.

"Shut up, *Jozo!*" she hissed, the intensity of her words clearing a gap between the two men. "The way to say it is 'do you *feel* me!'" She glared at the man. "So shut your mouth before I take that peashooter and shove it where the sun don't shine—I want to hear this!"

Sarah thumbed back over her shoulder before returning her full attention to watching the Hollywood group, both Julio and the Black Cat stepping back further from each other in surprise.

Julio pointed at Sarah with a quizzical look in his eye.

"This *woman*... she is the *American woman*?" Sarah heard Julio mumble confusedly, but she did not hear the Black Cat's response, if he had even made one.

Because Sarah was now openly and directly looking at the table where the stunning redhead sat with the boorish movie producer and his simpering entourage—as was almost every other person in the room.

They all saw as *la femme Circassian* put her head in her hands, her beauty quickly reduced to mud in a new flood of tears. The two big-time actors were sitting there with stunned expressions, their wives also close to tears at the humiliation being heaped on this beautiful woman—And the hot-shot movie producer just kept laying it on, his voice all hatred and mean.

"I could have had somebody better than you take the role," he yelled for the whole room to hear. "But *noooo!* You begged me for it! You said it was a role you were made for you... and so I took a chance... For what?"

The asshole looked about the club as if he were setting out the closing argument in some Hollywood legal scene.

"Have you even seen the first rushes?" He threw out his hands to the rest of the table and focused on the gay director. "Tell her! Tell her how pathetic they are!"

The director wilted in mortification, but nobody said a word. Sarah boiled as nobody even thought to challenge the old goat!

This hot shot needs a hot shot!

"Stay out of it," Sarah heard Julio warning the Black Cat from behind her. "Keep on the track—this is not *for your* business."

But the movie producer was only getting warmed up, and Sarah watched aghast as he violently grabbed *la femme Circassian's* upper arm, clearly hurting her.

"It's all your fault!" he began to rage. "And let me tell you something, you flat-faced bitch! If I go down because of this crap film, you go down!"

Sarah was aware that spats and tiffs between the glitterati are commonplace in joints like this and that most everyone takes them in their stride. But even the hot nightclub singer had now stopped as the spectacle of a star being shamed before her peers and public escalated.

One of the glam wives got up to leave, clearly at breaking point. Her husband, looking like he wanted to slug the movie producer creep, also got up abruptly—but they just up and left, hurrying out in embarrassed and angry impotence.

And *la femme Circassian* remained there... stranded, even as the others still present at the table withered; the gay director; the sycophant studio intern... It was as if they were all trying to make themselves smaller.

I know this type, Sarah thought to herself. She had seen his type in action before, the kind of guy who takes women to be their doormats, someone to wipe their dog crap on. To Sarah, this man was nothing more than an insecure egoist, a weak man who needed to cut others down to make himself look big.

I know you...

Sarah was now thinking back to her childhood. As a kid, she had seen two girls eviscerated in front of the entire school by a man who wanted everyone to know that he was the big boss. But all this man had been to Sarah was a bullyboy, some inconsequential head teacher who had decided he would make a screaming example of two children, and all because the odious man had thought they had been talking while he was preaching his own righteousness. Sarah remembered how that bastard's cowardly verbal rampage had crucified those two girls—destroyed them—and how nobody had done a thing to stop him, not even one of the other teachers, the so-called adults... And those two girls had never been the same again...

Sarah had been a kid back then, incapable of calling out the great brute to a well-deserved reckoning. But every now and then, when she found that she couldn't sleep at night, Sarah had thought about what that school principal had done, and she would think of the things she would have liked to have done to that pious bastard...

But now, here, in some strange small Budapest jazz club, Sarah was looking at a woman being completely degraded by a loud-mouthed clown and his sense of entitled self-importance. A woman was receiving a beat down delivered by someone from the gutter in the worst part of the entertainment world—And Sarah knew that the big-time actor, the one who had chosen to leave with his wife rather than confront an abusive man, would now always feel the same sting that she had felt over those two girls, two girls that nobody made a stand for... But not this time!

"Now look what you've done!" screamed the movie producer. He forced her—*la femme Circassian*—to her feet, the sheer violence of his sanctimonious fury cutting further welts into her arms as he held her in a vicelike grip. "See! You've totally ruined the evening!"

"Yeah, I can see that!" Sarah heard herself say. The joint went even quieter, the hot-shot movie producer caught short... "I can see how she's the one who has ruined the night," Sarah said, her jaw jutting out in defiance of the man's fury.

The aged brute looked at Sarah, his eyes displaying the dead heaviness of a shark, his anger turning cold.

"Who the... are you?"

But Sarah was not intimidated. She had looked into the predatory eyes of a real-life dogman and seen the horrifically distorted face of the animalized Agent John Smith baring down on her. She had communed with the awesome Sasquatch. This guy didn't even remotely frighten her!

Sarah took a step forward, oblivious to anyone else in the room. But then the woman, the object of this man's public scorn, held up her hand.

"Stop!" she said. "It's okay! We are leaving."

Sarah heard the woman's words but focused on the movie producer's dead eyes. She held his gaze, unwavering... but she had heard the woman's voice, and something triggered...

And then they were gone... The entire table got up and left as one, the blustering bellicose mumbling of the movie producer leading the way, his grip still firm and tight on *la femme Circassian's* upper arm. And this time, there was no catching of eyes between Sarah and the redheaded woman as they left...

Sarah held her ground as the movie producer and his remaining entourage scuttled out, though the incident had left a troubling sense of dread in her that she could not put a finger on. Eventually, the club's entertainment started up again with a subtle rendition of *American Woman...* and Sarah turned to see the Black Cat grinning sheepishly at her, the big man Julio nowhere to be seen.

"So, *American Woman*, that escalated and de-escalated quickly." His dry Etonian brogue trailed off a little. "Sorry about all that nastiness with that Croat idiot, but I think we were talking about you squatting some abandoned penthouse suite—Still interested?"

Sarah had all but forgotten about the Black Cat's red-bereted friend. She was tamping down a violent urge to vomit, but quickly managed to recomposed herself, aware that she was still the center of a number of looks from around the club.

"Sure," Sarah said, snapping warily back on to track.

"Good," he said. "But first, I have a question, eh?"

"What question?" Sarah said, her wariness growing.

"Do you trust your friends?" the Black Cat said, his face turning to a mask of soberness that seemed entirely focused on Sarah.

Sarah was taken aback by the forward, and even threatening nature of the question; it highlighted how alone she had become since her arrival in Budapest. She thought of Morning Star, and then of Tim Rogers and Daemon Skinner, and a tide melancholy emptiness washed over her.

"What friends I do have... or *did* have... I trust implicitly," she said quietly. "Not that it's really any of your business."

The Black Cat nodded.

"You will always have your friends," he said to her enigmatically. "Just be prepared for one hell of a climb tonight," he then added quickly with a laugh.

For some reason Sarah didn't feel the need to press the Black Cat further on what he meant by asking about her friends. She only felt the need to steady things. So they spoke a little longer, drank, and spoke again about nothing in particular before he calmly faded back into the city as the witching hour struck. Sarah had received what she needed from him, but was left wondering if she would ever see the Black Cat again; wondered if he had even become a new friend... wondered who he really was...

40

Some of Europe's nomadic classes style themselves as 'jet-set hobos,' others as 'international gypsies.' Most, as Sarah believed she now was, are just opportunists looking for that elusive rent-free lifestyle between road trips, people always on the lookout for squalid squats and flops while doing a shanty on the outskirts of society. But the idea of indefinitely crashing some Hungarian prince's long-forgotten penthouse, especially here in the heart of Budapest's party district, certainly had an appeal that touched a deeply latent sense of adventure in Sarah that she did not know she had.

Sarah had followed the Black Cat's directions and now presently found herself gawping up at an old apartment block of considerable vintage. She knew she had no head for heights, but figured scrambling up some five-story fire escape rig would probably be the worst of it—and that she could handle it.

After all, I'm the Mountain Daughter; climbing some dilapidated apartment block should be a breeze...

Sarah had stuffed a couple of chocolate bars, some biscuits, and two bottles of water into a cheap vinyl-like satchel she had bought, supplies for a planned night assessing the potential of the abandoned rooms that supposedly awaited her. Running water, she thought, would be a bonus, but unlikely.

Looking up at the building's exterior from the darkened cobbles in the street below, Sarah saw that the stately yet tarnished building revealed no seepage of light from the inside of its many high-cut and curtainless windows. She invested a further half hour in furtive observation to confirm that the general interior of the building was fully abandoned, and even derelict.

Looking around herself just to be sure no one else was around—or that no other *thing* might be lurking—Sarah became convinced that the building had everything anyone could wish for in remaining undetected during any attempt at ascent and entry. The building was just as Sarah's aristocratic friend had described it: an empty old nineteenth-century apartment complex styled in the grand architecture favored by Hungary's former upper echelons.

Straining for a better view, Sarah could also see that the high outer windows of the building's lofty penthouse were angled towards the interior. This gave the impression of the building looking imperiously outward and upward over the ancient city. The view from inside would be incredible, Sarah thought.

Beginning to feel truly tired, Sarah resisted the impulse to find an easier way up to the penthouse on the building's inside. *Who knew who or what might call the lower floors home...*

"In the decades since the end of communism, organized crime came to Budapest in their droves," Sarah's aristocratic chum had informed her at the jazz club. He had been sucking back yet another creamy round of brandy cocktails, all bought with Sarah's dwindling cash reserves.

"The worst of the worst that Russia had to offer made their way here, along with the Turks and assorted other bad guys."

“Still here today, in Budapest?” Sarah had asked nervously.

“All I know is that this penthouse has never been touched in decades, even though the building has changed hands many times—arms dealers, drug traffickers, and even a gang of nasty Bulgarian pimps.”

‘Bulgarian pimps’ had a ring about it that Sarah had found amusing in her slightly inebriated way.

“All these gangs had possession of the building at one time or another.” The Black Cat had given Sarah another of those mischievous winking looks that seemed part of his social DNA. “But they never touched it the top floor or changed it. They just left it as is—and now they’re all gone.”

This had pleased Sarah to know.

“So you would say it’s safe to crash there for a few days?” she asked, becoming increasingly convinced that such a place could be the answer to her long-term accommodation needs. “I mean, I’m not going to be stepping on the toes of anyone heavy if I doss down there on the sly, right?”

“Could be,” the Black Cat had said. “But there’s always that risk.”

“What risk, exactly?” Sarah had said, alarm bells once again going off in her head.

“Maybe the old owners will come back,” the Black Cat had laughed. “I’m not sure they would be entirely patient with some uninvited lodger—unless you had an interesting story to tell,” he added cryptically.

“A story to tell, huh? Over sixty years later, on the day I decide to move in?” Sarah had laughed. “You’re a guy with a sense of humor; I’ll give you that!”

But Sarah had wanted to know... just in case.

“Who owns the building now?” she had queried, caution in her eyes. “Any idea?”

“No one really knows,” the Black Cat had said, looking thoughtfully at his empty glass—and Sarah had ordered another expensive round. “I’ve heard talk about some Aussie chap... a long lost relative of the original owners or something. It’s said he’s planning to purchase the building through some *ghost* company.” That mischievous look had lit up his face again as he had emphasised the word *ghost*. “But that was a while ago, and I’ve heard nothing about any ghost or things.”

“You’re a funny guy,” Sarah had mused.

41

Many of the windows of Budapest's older districts are constructed in the traditional double-glazed style, with at least half a foot's worth of space sandwiched between two windowpanes fixed into typically enormously thick walls. An occupant is often forced to wrestle with both panes individually to access the outside, the same being true in reverse. In their haste to leave, the apartment's original owners must have failed to lock at least one outside window pane—a fact that the Black Cat's curiosity had established quite some time ago...

Sarah's climb to the top of the building was thankfully uneventful. It was an early spring evening, but there was a mild chill in the air under a cloudy night sky, chilled enough to make the metal climbing ladder cold to the touch.

The final rung gave Sarah access to three windows that offered a view into the penthouse's internal gloom. Reaching up on her tiptoes, Sarah could just see through the middle one. But it was the window to its right that Sarah had been told to look for, the fire escape's railing making a convenient step-up for a final heave of her body through the window's threshold once it had been opened.

Sarah assessed the task ahead with a wary eye. Even at these relatively minor heights, the thought of tempting gravity by balancing on a thin, rusted metal bar five stories caught Sarah short...

Some mountain daughter after all, huh!

But that was not what was gnawing at her at that moment. There was suddenly something else; a moment when one can feel eyes upon oneself... Sarah was having such a moment.

She looked wildly about herself, but Sarah could not locate the origin of whatever she felt looking at her... creature or human. It was just an unwelcome feeling. But recent events had imbedded in Sarah the wisdom of taking heed of these kind of feelings, and she found herself clutching at the broken dogman tooth that hung about her neck—but nothing manifested...

Spooked, Sarah shook off the brief fright. It was the first time since arriving in Budapest that she had experienced an episode like that, that sense of being stared at. Unnerving as it was, Sarah forced down the sensation and applied herself to the challenge at hand.

Getting into position, Sarah opened the window just as the Black Cat had said it could be done. She was not exactly in the best shape of her life, and tugging herself over the window's open sill was proving more than strenuous. As she found her balance and the ever-present fear of falling dissipated, Sarah twisted to sit on the window's exposed wide shelf and looked back out over Budapest's fairy-tale skyline. Her legs dangled out into the cool city air... and she felt so tired... so tired...

Sarah's mind drank in the scene laid out before her; the majestic domes that rolled within lowly illuminated clouds, their grandeur presiding over a humming symphony of distant city traffic; the bridges spanning the inky black of the Danube, all ablaze in fluorescent yellow lights; the high gothic spires of the nation's parliament, their misty shapes ghostly lit to the north like sentinels on the banks of that mighty river, its waters flowing like a persistent memory through deepest Europe's past and future; the far bank of the mighty Danube reaching up like a worshipping man to a fable in stone... and Sarah slumped in awe at the beauty of the Budapest's famed Castle District... And she thought: *What stories could be dreamed in a world such as this...*

42

"How do you run from something that will hunt you forever?" the voice said, and Sarah wrenched herself around, looking back into the room she had planned on claiming for herself. Its shadows were as deep and dulcet as the sound of the voice that had startled her out of her meanderings: *Had she fallen asleep?*

Sarah nearly fell, her eyes blinded as I groped for a handhold on the window's peeling frame—it was daylight!

"The Black Cat directed you here... to learn a terrible secret," the voice came again, but this time further away, deeper into the gloom behind Sarah. For some strange reason, Sarah felt, in that moment, that if she turned and followed the sound of the words, she would be lost... and yet, that voice...

Still unnerved, alert and even frightened, Sarah swung her hips over the window sill and lightly slid down onto the floor, her shoes making a muffled tap on the dusty parquet flooring as she landed. She looked up into what she thought seemed like small, darkly golden lights glowing from the room's shadows.

"I didn't mean to trespass or anything," Sarah said nervously. "I was told—"

"—You should know," the voice sounded again. "I have slept with dying kings and been the plaything of their queens; I have murdered at their command and know them to be murderers, the killers of children and the old; I know the darkness where they go to hide their crimes and the crimes they hide within; I know their most obscene desires, and I know their most shameful lies; You should know that I have listened to their dreams: And I can tell you; they are such a *disappointment!*"

Sarah felt glued to the spot as she made out the dark outline of a woman's figure standing amongst the apartment's sheeted furnishings. Her eyes struggled to adjust, but then she recognized who was speaking to her... the red hair, that voice... *la femme Circassian... Those iridescent eyes...*

"And there is so much more than this to tell you... Sarah, *Daughter of the Mountains...*" she heard the woman say.

She knows me! And I know her!

Sarah strained to take in greater detail from the outline of the mysterious woman speaking to her. She could dimly make out the same clothes the woman had been wearing at the jazz club only hours before, her hair the same radiant blush of crimson. But Sarah saw that she no longer wore the chocker that had made Sarah think of a dog collar; the thing was no longer fastened around her neck...

"Come closer," Sarah heard the woman's voice say, though it was as if her lips had hardly moved.

Sarah made a slight motion forward, but then she noticed something else that had not at first seen when she had first looked into the white-shrouded room. A free-standing easel with a small painted canvas stood isolated just behind the red-haired beauty, its disturbing image delicately illuminated by the soft morning light. Sarah could make out the harsh tones of a portrait; a portrait of a face, a face seemingly engulfed from behind in the frightful maw of some wolf-like beast... a dogman!

Sarah flinched. But she could see that the painting's hauntingly beautiful face belonged to the woman now talking to her... Inviting her...

Sarah murmured, "Who are you?"

Another voice, a much deeper male voice, answered: "Someone assigned to help you." Sarah gasped inwardly as the hulking bulk of the Ghost emerged from the room's deepest shadows to stand just behind the woman and the easel bearing her macabre portrait.

"You could have given me a warning," Sarah stammered, her focus returning to the amber glow of the woman's eyes, eyes that were looking at her intently.

The woman continued as if Sarah had said nothing: "The last time I stood in this room was in 1956, just before the godless Russians came and moved in to crush the Hungarian uprising." She paused as if remembering. "It was also the final time I saw my last husband, an honorable man; he who had been an officer in the German Army... But like all of them, he is now gone."

Sarah hesitated as she digested the woman's words, realizing that if what she had heard was true, then this strikingly attractive woman would have to be at least eighty years old. Sarah could make out the corners of the Ghost's mouth twitching in knowing amusement.

He said, "I know what you're thinking–"

"–That she's only about thirty years old..." Sarah countered, staring incredulously at the woman before her. "How can she possibly–"

"–You ask who I am?" the woman interrupted tersely. "I will tell you; I am the *Contessa Arzéna Lázár*... I am the first, the second, the third, the fourth... and as of this time in history, the fifth *Contessa* of that name!" The woman's eyes shimmered in the dawning of the day.

But Sarah was struggling to keep up. *It made no sense...*

Again, Sarah heard the rumbling words of the Ghost.

"The *Contessa* is better known today by her stage name, *La femme Circassian*," he said. "As far as the public is concerned, she is only the latest in a long list of talented women who have appeared under that name."

Sarah laughed. It was a tinny sounding laugh, the laugh of the mystified.

"How is that possible?" she said, her head slowly shaking in bafflement. "Surely you're talking about your..." Sarah struggled to think of the words. "...Surely you're talking about your ancestral lineage?"

She looked keenly at the woman's face—her pure skin, her lips... *those eyes*—all impossibly fine, impossibly young!

The woman answered in her melodic voice, only the slightest trace of a Hungarian accent in its smoothed syllables and consonants: "The world thinks I am the granddaughter of the famous post-war ballerina and spy who went by that name, and that I am the great-granddaughter of an interwar surrealist artist known by that same name..." She paused to nod as if confirming the truth of her words. "It is a game that people like me have to play."

"People like you?" Sarah queried, a strange fear beginning to fill her mind. "Who... or what are you?"

The woman took a step closer to Sarah, who involuntarily backed away, the small of her back jamming up against the sill of the window behind her. The two women stood looking at each other, studying each other, one trying to understand, the other trying to be understood.

"I am over two hundred years old," *la femme Circassian* eventually said. "And it has taken me all those years to find you, *Sarah Shaw... you* who the Forest People call *Daughter of the Mountains...*"

And then another voice came into Sarah's head from a connection deep within. It was a voice that she remembered, even cherished; but its familiar tone had a pleading edge to it: '*Help us...*'

"What are the Dogs of Budapest?" Sarah found herself saying, as if on auto.

There was a quietness in the air that greeted Sarah's question. Then she saw the Ghost move towards the *Circassian* from behind her and whisper something in the woman's ear, something that Sarah could not hear. The woman nodded as if in agreement and turned the full attention of her almost scary eyes on Sarah.

"We are," the *Circassian* answered. "We are the Dogs of Budapest... We who are born to hunt the wolves that roam amongst us."

Sarah thought back to the moment the question had first entered her mind, as if it had been placed there by the sasquatch from beyond the realms of reason or perception. She remembered how Morning Star had asked her how she had come by the name, but she had been unable to tell him, which had seemed to trouble him.

"You are the Dogs of Budapest?" Sarah questioned, unsure if she had heard correctly.

But it was the Ghost who answered.

"We are the last of them... The *Circassian*, me, Morning Star, and the Circassian's daughter."

"Morning Star?" Sarah asked. "He's part of this Dogs of Budapest thing?"

"Yes," the Ghost confirmed. "He's been at this longer than me, ever since an encounter in Vietnam."

"And you have a daughter?" Sarah asked, turning her attention to the *Circassian*. "What, she must be a hundred and eighty years old, huh?"

The Circassian turned to the Ghost, and a slight melancholy smile passed between them. But they did not answer.

"And now you have come into our world, *Sarah Shaw*," the *Circassian* added, returning her attention to Sarah. "And there is so much for us to discuss—for you to understand."

The *Circassian* moved even closer, the light of the beguiling room now fully illuminating her porcelain-skinned face.

"But first, I must ask you... do you trust your friends?" Importance was etched into the *Circassian's* words.

Sarah's first response was to think back to how the Black Cat had asked the exact same question earlier that night.

"I'm talking about the Deputy policeman and the animal-control worker..." the *Circassian* said softly.

"Yes, yes," Sarah confirmed, aware that Tim Rogers and Daemon Skinner had been the only people who had come to mind upon hearing the word 'friends.' "Yes, I trust them with my life... like you most likely trust Morning Star... and the Ghost."

A rueful soft laugh rumbled from the back of the room where the giant bearded man had retreated to.

The *Circassian* smiled.

"Good," she said. "Because they will play an important part in what will come, my dear."

The *Circassian* now placed a cradling hand on Sarah's flushed cheek, and Sarah could see the woman's thoughts forming into words as she looked into her amazing eyes.

"You are the new generation, Sarah... and so you must listen carefully to what I am about to tell you..."

Sarah didn't feel it at first, but a warm glow grew within her as she immersed herself in the words coming via the *Circassian's* silky voice. It felt like she was on the cusp of learning something miraculous, something that might make a senseless and violent world make sense... like she was about to learn how her own life could make sense...

"Tell me," she said.

Then the *Circassian* began to speak... and Sarah was lost...

43

Budapest, early February, 1945.

The dark symphony of warfare raging in Budapest's streets reached Johnny Kovacs' bombed-out tenement as a ghostly echo, drowned out by his chaotic and confused thoughts. Once again, he was poring over the manuscript, *Memoirs of a Traveling Muse*, the paltry light of dripping candles the only source of illumination.

He wondered at the cruel self-confession within the manuscript's pages—the callous substitution of a beautiful peasant girl in place of Kluge's lover, a woman he was now convinced was the elusive British spy, the *Circassian*.

Somehow, Kluge's woman had survived execution at the hands of the *Waffen-SS* even as her innocent stand-in had swung lifeless in a lifeless tree, the ever-present crows feasting on her death. Kluge had used this terrible sleight-of-hand to escape the wrath of the *SS* with his beautiful *táltos*... the substitute girl's mutilated face now appearing in many a dream since Kovacs' terrifying experiences in Russia's foreboding Pripet Marshes. The search for a lost unit of *Waffen-SS* killers had brought Kovacs face to face with something unimaginable.

But now he knew something else unimaginable. Kovacs knew who had really killed the unfortunate girl that he had seen hanging limp on that fateful day, and all to protect an unearthly being that was apparently centuries old. It was the last part of the mystery that now seemed too fantastic for Kovacs to believe.

Kovacs was not a religious man, nor even prone to the superstitions that permeated Hungarian culture, the people to whom he belonged. When he first read through the pages of the manuscript he had acquired, he thought it was the work of a madwoman, a bizarre exercise in self-delusion. And yet it continued to trouble his Hungarian soul.

Of all that he had absorbed in reading the manuscript, the one part that Kovacs' *could* fathom—and obsess over—had been the undoubted claim that it was the autobiographical account of a woman who referred to herself as *la femme Circassian*. To Kovacs, this was obviously the very same *Circassian* that the German Army had been trying to root out as an unlikely British spy on the Russian front—

But then the wolf-beasts had attacked, and Kovacs had barely made it out of Russia with his wits intact. That he was even alive now, deep in the destructive depths of the Red Army's siege of Budapest, was a miracle.

The Circassian? Why should she matter?

Kovacs was sure the manuscript was not any possible form of spy tradecraft, at least nothing he could make out. It simply was the laid down words of a life lived, words written by a woman who claimed to have lived that life—a life that was fundamentally esoteric in nature, even occult.

The manuscript disturbed Kovacs every time he read it, its shadowy passages weaving the latent fears of a supernatural presence into his waking consciousness, its stories from an ancient time that was so ingrained in those who shared his ancient Hungarian ancestry. By Kovacs' troubled reckoning, the author of this disquieting manuscript would now have to be at least two hundred years old, give or take a decade.

Impossible!

Kovacs looked over at the painted image he had been carrying with him since his fateful and terrifying encounter with human-like wolves back in 1943. The image still had the power to seize the mind, to overwhelm a man with a maddening mix of fear and desire. He considered the woman's ominously beautiful face, her head bizarrely encased from behind in the open jaws of a wolf-like creature seemingly intent on devouring her...

Those eyes! Kluge's woman... the Circassian...

A floorboard creaked, faintly audible over the crump of distant explosions. His survival instincts primed by the worsening siege, Kovacs froze: Had the latest Russian shelling breached the building as he had set about losing himself for the thousandth time in these fantastical memoirs?

Kovacs crept to the doorway, alert, pistol poised. His eyes widened at the approaching figures huddled in heavy cloaks despite the musty air: he almost swooned as he made out *Hauptmann* Kluge... and a slender woman clasping an infant to her breast. Her vivid locks peaked out from the hood's shadow, but those eyes—amber glowing in the gloom—they hit Kovacs with electric recognition.

The Circassian!

Kovacs first thought was to run, or shoot... or do both! It seemed beyond the fantastical—Just as he had once again pulled out the battered manuscript for yet another incredulous read, a man he had lost all contact with should now appear with the very source of his obsession—*in the flesh!*

"What madness is this?" whispered Kovacs when the couple and their child reached his door. "How did you know I was here—and *how* is *she* here?"

Kovacs pointed a weak finger at the woman holding the child. A humorless smile creased Kluge's worn face.

"It's an old habit. In these uncertain times, one needs to keep tabs on what one hopes are still reliable contacts."

"What do you mean by 'reliable contacts'?" Kovacs queried warily, still holding his gaze on the woman.

Kluge's smile disappeared, the severe manner of the commanding officer reasserting itself.

"We have both seen them—and we both know what they are capable of!"

It was true, and Kovacs knew exactly what Kluge was alluding to; that both he and Kovacs had witnessed the horrifyingly incomprehensible carnage that resulted from an assault by something that should not exist.

Kovacs continued to contemplate the woman, but he spoke to Kluge. "I thought I was going out of my mind," Kovacs confessed. "What were they?"

Kluge shook his head, and Kovacs broke his gaze off the woman's hypnotic face.

"I know that you thought that I had somehow arranged for the murder and disappearance of that missing *Waffen-SS* unit." Kluge looked severely at Kovacs, an imploring intensity causing his face to go rigid. "I did not kill those men; I did not order their deaths, nor did I make them disappear!"

"Then what happened to them?" asked Kovacs. "You never gave me any satisfactory answers at the time."

But it was not Kluge who answered.

"Those wolf-beasts that attacked," said the woman, her voice as melodious as her eyes were luminous. "They are what happened to your *SS* soldiers."

Kovacs tried looking at the woman more closely, objectively. But again he was engulfed in the preternatural effect of her eyes, just like *those* in the painting behind him. She didn't appear a day over twenty to Kovacs, despite the fine lines of haggardness that had crept into the surrounding skin that framed those amber lights.

She is impossible!

"Those things killed that Waffen-SS unit?" Kovacs asked hesitantly, aware that he was talking to someone who seemed of a different world; a warning surged through his mind...

She is the Hauptmann's woman...

Kovacs remembered back to the hurried retreat of the German forces soon after his incredible encounter with the beast creatures. The incident had effectively ended his investigation into the missing *SS* men, and it had also effectively ended Kovacs' career with the German military police. After what he had seen, his nerves were too shot for him to ever regain the former effectiveness that had made him a prized asset of the German military police. His final report had been an exercise in bland officious doublespeak, the language of the mediocre. He had mentioned nothing concerning the beastly apparitions that had looked and behaved like savage wolves.

The woman said, “No, you don’t understand what I am saying.”

Kovacs looked at Kluge and saw a creeping fear seep into his features. He looked back at the woman, the child swaddled in its blankets and huddling in her young arms.

“Tell me,” he demanded.

The woman looked at Kluge, and Kovacs saw him give her the slightest nod of reluctant approval.

“I am telling you,” she said, her soft, warm voice gaining an edge to it. “Those animals, those wolves you saw with human limbs and bodies; I’m trying to tell you that they *were* your *SS* men—that those inhuman beastly wolves *are* your missing *SS* men!”

Kovacs’ memory flooded his consciousness with the images of mayhem and gore, of the snarling savagery of the wolves that he had seen walk like men; his mind went into overload. He fought with his own thoughts and against the memory of those frighteningly human characteristics, which now came into stark and dreadful relief... and yet it all still refused to make sense to him.

“At least what was left of them,” Kluge offered, sensing the mental battle playing out within Kovacs.

Kovacs retreated shakily back into his bare and sparse room and sat down, Kluge and the woman following. He put his head into his hands, disbelief coursing through his veins, his entire being.

Kluge watched as Kovacs grappled with his mind.

“You wouldn’t believe some of the things they are doing in the camps,” Kluge said quietly.

Kovacs looked up at the woman and realized that she was somehow more beautiful and intimidating in the flesh. He pointed over his shoulder back at the lurid painting on display, its glowing eyes staring back at her eyes—eyes just as luminous, and maybe even more so.

"Are you her?" Kovacs asked as if trying to square an impossible story with an improbable reality.

The woman scrutinized the painting.

"It is a self-portrait," she said, eyeing the canvas. "It is me—something that overcame me in the Pripet Marshes.

She stepped back and gave her child a motherly hug.

"But it is nothing—a silly thing!"

Kovacs had, however, realized that a piece of the puzzle had fallen into place, confirming what he had suspected to be true.

"Then it is you; you are the British spy called the *Circassian*?" Kovacs said.

There was an difficult silence. The child in the woman's arms whimpered, and Kovacs suddenly felt ashamed.

"Really, it no longer matters to me if you are or are not a spy for the British," he said. "I just need to know if you are this *Circassian*... and if you are the one who wrote this manuscript?"

Kovacs reached over and held up the chunky collection of typed pages he had been reading through before Kluge and the woman had arrived. The woman inclined her head as if to inspect the bundle of sheets, but Kovacs could already tell she recognized them.

"I am the one they call the *Circassian*," she said quietly. "And that is my story that you hold in your hands."

Kovacs felt an enormous weight lifted from his consciousness, like a fog burning off in the morning sun.

He couldn't look at the woman, so he turned to gaze again into the amber eyes of her self-portrait.

"How can it be?" he mumbled as if to himself. "How can it be? –You would be over one hundred and fifty years old if it were true..."

Kovacs turned and peered back into the painted image he had carried for so long.

"I just need to talk to this woman," he said, pointing at the face locked in the wolf's jaws. "I need to talk with you about who you are..."

There was no answer, but Kovacs felt Kluge kneel beside him, both men looking into the painted amber jewels of light emanating from the *Circassian's* portrait.

"Do you believe in second chances, Herr Kovacs?" Kluge said.

Kovacs just shook his head gravely.

"What do you want with me?" he managed hoarsely, bowing his head as if to deny Kluge and this perplexing woman were really there.

An explosion rocked the burnt-out shell of the building, but Kluge steadied himself as the unfazed *Circassian* peeled back blankets to check on the mewling infant. Kovacs glimpsed a shock of strawberry locks before the child disappeared into her mother's enveloping coat lapels.

Kluge faced Kovacs grimly. "What you discovered in that godforsaken cabin, that is the horror that is hunting us now–not this cursed war–but something relentless in its need to hunt us and our child down."

“Those things, those unnatural beasts...” Kovacs shuddered violently. “I can still hear their infernal howling.”

The *Circassian* looked up from quieting the baby. “Old sins cast long shadows—this thing is more ancient than you can imagine.”

Kluge placed a calming, almost fatherly arm across Kovacs’ shoulder.

“This war that rages about us,” he said solemnly. “It is already over.” Kovacs felt the press of the former German officer’s hand. “But a new and more terrible war is just beginning... A war with terrible secrets beyond anything that humanity has ever faced.”

The *Circassian* followed on from Kluge’s black words. “What you saw in Russia was only the beginning, Mr Kovacs.”

An especially loud detonation erupted somewhere north, the walls quivering in tremulous sympathy with the *Circassian’s* dark warning. But Kovacs hardly noticed.

“And this is why we are here,” he heard Kluge say.

“Why?” moaned Kovacs. “Why have you sought me out now?”

The Circassian spoke: “We want you to keep the manuscript... to protect it. So our child might one day know who her mother was.” She took hold of the journal from Kovacs’ trembling hands. “Our child cannot possibly follow us where we must now go,” she said emphatically.

The baby began whimpering from the now closer explosions battering at the city’s crumbling walls. As Kovacs looked at the manuscript, Kluge looked keenly back at him.

"We have to flee this city before they find us," he declared, his protective gaze flitting between Kovacs and the *Circassian* holding their child. "But we dare not risk being caught in the net closing around us." He leaned in closer. "I know it is much to ask, especially with death at every door, but will you take our child and raise her in safety?"

Kovacs was astonished by the request. He eyed the innocent babe swaddled in its blankets and the protective warmth of its mother and knew he was not the man to take on the task Kluge was asking of him.

"I have never fathered a child or been a father to a child," he said haltingly... And then an idea came to him.

"What?" said Kluge, seeing the change come over Kovacs. "What are you thinking?"

Kovacs looked again at the *Circassian* and the baby she was holding and started to laugh.

Both the *Circassian* and Kluge were momentarily taken aback by the outpouring.

"I have a brother, just outside Budapest," Kovacs said. "He and his wife are planning their escape to America, even as we speak."

Kovacs seemed to become giddy at the thought.

"My brother and his wife have no children; they can take your child," he said with rising glee. "They can take her, and she will be brought up in America!"

Kovacs and Kluge began to laugh together, a bizarre sound in the middle of so much suffering and killing. They began to weep with laughter.

But the *Circassian* was not laughing; no tears of joy were forming in her eyes. She held out her baby and beheld its face. The two men stopped, profound realization at the sadness clouding the mesmerizing jewels that were the *Circassian's* eyes; for she knew this might be the last time she could ever behold her own daughter.

"Her name is Katarina," the *Circassian* said, holding the child out for Kovacs to take. "Time will tell if she is her mother's daughter, but you must promise to tell her of me, her true mother."

Kovacs took the child, the tragedy and joy of the moment mixing in his own emotions. He felt a great love overcome him, something inexplicable and unique in his experience. He saw Kluge, hope whelming up in the other man's face.

"Welcome to the family," Kovacs said as he peered into the pretty little face before him. "Welcome to the family, Katarina Kovacs... May you live a long and peaceful life..."

44

"I am dying," said the old woman, her cup of coffee having gone cold, untouched among the other three empty mugs belonging to the people she sat with. "And so my mother wishes for you to have this."

Sarah took a thick leather-bound tome from Katarina Kovacs' frail hands. The redoubtable woman had noticeably deteriorated in the months since Sarah had last seen her, her long, flowing, reddish white hair having thinned out and taken on a lackluster sheen. Sarah had since learned of the fate of Katarina's imposing mountain lodge; it had been burned to ashes in the aftermath of the destruction of the dogman Sarah now remembered as Broken Fang.

"And this too," Katarina continued. Her ever-present nurse produced a large envelope, which Katarina handed to Sarah.

"What is it?" asked Sarah, ever fearful of more unpleasant surprises and unknown factors.

"Do not open it now," Katarina answered. Let's just say that it is much-needed homework, something to help you put things into a better perspective."

"Is it about the work ahead of us?" Sarah asked.

"You will find it useful," was all Katarina would say.

Sarah felt for the broken tooth on the end of its chain, the chain that now hung more heavily around her neck than ever before. Its weight bore down on her all the more now that Sarah knew who and what the Dogs of Budapest were—the knowing was a terrifying burden. She was as close to the ultimate nightmare as any human alive could be.

Sarah looked about herself, at her companions. They were sitting together in one of the better cafés that populate Budapest's famous *Andrássy út*, the main avenue that runs through the heart of the city on the flat Pest side, and the site of the European continent's first underground metro. Opposite, visible through the extensive glass frontage of the café, Sarah could see the brooding structure of the Hungarian State Opera House, home of some of the greatest classical music ever composed. But it was the two young men sitting opposite her that had been taking Sarah's attention since first sitting down with them.

Deputy Tim Rogers and Daemon Skinner sat in black stoic silence, their eyes fixed on the cluttered table separating them from Sarah and the woman Katarina Kovacs. Sarah regarded them, happy to see them, yet troubled—these were not the friends that Sarah had left months ago. They were different, hardened... changed... They wore black, everything black.

"How long do you have?" Sarah said, her words meant for Katarina, but her eyes still coming to grips with the disquieting differences that had taken hold of the deputy and the animal-control worker.

"The doctors say months, maybe a year," Katarina sighed, but without a hint of self-pity "I don't think any of them really know—I have not inherited my mother's longevity, it seems."

Katarina's mother—la femme Circassian.

Sarah looked sharply at Katarina.

"I'm so sorry," she said, not knowing how to respond.

"Don't be," Katarina replied. "We have more important things to worry about today than the coming of my death."

Sarah placed the leather-bound volume Katarina had given her on the table and opened its hefty cover. A title page written in English greeted her, and she read: *Memoirs of a Travelling Muse...*

"They are the original accounts of my mother's life," Katarina croaked, a hint of emotion strangling the words as she spoke them. "You will find them helpful over the next few weeks, months, and even years."

Sarah slammed the book's cover shut!

"No!" said Sarah, mortified at the enormity of the gift. "Surely they belong to you... You should have them, not me, surely?"

Katarina studied Sarah for a moment, her eyes calm, her face serene.

"You spoke with my mother, did you not?" she said.

Sarah nodded and thought back to a month ago when she had encountered the ethereally beautiful red-haired woman with the startlingly hypnotic voice, the night Sarah had been scoping out an abandoned apartment as a new place to live. To Sarah's astonishment, the woman had been the same stunningly attractive woman she had witnessed being abused earlier that night in a shady nightclub; like as if their latter meeting had been prearranged; like Sarah's fortuitous introduction to a young English aristocrat had been an accident of fate; as if the upsetting and abusive scene she had witnessed unfold at the jazz club had been a random quirk of chance; as if her quest to lay claim to an abandoned penthouse had been mere happenstance in a city full of happenstance and mystery; as if all had led to an unexpected meeting with a woman called by others *la femme Circassian—she* who was the impossible mother of Katarina Kovacs...

There is someone already assigned to help you...

"Yes," said Sarah, looking back down at the leather-encased volume she had just closed shut. I spoke with her... She told me of the Dogs of Budapest and the *wolves* that they hunt."

"The *wolves* that *we* hunt," Katarina corrected her.

There was a warm smile for Sarah on the old woman's face, the kind of smile people usually reserve for family. It was a smile that said you're one of us now.

"And so you know who—or should I say *what*—my mother is?"

Sarah went quiet. For the last two months, she had holed up in the deserted apartment that the Black Cat had steered her to, a richly appointed set of rooms owned by the Kovacs family since before the Second World War. Sarah's immediate financial problems had vanished, *ah la* the *Circassian*; her living needs now bolstered by a healthy trust fund arrangement under the name Sarah Bergstrom, all linked to Katarina Kovacs' Hungarian business interests. Life for Sarah should have been everything anyone on the run could want it to be—safe, and financially secure. But Sarah had been troubled by the things she had learned...

"You've changed, Sarah," said Daemon. You're harder. The things you've seen are things we have all seen; we've all changed... but especially you."

Sarah nodded, understanding what Daemon was saying. She thought, if you only knew what I have learned since we last spoke.

Sarah, Daemon, and Deputy Rogers had been reunited only a half-hour before. It had, at first, been a joyous, if surreal, moment. The three of them had hugged and kissed. But it became apparent to each of them that something heavy now hung in the air between them. It was Rogers who asked the question.

"What did Ms Kovacs' mother tell you that has us coming all the way out here?"

Sarah looked sideways at the frail old woman beside her. Katarina gave her a nod, and Sarah thought about the woman that was called the *Circassian*. She had accepted that the woman might be Katarina's mother, but she was a woman obviously only in her late twenties or early thirties. It was something that Sarah had not yet fully come to terms with. But then Sarah still struggled to comprehend the enormity of living in a world where supernatural creatures battled manmade monstrosities in a life-and-death struggle of cosmic proportions.

Sarah had learned much in the last two months.

"There is a ring of traffickers at work in this city," Sarah began slowly. "This ring has been operating in Europe since the early 1950s. It provides a food source to sustain a stable of artificially manufactured hybrid creatures, creatures that are a DNA cross between humans and the creature we call a dogman."

Sarah let her words sink in. Rogers and Daemon stayed quiet, a fearful intensity filling their eyes as they absorbed what Sarah was saying. But Sarah was counting on their combined experiences ensuring that they would take her seriously.

"I have been told that the food source this group provides for these creatures are living human beings."

Sarah paused ominously as Daemon and Rogers looked at each other, their expressions unchanged. *Hardened...*

"Morning Star had suggested as much when he came to us with this idea that we join you in Europe," said Daemon.

Rogers nodded and added, "He asked us if we were willing to take the fight to the people who had kidnapped us back in Oregon—we said *hell yeah*!"

Sarah smiled. Deputy Tim Rogers might have grown and matured over time, especially since their discovery of the hideously butchered remains of two Homeland Security agents all those months ago—because hairy encounters with a rancid dogman and the fearsome sasquatch will do that to a person. But Sarah felt oddly reassured that there was still some of that good ol' boy left in Rogers, something Sarah was depending on for the task ahead.

However, Rogers' mood remained dark, even cautious. Sarah could see he wanted to say something; she inclined her head for him to continue.

"Morning Star suggested that we read Detective Lee into the program... to get some *intel* on who we might be dealing with," he said, his voice dropping into hushed tones. "Morning Star gave the detective a name that he said he got from some guy called the Ghost."

Sarah's brows lifted at the sound of the name, and she glanced at Katarina... *And some of the worst monsters are human...*

"I know this *Ghost*," Sarah said. "He's part of the team we'll be working with—What did Detective Lee find?"

"Lee's checking out of the name that this Ghost guy gave us turned up some pretty interesting stuff, stuff about some kind of porno movie producer," Rogers said.

"A man called *Dorgan Silasi,*" Sarah confirmed and saw that Katarina was giving her a cautious but knowing look.

The old woman checked her watch.

"They will be here in the next two or three minutes," she said to Sarah cryptically.

Daemon leaned in, seemingly oblivious to Katarina's comment, and said, "Lee told us this guy's got some heavy connections with the Russian mob. Lee suggested we make a pass on any ideas about going up against this guy."

Sarah regarded both of her friends and then looked directly at Daemon.

"Do you remember when we first met, Daemon?" she said.

Daemon answered: "Sure, how could I forget!"

"You told me then that—and I quote—*that there is a war going on...* Remember?"

Daemon sucked in a deep breath, nodding, and Sarah turned to Rogers.

"And you?" she said, her mouth hard and firm. "Are you still sworn to protect and serve?"

Rogers bulked at the question.

"Of course!" he snapped.

"Then listen up, the both of you—because in less than two minutes, this so-called movie producer *Dorgan Silasi* will walk into this café on the arm of a woman so beautiful it'll hurt you!"

Rogers and Daemon flinched in confused apprehension at the name *Dorgan Silasi* and the abstract idea of meeting a true beauty. They shared puzzled looks, bewilderment spreading across their faces.

"This man, this porn king you are about to meet—" Sarah let her words hang. "This man is a wolf! He's the worst of his kind, and it's time he was hunted down and taken out!"

Sarah smiled inwardly as her two friends exchanged worried glances with each other.

"By *wolf*, you don't mean he's an actual morphing werewolf or something?" Daemon asked warily. "He's not going to change into an actual *werewolf*, is he?"

Sarah couldn't help but smile.

"No, this guy is all too human, and that's what makes him one of the most dangerous beasts out there," she said, her seriousness returning as she spoke.

Sarah realized that her two friends were about to undergo a baptism of fire in a war that was not being fought with guns and bullets but with cunning and resolve. *La femme Circassian* had already fully briefed her on what she expected Sarah and her friends to do. Now, it was her turn to brief Rogers and Daemon.

"Pay attention, guys," Sarah continued. "Because the woman accompanying this Dorgan Silasi monster is Katarina's mother, the *Countessa Arzéna Lázár*... also known by her stage name *la femme Circassian*..."

Sarah paused. She could see her two friends doing the calculations, grappling with the idea of a woman, who must be at least a hundred years old if she was Katarina's actual mother, being 'so beautiful' it would hurt them.

Sarah felt the imp of the perverse take hold.

"I can see what you two are thinking, but rest assured that this is a woman who *claims* to be over two hundred years old—" She held up a restraining hand as she saw their mouths open. "But you will see that she looks hardly a day over thirty!"

Sarah's hand remained firmly uplifted, her frown brooking no dissent at what she had just said.

"And given what we all now know is out there, this is hardly the most difficult concept either of you have had to deal with in the last few months, if you get my drift."

She watched Daemon and Rogers cope with the notion that a two-hundred-year-old woman could be a great beauty... or even two hundred years old!

"She speaks the truth," Katarina said, her voice hollow and fragile from beside Sarah. "It is not necessary at this time that you *believe* this, only that you have been *told* this. The day will come when you will *understand* these things more fully."

Sarah could see a light switch go on in Daemon's eyes, always the one to keep an open mind on all things weird and supernatural. But she also noted the reluctance in Rogers' confused expression.

"Tim," Sarah said softly, even compassionately. "We have come too far, you and me, to stumble over this—After everything we've seen, is it too hard for you to believe that there are people in this world who still live to fantastic ages?"

Rogers stroked his chin, a skeptical frown creasing his forehead.

"Actually, Sarah, I'm more worried about meeting this Dork-an-*Salatsky* guy—whatever his name is—especially after what I heard Detective Lee say about him." He gave Sarah a worried flick of his hand. "They don't even let me carry a gun in this country."

Sarah couldn't help but laugh.

"Don't worry, Tim," she smiled. "We're being covered by one of the most lethal killers on the planet." She leaned in all conspiratorial. "This *Silasi* guy might be a predatory wolf, but if he tries anything stupid, then our Ghost will put a bullet through his skull before he can say—"

"—The Ghost is a real guy!" Rogers snorted. "I thought Morning Star was being all *metafickle* or something when he talked about there being a ghost thing or whatever!"

Rogers swivelled his head, as did Daemon, as if trying to determine where Sarah's ghostly sniper might be covering them from. Both seemed to be expecting to find the tell-tale signs of a red laser sight strobing through the Hungarian air.

"My mother would never put us in danger," Katarina protested. "You have nothing to fear from this meeting. The man Dorgan Silasi believes he is coming to meet with a wealthy independent American film investor who is interested in rescuing his failing movie project."

"You?" asked Daemon of the old woman.

"No, that would be me," said Sarah. Katarina is here in her capacity as a former and well-known Hollywood entertainment lawyer."

Rogers and Daemon saw an uncharacteristically dangerous glint begin to glow in Sarah's eyes.

"Today, I am a young American woman who has recently inherited a sizable fortune due to a most unfortunate death in the family," she said. "And in my grief, I am looking to put my money into something exciting and glamorous."

Katarina added, "A young and impressionable woman with money is something this Dorgan Silasi has never been able to resist." She cast a wary eye over the two young American men. "My mother has been cultivating this set-up for the last year, and all that was missing was someone believable to play the gullible movie investor."

"And then a young American called Sarah came along," finished Daemon, a perceptive smile on his lips. "This is becoming real interesting–So, what's the plan?"

Sarah shrugged her shoulders, starting to work herself up into the role of a spoiled American heiress, someone looking for adventure in the glam world of European cinema.

"The plan is that we're just three silly little rich kids with too much money to spend for our own good," she said, her voice taking on a giggly sound that had Rogers blinking in concerned disbelief. "Daemon, you're my surly little brother who didn't get daddy's dough." She fixed Rogers with a playful smirk. "And Tim, you're my jock toy boy with a roving eye for the Hungarian babes when my back is turned."

Sarah gave a satisfied sigh and sat back, enjoying the consternation breaking out on Rogers' face.

"Your toy boy?" Rogers hissed, his face reddening.

"I always figured you for a toy boy, or at least a boy with toys, Deputy Tim," Daemon grinned at Rogers. "Shouldn't be too hard for you to pull that one off."

Rogers was about to respond when Katarina cut them off.

"They are here," she said.

Sarah had already seen their arrival, and it sobered her that she would once again lay eyes on the man escorting Katarina's mother into the café.

The worst of the worst...

She watched as her friends turned to look at the unlikely couple, their progress already receiving looks of recognition from other customers scattered about in the café. She saw

Rogers' and Daemon's mouths go slack at the sight of the woman... *because men are so predictable.* But Sarah was focused on the old and tired-looking man being guided to their table by the extraordinary beauty at his side; *Dorgan Silasi*—a man she had last seen publically humiliating *la femme Circassian* in a seedy little Budapest nightclub.

The Wolf of Budapest...

An intangible darkness came over Sarah. She snarled inwardly at the sight of the man, an aged body encased in a dark grey suit of uncertain vintage, shoes polished to a mirror shine.

This is going to be fun...

Sarah watched *la femme Circassian*, the *Contessa Arzéna Lázár, the Fifth,* spread her radiance, piloting the decrepit old movie producer as they shuffled through the admiring glances that now followed them. She felt annoyed when Rogers rudely stole a quick sideways look at Katarina as if he could still not accept that the refined creature approaching them could actually be the older dying woman's mother. She took in the wounded look in Katarina's eyes... Sarah would speak to Deputy Tim Rogers later regarding his manners...

The *Circassian* glided forth, immaculately dressed in a grey business suit, her face perfect and glowing under the café's warm lighting, their defuse glimmer lending a deeper shade of red to her elegantly coifed tresses. Sarah noticed she was again wearing a rough dog collar, the same brutish-looking leather choker she had seen encircling *la femme Circassian's* throat on that fateful night at the jazz club; its metal leash ring glinted in the café's dull light.

But Sarah's heart ached as she realized the *Circassian* had offered no recognition towards her dying daughter as they approached—not even the most subtle nod of acknowledgment. Sarah had been warned that a level of *tradecraft* was essential in the dangerous game she now played. However, this studied indifference by *la femme Circassian* to Katarina seemed too unkind given the circumstances, even if the stakes were as high as Sarah knew them to be.

La femme Circassian... Your daughter is dying... You are too cruel...

"You're late!" Sarah said curtly, the sharpness in her voice startling the sallow Dorgan Silasi. Even the unflappable poise of *la femme Circassian* took pause. The couple stopped, and Silasi looked up from his shuffling feet as Rogers and Daemon broke off from their ogling.

The *Circassian,* recovering her composure almost instantaneously, casually inclined her head. The circular O-ring on her collar swung lightly, its shiny metal tinkling out a mischievous light.

"It is always the same with the Americans," she cooed into Dorgan Silasi's waxy ear while fixing Sarah with a territorial look, the melodious sound of her voice further enrapturing Sarah's male friends with its playful tones. "Time is money, and money is time... no?"

But Sarah was paying her no attention, her concentration squarely fixed on the old movie producer at the *Circassian's* side. She imagined her eyes burning a hole through the man's ugliness. This was the man, the alpha in a pack of animals that were trafficking in human flesh. Sarah had waited for this moment since she first learned who and what the *Dogs of Budapest* hunted.

Sarah was now one of those dogs... She fingered Broken Fang's jagged tooth on the end of its chain, felt a surge of adrenaline, and wondered if this is what it feels like to be *alpha.*

Let the hunt begin...

The *Circassian* and the Ghost had already taken the time to instruct Sarah in the tactics and traditions of the old ways of hunting wolves with dog packs: The swift sighthounds bred for the catching and cornering of fugitive wolves (Morning Star); the brutal and large mastiffs to help bring down the wolves (the Ghost); and the scent hounds to track down and root out any wolf or wolf pack at large during a hunt—this was the *Circassian*: And now it was also Sarah.

At first, Sarah had been horrified to be associated with a mindset that called for the organized hunting down of any creature, let alone another human. But she eventually came around to the *Circassian's* way of thinking.

These are the worst of the worst! A day of reckoning is coming for you, old man... And your wolves...

Knowing that he hovered incognito nearby, Sarah thought of the Ghost and silently pondered how cathartic it would be if he simply took the movie producer out now with a single shot... But that was not the *Circassian's* plan—at least not for now.

A day of reckoning is coming...

Sarah let her eyes boil welts in Dorgan Silasi's psychological skin.

But the old brute was giving back as good as he received. She could feel the chill of the man's meanness, the same malevolent spitefulness she had seen him so publicly exhibit that night in the jazz venue. He was looking closely at her, studying her... recognition starting to bloom in his eyes.

"May I introduce—" the *Circassian* began, but Dorgan Silasi interrupted her with an impatient and discourteous wave of his hand.

"We have met before, have we not?" he said to Sarah carefully.

The evil that Sarah saw in his eyes pierced the space between them. She heard the tone in his voice, the same curtly punctuated tone she had seen him previously use to exenterate the *Circassian's* dignity. But this time, she heard it up close. She felt the red mist of anger begin to fall across her thoughts just as the *Circassian* turned her smile on the object of Sarah's growing rage—

"—Darling! I told you this before we arrived!" the *Circassian* laughed musically, and Rogers and Daemon resumed their gaping. "This is the brave young woman who came to my aid when you were *such a pig* to me at the jazz club... Remember *darling*?"

The old goat's eyes sagged momentarily, and then they lit up; he even smiled... It was the most dangerously disconcerting thing Sarah had ever seen another human being do.

"*Ahhh!*" he breathed, and a fetid wafting of his stale breath filled the air. "Yes, I do remember..." He nodded, his aged neck muscles tensing and knotting. "Most definitely I remember..."

End of the first series in *The Cryptid Dossier: Confidential Case Files 1-4* by Quell von der Umbra.

If you enjoyed these four combined instalments from the first series please feel free to leave a review on Amazon. All feedback is greatly appreciated.

About the author...

'**Quelle von der Umbra**'* is the penname of a former intelligence asset come whistle-blower who practices the art of '*fictionalize to publicize*' in exposing the sinister and beastly forces that lurk in the shadows of our world.

He lives in seclusion at an undisclosed location, his true identity only known to a few people, some of whom he writes about in his ongoing series: *"The Cryptid Dossier: Confidential Case Files"*

Visit **cryptid-dossier.com** for more information on the fascinating world of **Quelle von der Umbra**.

This first print edition
is dedicated to my
Mother

*Please note that 'Quelle von der Umbra' is a fictional person created by the author of the "Cryptid Dossier" series.

Printed in Great Britain
by Amazon

43599014R00196